Hotel Mamie Stover should go down in history as one of the most ingenious inventions of the twentieth-century mind. Mamie Stover herself, the clever businesswoman with all the natural assets who made her way into the history and hearts of servicemen in THE REVOLT OF MAMIE STOVER, has now come up with the secret of happiness for tired couples, tired single men, and even—upon occasion—tired virgins. To be specific, Mamie has opened a brand-new hotel in Hawaii that, without any advertising whatsoever, is always filled to capacity. Why? A national magazine hires Jim Madison, who knew Mamie during the war, to ferret out the answer to that fascinating question, and you—after your first glimpse of Mamie's monumental proportions—will find yourself breathlessly tagging along with him.

On the secluded island where Hotel Mamie Stover is located, Jim learns that Mamie is offering the tourists who come to Hawaii just what they really came for. Encouraged by lectures to participate in the art of love as it was practiced by Hawaiian princesses, they are given new vitality by means of massages, amatory foods, and exhilarating sports. They are provided with perfumes and diaphanous clothes, and are completely protected from the usual fears and worries by all kinds of remarkable arrangements. Is there a catch? Does illusion triumph? What kind of piece does Jim Madison write for his employer? In HOTEL MAMIE STOVER you'll learn the answers to these questions and many more —and perhaps find out what kind of person *you* really are as well.

HOTEL MAMIE STOVER

WILLIAM BRADFORD HUIE

Hotel Mamie Stover

Clarkson N. Potter, Inc. / *Publisher*
New York

CHAPTER ONE

In which we meet Jim Madison and
Mamie Stover who, for the second
time in their lives, have been brought
together by fate for one week. And
we begin learning about the new kind
of sex : *like-sex*. 1239345

Hawaii : 1955

UNDER LATE-AFTERNOON sun on the island of Maui a man and
a woman walked together along an isolated beach. The man
was the novelist, James Monroe Madison, the woman was
Mamie Stover.

Mamie's hair was tucked into a swim cap, and her terry
cloth wrapper reached halfway between her hips and knees.
The wrapper had pockets into which Mamie thrust her hands,
and she walked barefoot with the peculiar confidence of a
woman who knows that people will pay to watch her walk.
Other than the wrapper Mamie was naked, for she disliked
bathing suits, particularly bikinis.

"The decent way to tan is naked," she said. "I advise
women to tan naked,and not wear even a finger ring in the sun.
A woman's body looks indecent when she lets the sun stripe it."

Jim Madison smiled at Mamie's defining decency. He knew
why she liked to tan naked.

Mamie now tanned naked because during the Second
World War, while she was a whore in Honolulu, economics
forced her not to tan at all. Men headed for, and returning
from, Pacific islands wanted milk-white skin; so Mamie, in
her come-on walks at Waikiki, wore ankle-length Hawaiian

7

muumuus and sun hats and advertised that she kept herself milk-white "all over . . . with just a healthy suggestion of rose-tint."

From 1942 to 1945, on most days, especially on weekends and paydays, by 11 A.M. hundreds of service men were on the beach. Near noon, like a cabaret crowd anticipating the floor show, the men stopped swimming and sat down. Sometimes they were disappointed, but more often, exactly at noon, "Mamie's Walk" began.

She always started east of the Moana Hotel and walked past the Moana and the Outrigger Club towards the Royal Hawaiian Hotel. She always wore a different-coloured, dia-phanous *muumuu,* a different sun hat, dark glasses, and clogs which accentuated her six-foot height. Her gold-blonde hair was always dressed differently, fastidiously. She never paused, never spoke, never smiled, never gestured. She only walked, naturally and proudly. She walked on the beach like Gypsy Rose Lee walked on a stage when Gypsy was strip-teasing. Except Mamie was taller, blonder, more striking than Gypsy, and Mamie had a natural sway-and-swivel. Always Mamie walked between the men and the sun-reflecting water, and the men watched her rhythmic, veiled movements. Her natural walk had the effect of making each man feel, even though he could not clearly see, that she was naked under the *muumuu.*

Mamie's Walk was deplored by the church, explained by science.

As to the church : the day Jim Madison first saw Mamie's Walk was in 1943 and he was lying in the sand beside a Methodist chaplain from Chattanooga, Tennessee.

"You remember, Chaplain," Madison remarked, "the New England missionaries imposed the *muumuu* on near-naked Hawaiian women to make them less attractive to sailors. A century passes and Mamie uses the *muumuu* to attract sailors."

The chaplain shook his head. "It's the way of the church. We promote sin by trying to discourage it."

As to science, Havelock Ellis : "Rhythmic bodily movements

arouse the male even more than bodily proportions. This is especially true of a certain rhythmic, slightly swaying walk which cannot be acquired or cultivated, but which is natural in a few rare woman. That such a woman, merely by walking before them, can arouse normal males is unquestioned."

As Mamie began each walk at Waikiki, the fighting men began and passed along a rhythmic cadence count:

> One ... Two ... Three ... Four,
> Mamie's ... What ... We're Fighting ... For.

Or:

> One ... Two ... Three ... Four,
> Mamie ... Is ... The Perfect ... Whore.

Or:

> One ... Two ... Three ... Four,
> Mamie's ... The Whore ... That We ... Adore.

There were scores of these couplets: GI poets competed in their composition. Early in the war the couplets were derisive; but as the war aged and disillusion spread, the couplets and the tone of the chanting began to evidence a barrack-room affection for Mamie. She was like *Lili Marlene* and *Mademoiselle from Armentières,* except she was real. And she was one profiteer who didn't pretend to patriotism. She was one sex symbol who stood ready, the men said she lay ready, to soothe what fevers she kindled. So, late in the war, when the men chanted "Mamie's ... What ... We're Fighting .... For," more than a few seemed to believe it.

To Mamie Stover the war was opportunity. She came from nowhere in the Mississippi Delta: her father was a lecherous, no-account barber. At seventeen she won a beauty contest and a one-year film contract. She was deflowered and rejected in Hollywood, and she saw the war as her chance to attain happiness. In Hawaii she found a million bored traveling men with money, and in the best tradition of American ingenuity she fashioned an apparatus for diverting them.

In the middle of a large, empty room she erected a Bull Ring—four Pullman-size adjacent compartments each with a

9

red couch—and she moved determinedly from couch to couch while her servants shuttled men in and out. The fighting men said: "Never in the course of human intercourse have so many men paid so much for so brief an encounter with one woman." Accepting only cash, evading taxes, playing the black market in whisky, and riding the avalanche of inflation, Mamie accumulated half a million dollars.*

"I think it's immoral for a woman not to accumulate money during a war," Mamie explained. "When men are throwing twenty-dollar bills away like empty beer cans, a woman ought to be busy with a basket."

Many an American, long after he had reoccupied his niche on the mainland, long after he forgot his battles, remembered bered watching Mamie walk at Waikiki, remembered chanting "One... Two... Three... Four" as she walked, and remembered standing in line at Mamie's Place and paying his money for his turn on a red couch with the woman who embodied all the rose-tinted skin, all the gold-blonde hair, all the luxury-model breasts, all the foam rubber buttocks, and all the race-horse legs which had been pinned up over every bunk in the war.

Now, in 1955, Mamie was thirty-five and a millionaire. With her partners, Jesus Portales and Monty Whitaker, she owned two enormously profitable enterprises. One of these was the night club, Mamie's Luau, at Waikiki; the other was Hotel Mamie Stover, eighty miles from Honolulu, on the island of Maui near the old whaling port of Lahaina. It was on the beach at Hotel Mamie Stover that Mamie and Madison were walking.

They walked together like a man and woman who, at some earlier meeting in their lives, have associated sexually. This meeting for Madison and Mamie was one week in 1939. They met on the freighter which brought her to Honolulu. She was nineteen, defeated, broke. He was twenty-six, despairing after

* How Mamie made her wartime fortune is detailed in the novel *The Revolt of Mamie Stover*.

the collapse of his first marriage. During their week on the freighter they used one another against loneliness. They didn't fall in love but they came to care what happened to one another. He urged her not to become a whore and offered her money to return to the mainland. But she insisted that, having been rejected in Hollywood, whoring was her only chance to "be somebody." Thereafter Madison befriended her several times in Honolulu; but after the war and his marriage to Emily Barham, he saw Mamie rarely . . . only to nod to her in a bank or wave to her in a passing car.

But he had never lost interest in Mamie as a woman with whom he had shared loneliness, and as a physical, social and financial phenomenon. To his publishing and motion picture associates, in London, New York, Rome, or Beverly Hills, he often recounted how this talentless girl, rejected by picture producers, with nothing but an erotic walk and a will to wealth, with no windfall from any rich husband, had started in a Honolulu whorehouse, and in the revolutionary years 1940–55 had become a millionaire tourist attraction.

With the device of a telephone call, Fate had now sent Madison to Maui to associate with Mamie for a second week in their lives. Several days earlier, in his home in Pacific Heights, overlooking Honolulu, Madison had taken the call. He heard the voice of the New York operator.

"New York is calling Mr. James Monroe Madison."

"This is he."

"Hold on for Mr. Cullen."

Nick Cullen was editor of *Vacation* magazine: that slick, 230-page, technicolored, monthly guide to far-off adventure. In 1950, for *Vacation*, Madison "revisited" the Chattahoochee Valley in south Georgia where he was born, and wrote that familiar story about the novelist who roams the earth, who now lives far away on an island hilltop, but who comes "home again" to walk the "ancient red hills and quiet green valley of his birth."

"How are you, Jim?" Nick asked.

"Fine, Nick. You?"

"Not too bad. What are you doing besides writing money-making motion pictures?"

"Working. I got back from Beverly Hills three weeks ago. My wife has taken the children to visit her mother in England. I have to deliver a novel on Labor Day. Same old seven-mornings-a-week grind."

"How about something for me? Something you can knock out in a few days?"

"Like what?"

Nick Cullen cleared his throat. "Now that statehood is assured," he said, "we are devoting an entire issue to Hawaii. We'll have all the usual stuff: Diamond Head, Waikiki, volcanoes, pineapples, sugar cane, Pearl Harbor, descendants of Yankee missionaries, grass skirts, and surfboard riders. But I want one fresh piece . . . offbeat, brassy, irreverent."

"And you want me to sing off-key?"

"Yeah. I want you to present Mamie Stover."

The line went silent for a moment as Madison tapped his desk, bit his lower lip.

"Let's not do it, Nick," he said. "I have neighbors who rent land to Mamie. I'll embarrass them if I publicize their profits from her."

"You're big enough to risk that," Nick Cullen argued. "Mamie has become a force in Hawaii. Of the 110,000 tourists who visited Hawaii last year, 9,847 stayed an average of eight days each at Hotel Mamie Stover for which they paid a total of 2,954,162 dollars. Telling the story of Hawaii in 1955 without mentioning Mamie would be like telling the story of France in the eighteenth century without mentioning Du Barry."

"If Mamie has become a force," Madison said, "she's still an indecent force. Of course she has quit whoring. She's rich, and there are no whores in Hawaii any more. But Mamie's still selling the idea of sex. They say she's reviving paganism, that she encourages adultery, that she's a threat to the family. If I publicize her, my wife will say I'm being unfair to our

12

kids. I'll probably be accused of aiding Communism by 'hacking away at the foundations of free society.' "

Nick Cullen, in New York, squared up to his desk. He knew what he wanted.

"But, Jim," he said, "you don't aid Communism or mistreat your kids by answering questions about our society. That's all I'm asking you to do. Why, despite her having been a whore, is Mamie so attractive to tourists? When 110,000 Americans spend their savings on a dream trip to Waikiki, why do thirty-seven per cent of them dine at least once at Mamie's Luau? After only four days in Hawaii why do ten per cent of them leave Waikiki, check out of world-famous hotels, and go to a remote, unadvertised hotel on Maui? What does Mamie offer that other innkeepers don't offer?"

"There is one answer to all those questions," Madison said. "It's what Mamie calls *like-sex*. You know what love-sex is. That's where partners have sex because they say they love each other. You know what money-sex is. That's where one partner buys the other. Those are the two old kinds of sex. Waikiki has always attracted sex-hunters, women as well as men. But the Air Age hunters don't stay long enough to find love-sex. And money-sex is unavailable. So today's hunters aren't finding much sex of any kind at Waikiki, and they are disappointed. Mamie offers to help them. She offers a new kind of sex. Like-sex. In like-sex you don't need love or money. Travellers are brought together and encouraged to try to *like* one another enough to have sex for a night or a week. So the sex-hunters are deserting Waikiki, flocking to Mamie's hotel, and she's teaching them like-sex. That's why Waikiki loses so much business to Mamie."

Nick Cullen winked at his secretary who was listening and recording the conversation.

"You've just written our story, Jim," Nick said. "I want to know all about like-sex. I want you to escort *Vacation*'s five million readers on a search for like-sex: an evening at Mamie's Luau, a week at Hotel Mamie Stover. Introduce us to our sex-hungry travelling companions: make us feel what they seek, what they find. Introduce us to Mamie : make us feel what she promises, what she delivers. It can be great, Jim."

The argument continued, Madison resisting and Cullen selling, and Nick Cullen won because he had caught Jim Madison when he was tired, when his wife and two children were away from him; and Cullen had caught Madison on a day when at 4 A.M. Madison woke up doubting that the novel on which he was working was any good. Cullen was offering Madison a holiday from that novel, from the torture of facing blank pages alone . . . and Cullen was offering him ten thousand dollars to take this holiday.

So before the conversation ended, Cullen had winked three times at his secretary, each wink marking some decline in Madison's resistance. When Cullen cradled the telephone he stood up, exhaled, grinned and rubbed his hands together.

"Jesus, we're lucky !" he said. "Our readers are tired of Waikiki, grass skirts, hulas and volcanoes. They see it all the time on TV. Mamie Stover and like-sex will give us something to sell that TV can't touch."

What really caused Madison to agree to write the story was a question he had to ask himself. Hadn't he once used Mamie for like-sex? During that week on the freighter, back in 1939, hadn't he clutched Mamie, used her against his loneliness, without having loved her? So if she was now an indecent force wasn't he partially responsible for her becoming such a force? Perhaps even more responsible than his neighbors who rented land to her?

Madison began his research by visiting Mamie's Luau at Waikiki. Then he flew to Maui; and at Hotel Mamie Stover, in swim trunks, he joined Mamie on the beach. They had walked more than a mile, talking, and they had now reached a dangerous area which was off-limits to the hotel's guests.

"You look tired, Jimmy," Mamie said.

"I am tired, Mamie. Forty-two birthdays plus the airplane disease. Every producer I write for wants to make his film in London or Rome or Hongkong. Every publisher wants me to visit Africa. Too many airplanes, too many miles, too many hotels, too many people. And Oahu (Honolulu) doesn't seem like an island to me any more. It's not restful; it's restless. With statehood it'll be no place to live, just another Los Angeles suburb with supermarkets and traffic problems."

"Has your wife been good for you?"

"Wonderful. All writers should marry Englishwomen.* They are the only women left who are conditioned for absentee husbands. They manage homes, families, places in society, all with no more than a weekly report from the absent spouse."

"They require a bit more than that, don't they?" Mamie asked dryly. "Don't they own the insurance policies, the home, the income, the church, the country club, and don't they expect the husbands to visit them often enough to keep them pregnant?"

"Yeah. I guess that's true."

At Mamie's favorite spot for swimming she slipped off the wrapper, lifted her arms, and said: "Speaking of age, Jimmy, is this the way I looked to you sixteen years ago on the freighter?"

Standing naked under a man's eyes, Mamie was as confident as an artist's model. She swam every day in rough water to firm her muscles. Her breasts were as high as ever: not once in her life had she worn a brassière. She never drank or smoked; she disciplined her diet like a Channel swimmer. Twice daily she was under the hands of Hawaiian masseurs.

"You look magnificent, Mamie," Madison said. "You haven't gained an ounce."

"Two pounds in sixteen years."

The only change Madison noted was in her face. It looked bonier, like a high-fashion model's. Her lips and cheeks had lost their youthful pout, and this gave her a more triangular face since her gray-blue eyes were set far apart. There was harshness in her eyes and in the line of her jaw, but no more,

* Madison's romance with Emily Barham in wartime London is detailed in the novel *The Americanization of Emily*.

15

Madison thought, than he was accustomed to seeing in women who are successful in show business.

Mamie joked : "Is this the pose you want for *Vacation* ?"

"We'll add an hibiscus bloom or two."

Mamie raced into the surf and dived under a breaker. Madison followed. He was a good swimmer but no match for Mamie, so he didn't try to keep up.

For the average swimmer this beach is perilous. Fifty feet seaward the ocean floor begins dropping down precipices and steep slopes until the water becomes four miles deep. The "island" of Maui is a peak in a volcanic mountain range. If the water were air, and if you stood on the ocean bottom and looked up towards Mamie's beach, it would be like looking at the Matterhorn from Interlaken or at Pike's Peak from Colorado Springs. As things really are, Mamie's "beach" is a lofty ledge. This creates an undertow which sucks and pulls, and only strong swimmers should risk it.

Mamie enjoyed risking it. As men enjoy racing cars, or scaling cliffs, or fighting bulls, Mamie enjoyed swimming powerfully and naked against this primeval force. It made her feel like a positive particle in a universe. She had left the safety of a ledge to challenge an element twenty thousand feet deep. Below her were tons of voracious marine life including the whales which once lured white men to Hawaii. Above her, in the distance, she could see Puu Kukui, one of the two peaks which dominate Maui. She respected vastness and mystery, and she liked to feel her blood surge, her long body strain in conflict with the undertow.

Today, however, deep in her viscera, Mamie felt a knot of uneasiness. The knot had been forming since the previous evening at Mamie's Luau when her publicity agent, Leo Hirshman, came into her dressing room and told her that Jim Madison was waiting to see her.

"Madison brings us opportunity and a problem," Leo told her. "He's been assigned to put us in the statehood issue of *Vacation*. In that beautiful Travel Bible, Mamie Stover can stand tall and invite all good vacationers to come to Mamie's

Luau and Hotel Mamie Stover and find REAL Paradise in the Pacific."

"And Madison wants to write it?"

"That's what he says. I talked with him while he watched your act. He'll have five million readers on the Mainland, in Canada, in Australia, all the places our customers come from. It's a press agent's dream."

"Have you told Jesus and Monty?"

"Jesus talked with Madison. Jesus is being cagey. He told Monty."

Mamie sat down.

"What exactly does Madison want from us?"

"He wants to know all about our operations. He wants to pretend he's a guest and visit the hotel for a week. He wants some pictures. And of course he wants to talk a lot with you."

Mamie was worried: "He can hurt us, can't he?"

"It depends," Leo said. "He can bring us more dough. Whatever he writes, even if he denounces us for running a new-model whorehouse, he'll send us customers. But how much trouble he'll bring us . . . that's the question. Mamie Stover in the statehood issue of *Vacation* . . . that's a sight that's bound to upset digestions in banks and pulpits. The immediate problem is that he's waiting to see you."

Mamie walked across the room on those long legs.

"Tell him this, Leo," she said. "Tell him I'm flattered he's writing the story. Tell him we'll co-operate completely. But tell him I'm not feeling well and I'm flying back to Maui now. Ask him to talk with Jesus and Monty, and ask him, please, to wait and see me at the hotel."

Mamie returned to Maui and conferred by telephone with her partners. The problem had many angles. Because holiday travel is Hawaii's life blood, *Vacation* magazine is a business publication in Hawaii. Mamie in *Vacation* would embarrass the missionary families who, in fact, were "in business" with Mamie since they controlled the land she used. Could anyone stop Madison? If Mamie and her partners refused to co-operate, wouldn't Madison write a story anyway? If Madison

17

could be induced not to write the story, wouldn't the magazine send someone else? And finally: Mamie wanted her picture in *Vacation*. She wanted to read Madison's judgment of her. For Jim Madison was the only man she had ever trusted.

Mamie turned to look at Madison as he swam behind her. His close-cropped brown hair was thinning; his temples were gray. His body was tanned, still strong, but it evidenced those years in airplanes and hotels. His eyes were humane, filled with the melancholy of men who labor in loneliness to understand, who lack the comforts of religion, who doubt and yearn and strive to communicate. The wrinkles at the corners of his mouth were from the smile he often employed. He found life generally sad and absurd, and the smile was his sympathetic comment. For this some people said he was cynical. But he insisted he wasn't cynical, that his smile expressed only perplexity and a desire to move on without argument or analysis.

Mamie remembered her first months in Honolulu when she began whoring to accumulate cash. She telephoned Madison and begged him to keep her money for her. As a prostitute she couldn't bank money: it would attract demands. She had to hide cash from cops, madams, rent collectors, tax gatherers. Madison didn't want to keep it. He didn't like men who safeguard money for whores, but he let her persuade him. She wouldn't have trusted her father with that money, but she delivered it each month to Madison. When she was ready to begin her black market maneuvers, Madison returned it all.

That, oddly, was another disturbing angle. A man who can be trusted to return a whore's money will make honest judgments. Mamie had never cared about other people's judgments of her. She cared about Madison's. Because she wanted Madison's good opinion, his story could hurt her feelings as well as her business.

As she swam towards the beach Mamie suddenly faltered against the undertow. She gasped, sucked in salt water, lunged frantically. Perhaps she would have made it on her own, but she was relieved to feel her hand gripped as Madison, with

surprising strength, pulled her to safety. They walked from the
water with Mamie holding on to him, coughing.

She was still shaking as she slipped on the wrapper.

"That's never happened to me in the water before," she
said. "I suddenly felt over-matched. I'd have drowned except
for you."

"You weren't in real trouble," he said. "You just momen-
tarily lost your nerve."

As they walked towards the hotel it was Mamie who was
tired and Madison who was refreshed.

"Jimmy," Mamie said, "you and I were friends once. I'm
still your friend. Are you still my friend?"

"I'm still friendly," Madison said. "But you and I are not
the same as we were in 1939 and '40. Then you were alone,
unprotected and broke. I was alone. Since then I've become
a husband and father. And you've become rich and a 'force.'
So you and I may be friendly, but the situation isn't the
same."

Mamie slipped her arm through his. "But you understood
why I whored during the war. It was my chance to be somebody. You understood that, didn't you?"

"I understood why you felt that way. There were many
whores during the war. The sexual ones were the easiest to
forgive."

"I'm not a whore now. I haven't been for ten years."

"What are you now?"

"I'm a hotel keeper. Since the war I've tried to educate
myself. I've read books and I've travelled. I decided that while
I was making money I also wanted to help people. With my
experience I can't be a wife or mother or social worker. So I
designed this hotel. There's nothing in the world like it. It
helps the Hawaiians who live here and work for me, and it
helps most people who come here."

Madison looked at her and grinned. "Don't *you* disillusion
me, Mamie. Don't you start pretending to help people."

Mamie felt herself faltering against Madison's disbelieving

grin just as she had faltered against the undertow. She said:
"There's nothing wrong in helping people, Jimmy. I can
afford to help people now. Sure, I'm making money. I love
money. You know that; I was always honest with you about
it. I like to look at money and feel it. You remember that night
at your house in 1940 when, all in one bundle, you gave me
back my first year's money? Twenty thousand dollars! Remember how I touched those new hundred-dollar bills and
laughed and cried? Remember how scared-to-death I was to
take that money out of your house to buy that whisky from
that Merchant Marine captain? I doubled that twenty thousand dollars in a month. Since then I've made lots of money
and I'm not ashamed of it. I'm sorry I had to whore for some
of it, but I'm glad I got it. And now I'm helping people . . .
I really am . . . and before you leave Hotel Mamie Stover
you'll agree that I am."

CHAPTER TWO

In which we turn back to the previous evening when Jim Madison,
after accepting the assignment from
Vacation Magazine, visited Mamie's
Luau to begin his research. We meet
Portales and Leo Hirshman and learn
trade secrets. We watch Mamie
entertain at the Luau, and we reflect
on how Hotel Mamie Stover is
promoted.

To VISIT Hotel Mamie Stover on Maui you must first visit
Mamie's Luau at Waikiki. Only by being impelled to visit
the Luau do you become a prospect for the Hotel.

Mamie and her partners have charted what they call the
Standard Hawaii Visitor's Experience. They have broken the
Civilian Visitor down into four types: Types Able, Baker,
Charlie, and Dog. The Ables are married couples 30–55 years
old; the Bakers are lone women 28–45; the Charlies are lone
men 30–55; and the Dogs are all others, mostly retired
couples who spend little and are therefore of no account.
Mamie and her partners can show you with charts what type
you belong in, how you will feel every hour in Hawaii, how
much money you will have, and how you can be induced to
spend it.

Whatever your type, every non-military visitor to Hawaii
performs an identical A-Day (Arrival Day) ritual. (Remaining
days of your visit are A-plus-1, etc.) You have left your niche
on the Mainland. You have assets or you wouldn't travel so

21

far. By plane, car or train you have reached Los Angeles, San Francisco, Seattle or Vancouver, where you have taken ship or plane.

If you have taken ship, at 7 A.M. on A-Day you are at the rail, and Diamond Head is off the starboard bow. It looks like what you saw on TV. You are being served breakfast on deck so you can look. The loudspeaker interrupts *Blue Hawaii* to describe what you see. The ship moves past the hotels at Waikiki with every passenger sipping coffee at the starboard rail, looking. Four miles farther, the ship noses towards the pier. You hear the band on the pier playing *Blue Hawaii* and you see the hula girls. As you step from the gangway a girl rustles grass against you, gives you the smiling *aloha*, and drapes the *lei* around your neck.

If you have taken the plane it's the same except faster.

Three chances out of five you arrive as a member of a "conducted tour" and you move by the conductor and by the coupons. You ride four miles through California-like traffic to your Waikiki hotel where another grass skirt hands you an ice, you are booked in, shown to your room, from whence you must rush to buy a costume. Men must have sandals, duck pants and *aloha* shirts. Women must have sandals and *muu-muus*, nothing else, no stockings, pants, girdles or brassières. For the show-offs there are sarongs and grass skirts for women, and wrap-around shorts, called *lava-lavas*, for men.

The pressing event is the hotel's *luau* for which you have been charged eight dollars a head and for which you report, camera in hand, at 5 P.M. The place is a portion of the hotel lawn, under palm trees, near the beach. You note how quickly Mainlanders have become Islanders. All the Ables, Bakers, Charlies, and Dogs are in costume, *leis* around their necks, with cameras cocked to show the neighbors in Kansas City. A procession begins. You are not part of it: you photograph it. A "native Hawaiian" blowing a conch shell is followed by four other "natives" bearing a pig's carcass to the barbecue pit. Except this pit is an *imu*, and while you click your shutter the "Hawaiians" fill the pig with hot coals and bury him.

While the pig cooks the band plays *Blue Hawaii*, and all types start consuming tall, colored, rum drinks with romantic names. Two "real Hawaiian" girls in grass skirts move from Able male to Able male, then to the Charlies, posing for snapshots with their arms around each man, after which they hold out little brown hands for dollar tips and move on. The music gets louder, the party gets drunker, and several Able women, along with a Baker, start trying to hula. (If they have come by ship they have had lessons *en route*: HALF THE FUN IS GETTING THERE.) The laughs get lustier, the sun goes down, the pig is disinterred, and all types begin grabbing fruit, fish, and half-cooked fresh pork.

As the moon rises, a few Able men try to hula. Everybody grins. One Charlie wears a flower over his ear. A few Able women, plus a Baker or so, get reckless. Behind a palm tree a Baptist matron from Omaha gets kissed by an Able male to whom she is not united in matrimony; and a Baker schoolteacher from Atlanta entertains a lukewarm proposition. That there is some yearning for abandon is disclosed by what the Japanese charwomen find in the nearby powder room next morning. The holiday women, if they dare to do like the real Hawaiians, will come to the *luau* naked under the *muumuu*. But few of them dare. However, during the *luau*, one wanton strips off her brassière in the powder room and leaves it. Others notice and imitate. The charwomen never have to buy brassières for themselves: they gather them, launder them, and sell the ones they can't use.

Just before midnight an Able male from Terre Haute, by rash action, learns that a brassière has been jettisoned; and he utters the remembered remark of A-Day:

"Goddam! No wonder those missionaries put these *muumuus* on Hawaiian women and then sired so many goddam kids! The *muumuu* makes everything so accessible!"

At midnight it ends: an authentic Hawaiian *luau*.

"Well, when they get to bed after that first *luau*, a lot of Ables, Bakers and Charlies ain't feeling so good."

The speaker was one of Mamie's partners: Jesus Portales (He-Soose Por-TAL-es), the Portuguese-American manager of Mamie's Luau. His father was brought from Portugal to work Hawaiian cane, but Jesus graduated to "entertainment." He operated whorehouses until they were disallowed in 1945. He looked like a middle-aged gypsy horse trader, yet he had a home for his numerous family in the new-rich Honolulu suburb, Kahala. He was in his office at Mamie's Luau talking with Jim Madison and Leo Hirshman.

"Three hours after that first *luau*," Jesus continued, "at 3 A.M., these Ables, Bakers and Charlies are awake. They can't sleep. Rum and fresh pork have always disagreed with them. They've got indigestion or palpitations, and they're trying to find the Alka-Seltzer. And they get to thinking what-the-hell. A *luau* ain't a damn thing but a cookout. Ain't nothing happened at Waikiki so far that couldn'a' happened on Saturday night in a backyard in Toronto. Since they can't sleep they notice that the hotel is just another hotel, that 'world-famous' Waikiki is just another beach. They decide that those hula girls learned to hula in Brooklyn, which they did, and that those 'native Hawaiians' are just like Hollywood Indians, which they are. They realize that those girls in grass skirts at the *luau* who were hugging men for snapshots were grabbing tips to turn over to some swarthy sonofabitch like me who owns the grass-skirted model concession. So the Ables, Bakers and Charlies try to get back to sleep, but they halfway figure that if they hear *Blue Hawaii* one more time they'll throw up."

Madison was wearing a white linen suit, a blue shirt, a blue tie. After dinner that evening he had driven from his home to the Luau.

"That sort of disillusion is universal," Madison said. "Most little-travelled people feel it wherever they go. They drink too much, eat unusual food, try to sleep in strange beds, wish they were at home."

"Sure," Jesus agreed. "That's right. But they feel it worse here because they expected more. This time they haven't taken a little drive on the Mainland. This time they've laid out real

24

dough. They've travelled thousands of miles to the Paradise of the Pacific. They don't know exactly what they expected to find, but goddam, they didn't expect it to be heartburn and just another cookout."

Leo Hirshman said: "TV has added to the disenchantment because TV makes everything familiar ... particularly to the small-town, small-city-suburban folks who come to Hawaii. Our Standard Visitor has seen pictures of hula girls. He has seen Diamond Head, *luaus*, palm trees, and Waikiki beach so many times on TV that when he gets here he takes one look and says 'oh, hell, I've seen it before.'"

Madison remembered Nick Cullen on the telephone: "Our readers are tired of Diamond Head, Waikiki, hula girls: I need something fresh, irreverent—like Mamie Stover."

"I understand that," Madison said, "but my question is: does your Standard Visitor become disenchanted more rapidly in Hawaii than he does in Las Vegas or Miami Beach? Those places are even more familiar."

"Disenchantment comes quicker here," Leo answered, "and it's more desperate. On the mainland when a holiday-maker gets bored he knows he can hop in his car and drive five hundred miles to some place else. He can fight boredom with motion. He can't do that here. This is an island. He has paid big dough to come here for two weeks. He knows he can't move, so when he gets bored he gets desperate. That two weeks begins to look like a jail sentence."

Madison said: "He can travel here, too. He can visit the Outer Islands."

"Sure," Leo said. "The tours take him to Hilo and show him a volcano. A volcano is interesting only when it's active ... like when he saw it on TV. Now he looks and it's inactive, so what-the-hell, it was better on TV for free, Kauai and Kona are minor-league Waikiki."

As he listened to Leo Hirshman and Jim Madison, Jesus Portales smoked his heavy-bowled Oriental pipe and calculated. He smelled trouble. The land in Hawaii is owned by several self-perpetuating Anglo trusts. These trusts never sell land;

25

they lease it and control its use. Jesus and Mamie were not land-owners : only rich lessees. Lessees prosper at the pleasure of lessors. Jesus's father, like all Portuguese laborers brought to Hawaii, was classified as non-white. In 1947 Jesus persuaded the Anglo trust officers to reclassify Portuguese as "white." This enabled him to lease land for his big home in Kahala, which was restricted to "persons of Caucasian descent."

So Jesus Portales had prospered, had even become "white" by knowing how to please Anglo trust officers. Before and during the war his whorehouses were on land leased from a trust founded by missionaries. The officers of the trust were respected Congregationalists. Jesus pleased them by paying them more rent each year and, especially, by assuring them that whorehouses were necessary in order to segregate inevitable sin and thereby safeguard the community's health.

After the war the trust officers were troubled. Their consciences would no longer permit whorehouses. Jesus helped them. He and Mamie devised a new mode of operation : Mamie's Luau and Hotel Mamie Stover, institutions which were not whorehouses but which could still pay high rent. The trust officers were satisfied. In fact, it was for this service that they promoted Jesus to "white," accepted fifty thousand dollars from him in advance rentals, and allowed him to move to Kahala.

Jesus bit hard on his pipe stem. Madison's proposed story would embarrass the trust officers. So the story would not be written; and if written, would not be published. As a tactic Jesus was co-operating with Madison, answering his questions, discussing the obvious. Next day Jesus would pass the word to the trust officers. A trust owned the land on which Madison's home was built. Two trusts were advertisers in *Vacation*.

Jesus lifted the heavy pipe from his teeth and said : "Remember, Mr. Madison, Mamie Stover's organization does not own the land on which we operate Mamie's Luau and Hotel Mamie Stover. We lease land from trusts. In order to obtain capital to develop Hawaii as a great state, the trust officers expect us to collect more dollars from tourists every year. But these trust officers are Church men. They restrict us lessees as to how we can collect tourist dollars. We can't operate slot machines, or crap tables, or horse races, or dog races, or jai-a-lai. We can't sell easy divorces. We can't sell whores, or naked French chorus girls, or big-name comedians telling dirty jokes. So we get no gamblers or sporting crowd or big-city easy-spenders. Then consider our other limitations. We got no Disneyland, no theatre, no skyscrapers, no Lincoln's Monument. So Hawaii gets no kids or free-spending young folks. The youngest man tourist we figure on is thirty; the youngest woman is twenty-eight. And these are Budget People—church members, middle class suburbanites, small-town Ford and Chevrolet drivers, and the folks who have already seen 'every-thing' on TV programs. What have we got to sell them? We got a beach, and this is a long way to travel for a beach. We got Hawaiian music, and our Standard Visitor has already got it running out his ears—records, radio, TV. We got the hula, and the hula won't make nobody a dime any more. A girl comes in here and wants to hula for me, I kick her hulaing tail out of the shop. This means that by Arrival Day-plus-3 or -4, us trust officers and lessees who need tourist dollars to develop a great state, we got a lot of bored Ables, Bakers, Charlies and Dogs at Waikiki, all dressed up in *muumuus* and *aloha* shirts, looking for 'romance' with ten long days to go."

Madison grinned. Then Leo Hirshman grinned. Jesus remained solemn, then he grinned.

"And that's where you come in," Madison said.

Jesus corrected him. "That's where Mamie's Luau comes in. Of course sixty-three per cent of the visitors never come here. They got no coupon for us : we don't co-operate with the tours. Ables, Bakers and Charlies have to lay out cash to see Mamie. They can't see Mamie on 'free TV in every room.' We don't get the satisfied folks or the ones on tight budgets. We get the ones who are itching for romance, and who brought along a few extra dollars."

27

"And to relieve this itch what do you give them that's permitted by the consciences of your rent collectors?"

"We invite you to see for yourself. But first, what did you see as you approached Mamie's Luau tonight?"

"Your sign, of course."

"Fifty feet high," Jesus said. "When Mamie is wearing four-inch heels and has her hair on top of her head, she stands six feet and seven inches tall. The First Lady of the Islands. On that sign she stands fifty feet tall. The bored Ables, Bakers and Charlies see that sign, and they figure maybe Mamie can show 'em something they're not tired looking at. What did you see when you got closer?"

"You've multiplied all the Polynesian props," Madison replied. "More totem poles, more war canoes, more fish nets, more red and yellow flowers, more gas jets burning in pools, more soft yellow lights, more bamboo, more *luhala* mats. And your entrance is the Inlet of Desire."

"And when you passed through our Inlet of Desire," Jesus asked, "what did you hear? *Blue Hawaii? Sweet Leilani? Song of the Islands?* No. You heard drums! We got no Hawaiian music here. There's not a steel guitar in the shop. Just drums. And no hulas. Just Tahitian love dancing: a man and a woman, bumping and grinding, getting worked up to enjoy *real* island love under a palm tree. Feel those drums!"

The three men sat quietly, glancing at one another. Even inside the partially soundproofed office Madison could feel those big drums. Boomp! Boomp! Boomp! Like a human heart.

"Our Ables, Bakers and Charlies," Jesus said, "relax in big bamboo chairs. They drink Passion Punch. They watch drumbeat dances. They see women with flowers in their long hair, hanging down their backs. They see men with flowers stuck behind their ears. They eat food which won't give them indigestion and which they believe is seasoned with sex stimulants. Leo Hirshman spreads that rumor. Then our guests are ready to see Mamie."

Leo Hirshman looked at his watch. "We can see Mamie in two minutes," he said.

Jesus Portales remained in his office to telephone his partner, Monty Whitaker, while Leo Hirshman led Madison to a table in the corner of the Aphrodisia Room of Mamie's Luau. Madison could see the "intimate" circular stage with the stage-level "Mamie's Walk" pushing out into the crowd. The Samoan drummers formed a half-circle on the stage, sitting on the floor or on low stools. The drums were silent. The crowd stirred expectantly.

"Haven't we met before, Leo?" Madison asked.

"I didn't think you'd remember," Leo answered. "It was at Universal in '47. I pushed a picture you wrote: *Swamp Fever*. We sat in a couple of meetings together. I went over the wall in '48 and landed here with Mamie."

"You like it here?"

"Love it. I got the house in Kahala, too. I've also been reclassified as white. My wife and kids are happy. I like Mamie. She drives like a freight train, but she's got brains. And she's not as selfish as the average show-business bitch."

Leo was forty-three, and from Chicago. He left North-western University in '32 to become assistant press agent for a fan dancer named Sally Rand at the Chicago World's Fair. Madison sympathized with him. For Madison knew the faces of publicity agents: the too-puffy face, anxious lines, tight corners of the mouth, caused by too much concentration on how to sell "entertainment" to an increasingly bored "market." Madison also saw Leo Hirshman as a man who had found security for his family far from the tough markets of Chicago and Los Angeles, and who wanted to keep it.

The Samoan drum leader smote his drum. House lights went down. Stage lights came up. A voice said:

"Ladies and gentlemen ... Mamie's Luau proudly presents The First Lady of the Islands ... Miss Mamie Stover!"

Applause built up. Drums thundered. And there she was, towering on four-inch heels, under a yellow spotlight. Wide yellow straw hat. Blazing silk *muumuu* which covered her nipples and reached her ankles. The *muumuu* was tight from her waist to her knees. Her gold-blonde hair hung low on her shoulders. The Samoan drums beat the same "One . . . Two . . . Three . . . Four" cadence the troops chanted, and Mamie walked.

To continuous applause and drumbeat she moved forward from the stage along the elevated walkway to the center of the room. Haughtily, she towered over raised faces. Then she executed her bread-and-butter movement. Slowly, gracefully, she turned that sway-and-swivel rump to the crowd and walked away, upstage, with the spotlight focused tight on her rump. The crowd yelled and whistled.

"There it is, Jim," Leo said. "You can't see *that* on television. That's the most saleable tail on earth. And I'm an expert. I've been selling tails since the Chicago fair."

Madison said: "That red silk looks like it's painted on her. How do you get it so tight?"

"Old trick. We started it in pictures the minute TV competition began to hurt. Of course she's got no pants on, and just before she pulls on the *muumuu* she rubs a little spirit gum on each cheek of her tail."

As Madison watched, Leo continued:

"Remember that trick we used with your girl in *Swamp Fever*? We pulled off her pants and rubbed glycerine on her tail. Then we put that thin, loose dress on her, let her splash around in the swamp with that Heavy who was trying to rape her, and as she struggled up out of the water we threw a tight spot on her tail and the camera caught it close-up with glycerine and water holding that thin, wet cloth to her skin. I always thought that shot made the picture."

After more maneuvers, Mamie responded to pleas, came back to the end of the walkway, and repeated the upstage walk.

"I'll just say this, Jim," Leo said. "I don't believe there's a man alive whose balls haven't turned to chalk who can watch Mamie Stover's tail without feeling *something*."

Her final trick was to stand downstage and let the lights go down in front of her and come up behind her. She loosened the cords which held the *muumuu* tight around her waist and knees, and let the *muumuu* fall free like a shift. This put her body in shadow under the silk as she executed several movements. Then all stage lights came up, and to applause, whistles and yells, she gave them her only smile. Instead of bowing she threw her arms high and waved.

"She'll be back in ten minutes," Leo said. "As soon as she changes and we sell another round of drinks."

"Why doesn't she smile more?" Madison asked.

"It'd be wrong for her," Leo said. "No grinning woman can be a successful sex symbol. Mamie must always look, not haughty, but aloof. She never smiles but once, and that's just a slight, amused smile ... not a wide, toothy grin."

"Does she try any singing or dancing?"

"Never. Mamie's act is just to *be* Mamie Stover and then *appear*. When you've got a talent who can fill the house just by *being* and *appearing*, you don't mess around trying to teach her to sing or dance or recite the Gettysburg Address."

"Does she strip?"

"No more than you saw, just loosening a cord here and there to assist her appearance. Stripping is too common for Mamie. She's a lady: the First Lady of the Islands. She's a millionaire. She's wholesome. She doesn't drink or smoke. She's not tough or common. She's always beautiful and in good taste. She doesn't make one vulgar movement: no bumps, grinds, nothing that she wouldn't do on a beach or in a living room. Even that big rump-view walk that brings down the house is just her natural, God-given walk. She's not trying to wiggle her tail, that's just her natural walk ... and it's a joy to behold and tell your neighbors about."

"That brings me to your job, Leo," Madison said. "How do you publicize her?"

"Well, it's like the Rockefellers," Leo explained. "You remember how Ivy Lee was hired just to keep the Rockefellers *out* of the papers? My job is like that. Mamie's publicity must be word of mouth...real subtle. The kind that reaches the customers but won't be heard or seen by the home folks who never come to Waikiki. We start with a knowledge of history. The only women who are remembered are whores and saints. Any others who are remembered are freaks : like Mrs. O'Leary because of a cow. Okay, Mamie Stover, thank God, is a famous whore. That is, she *was* a whore. But that was back during the war when everybody was making money in ways they'd just as soon not be reminded of. And Mamie was a successful whore. That word *success* makes everything all right. It's unsuccessful whores who foul up the oldest profession. Okay. We encourage speculation about how many men Mamie took on during the war. Ten thousand? Twenty thousand? It doesn't matter just so it's discussed in thousands. It makes Mamie sound patriotic : like a super USO girl. I found a report in some book that Du Barry had had nine thousand men before she became the king's favorite. I encourage comparison ... Mamie and Du Barry, see? I found that one of the early Popes estimated that twenty-three thousand intercourses were 'normal' for a woman in a lifetime. The Pope and Mamie, see? So we've got Mamie rumors circulating around the world : every tourist hears 'Mamie talk' on the ship or plane coming here. Just to make sure, we grease airline stewardesses and ship personnel, and they mention Mamie to every Able, Baker and Charlie who looks like a prospect for us. But Mamie's picture, just like the Rockefellers', never appears in the papers or on TV. This serves two good purposes. Nobody sees even Mamie's picture without paying, and by keeping her out of the papers and off TV we avoid irritating the Church crowd who own these islands."

Madison said : "So I suppose you and Mamie and Jesus and Monty Whitaker, all of you will regard me with some apprehension?"

Leo Hirshman lighted a cigarette and raised and lowered his thick brows. Madison thought he looked like a physics professor pondering the binomial theorem.

"You pose a problem," Leo said. "None of us knows exactly

how this Church crowd is going to react to all the prestige and publicity of statehood. Mamie Stover standing tall in the statehood issue of *Vacation*..."

Leo paused, manipulated his brows again, lowered his voice. "Just between two old show-business buddies, Jim," he said, "let me say this. You scare the hell out of me. I hope to God you'll look and think and then stop. Find out everything you want to about us. Base a novel on us sometime. But kill this *Vacation* thing for us. You don't need the dough. I'll thank you. My wife and kids will thank you."

"I can't promise that, Leo," Madison said. "But I'll think about it."

Madison picked up a four-page brochure advertising Hotel Mamie Stover. The brochure lay on every table at the Luau.

"Is Mamie's Luau," Madison asked, "the only place in Hawaii, or on the Mainland, where you advertise the hotel?"

"That's right," Leo said. "By word of mouth only, every prospective guest of the hotel hears about it either on the Mainland or *en route* to Hawaii or after he gets here. He comes to Mamie's Luau. Here he sees Mamie and he reads our brochure. If he wants to go to the hotel, he fills out the Guest Application Card, hands it to one of our Hawaiian hostesses. Either Mamie or Monty Whitaker or one of their assistants is here from noon to midnight to confer with prospective hotel guests. To become a guest, an applicant must be interviewed here, and approved. He must understand what the hotel is, sign a release, pay for a week, get his registration papers. No stranger on Maui can approach the hotel."

"The hotel sounds like an A-bomb laboratory," Madison said. "The process sounds like joining the Army."

"It's a very special hotel."

As Madison began reading the brochure, Mamie made her second appearance. She was her full six feet seven inches tall, with spike heels and her gold-blonde hair piled high and topped with a red hibiscus bloom. She wore a high-necked, skin-tight, jet black, shining silk, Chinese dress, split on both sides almost to her hips. Sheer red silk stockings came halfway up her thighs; and as she walked and turned, thigh-skin could be glimpsed above the stockings.

"Doesn't she ever show them more skin?" Madison asked. "A sarong? A bikini?"

"Oh, no," Leo explained. "Public nakedness is too vulgar for Mamie. Our Tahitian dancers expose skin. Mamie is luxurious and wholesome. We promote the hotel as a wholesome retreat where mature adults have fun. Mamie does good, helps people to healthier outlooks. Remember how all the great evangelists have been reformed drunks and fornicators? Well, Mamie is sort of an evangelist. Mamie's hotel is for her just what the Los Angeles temple was for Aimee Semple McPherson. Mamie works to preserve Hawaiian Culture, teaches the Spiritual and Physical Health of the islands. But . . . you mentioned a sarong. A sarong would be wrong for Mamie. A sarong hangs loose around a woman's hips. Mamie, to communicate for maximum impact, needs that beautiful, luxurious, shining silk glued to that million-dollar tail."

While Mamie walked, Madison read the brochure.

The brochure's entire cover was Mamie full-length, with earrings, looking regal, aloof, wholesome and evangelical in the long, graceful Hawaiian dress called a *holoku*. The First Lady of the Islands invited a "carefully selected" and "rigidly restricted" group of "mature, sophisticated" people to be her guests at her "home" on a REAL, REMOTE island. Mamie, in her "home life," was laboring to preserve "Hawaiian Culture" in the Age of Atomic Anxiety. Even her height marked Mamie as "truly Hawaiian in spirit" because the queens and princesses of Old Hawaii had all been six feet tall.

Inside the brochure Madison read:

It was these tall, magnificent Hawaiian princesses, with their zest for living, who captured the hearts of the intrepid white men who braved perilous seas to reach Hawaii in the 19th Century. The proud men who most appreciated these magnifi-

34

cent Hawaiian princesses were Mark Twain, Jack London, Herman Melville, and the gentle Robert Louis Stevenson. Mamie Stover is the spiritual daughter of these remarkable women, trying to preserve their arts and their wholesome, zestful attitudes toward human life.

. . . The Hawaiians were the happiest people on earth. They enjoyed true peace of mind and peace of soul. All but a few of them are gone now: annihilated by Yankee Calvinism and Yankee Materialism. The few who survive, including the personal servants of the last princesses of Hawaii, now live with Mamie Stover in a remote, protected Paradise . . . like Shangri-la.

. . . The Old Hawaiians believed that sexual intercourse is the Beautiful Adornment of Life. Therefore the principal business of each day for both men and women was to strive to make themselves more attractive to the partners they had chosen or would choose. A man, through feats of strength, skill at games, rhythmic movement, or bodily adornment would try to make himself more attractive. A woman each day would strive to learn new secrets of giving sexual delight, and she worked at making herself more attractive through diet, adornment, lotions and perfumes, and graceful, rhythmic movement.

. . . The Hawaiians, in short, believed that the prudent individual, striving for the full life, should conduct himself, discipline his actions, towards the end of sexual prowess, sexual attractiveness, and sexual longevity. Hawaiian princesses boasted, not of riches, or temporal power, or places reserved in Heaven, but of being able to make love zestfully and often at sixty . . . and of being able to give indescribable ecstasy to their partners.

. . . Mamie Stover is one of the most disciplined women on earth. She both practises and preaches discipline. She neither drinks nor smokes. Her food is selected, prepared, and portioned each day by survivors who attended Hawaiian royalty and who understand the relation of diet to sexual prowess and longevity. Mamie and her guests swim each day in live, active water, after which they are massaged by the last Hawaiians who know the ancient Polynesian secrets of oils to keep bodies lithe, youthful and delightful. Mamie has servants versed in both Polynesian and Oriental secrets of aphrodisia; she has one priceless, eighty-year-old servant who has done nothing in all her life but study the effects of delightful stimulants to be released in the air over couches.

. . . Anthropologists tell us that because they so valued sexual delight, the Hawaiians possessed the greatest sexual skills of any people on earth. And it was this which caused the Hawaiians to be exterminated. For the cold, mirthless, Puritanical people who travelled from New England to "Christianize" the Hawaiians possessed no sexual skills and refused to strive to give sexual delight. The Hawaiians were neither "aided" nor "converted." They were dispossessed and exterminated by sexually frustrated Yankee missionaries and Yankee tradesmen. Now Mamie Stover, a transplanted Mississippi belle, is fighting the final battle to save Hawaiian culture from final eradication.

. . . What precious little remains of Hawaiian culture may yet save this tired, bored, all-dressed-up-and-nowhere-to-go, machine-crucified world of the twentieth century. Mamie Stover understands how Mainland society is beset by divorce, sexual frigidity, guilt, alcoholism, delinquency, and frustration. At Hotel Mamie Stover the surviving Hawaiians help their stricken white brothers and sisters. These last Hawaiians are modest, simple people. They cannot tell the world how to make a Better Mouse Trap or a Bigger Bomb. They can tell the world only how men and women can function sexually with the most mutual ecstasy for the longest number of years.

. . . A final word : the magnificent, six-foot-tall Hawaiian princesses, with their prowess and sense of rhythm, could derive and give more sexual pleasure between fifty and sixty than at any other time in their lives. The Hawaiians looked, not to youth, but to maturity for sexual delight, and a woman less than thirty was regarded as a novice more to be instructed than enjoyed. For this reason Hotel Mamie Stover will accept as a guest no woman under twenty-eight and no man under thirty.

. . . Hotel Mamie Stover prefers married couples as guests but it also welcomes single men and women. If you desire to visit the hotel, at rates to be agreed upon, fill out the attached Guest Application Card and hand it to a hostess. Sometime during the evening the hostess will escort you to a private up-stairs lounge here at Mamie's Luau. There you will confer with Mamie or one of her associates.

. . . To Mamie's regret, facilities restrict the guest list to one hundred men and one hundred women.

Madison chuckled at each paragraph, and when he finished reading he laughed heartily.

"Leo," he said, "I have a slogan to suggest. COME TO HOTEL MAMIE STOVER AND FIND PEACE OF MIND, PEACE OF SOUL, AND A PIECE OF TAIL."

"As a matter of fact, Jim," Leo replied, "that is the hotel's slogan, except we express it: PEACE OF MIND, PEACE OF SOUL, AND PEACE OF BODY."

As Mamie left the stage, Leo leaned over the table to Madison and said: "Jim, before I tell Mamie you are here, let me ask you one more favor as an old show-business buddy. Now you know me and Jesus. We're just a couple of hard-working characters trying to get along. We like this business because we're doing *well*. But Mamie's different, and so is Monty Whitaker. Mamie and Monty like to feel they're doing *good* at the hotel. You get what I mean?"

"I believe I do," Madison replied. "It appears to be a new twist on the old story about the missionaries. The missionaries came from New England to do *good* and instead did *well*. Mamie and Monty have already done *well*; now they insist on doing *good*. Is that it?"

"That's it," Leo said. "And you know, what-the-hell, maybe they *are* doing some *good*. In any case, be friendly with them, will you? For an old buddy's sake?"

"I'll try," Madison said.

As we have seen: at this point Leo Hirshman went to Mamie's dressing room and told her of the *Vacation* project and that Madison wanted to see her. Mamie, to gain time to confer with her partners, asked Madison to wait to see her at the hotel. Madison, as we shall see, then went to "an upstairs lounge" at Mamie's Luau to meet Monty Whitaker, manager of Hotel Mamie Stover.

CHAPTER THREE

In which we meet Monty Whitaker,
manager of Hotel Mamie Stover, and
watch him select Elaine Shelby, of
Richmond, Indiana, to be a guest at
the hotel and a prospect for like-sex.

JOHN CHARLES FREMONT "Monty" Whitaker was different
from his partners, Mamie Stover and Jesus Portales. Mamie
and Jesus were born on the wrong side of the tracks. But
Monty was born Anglo, Congregationalist, prosperous and
respected.

His grandfather and father were innkeepers at Waikiki in
the "grand days" before the First World War and between
wars, the days when Waikiki had class and quality, when
Honolulu was strictly segregated, when Yankee trust officers
drew lines and told everybody where to stand and when to sit,
when two hundred whores entertained soldiers and sailors in
a policed area five miles from Waikiki, when no whore ever
saw Waikiki much less walked there, when Waikiki hotels
were for the elegant Few from Philadelphia and Cleveland and
San Francisco and Vancouver and London and Rome and
Berlin.

In those grand days the Whitaker-owned hotel, the graceful,
two-story Lunaliho, was quiet and beautiful, with the whitest
portion of beach and the most dramatic view of Diamond
Head from its terrace. Guests arrived by ship for a month or
a season, and the Whitakers were respected men, proud of
being efficient inn-keepers.

When Monty Whitaker went to Stanford University in

1937 to take his degree in business administration, the Depression had hurt Waikiki. His family was feeling the pinch. But his future appeared secure. He'd join his father at the Lunaliho and one day succeed him as host.

But the war brought masses of soldiers and sailors to Waikiki. It brought Mamie Stover. And on an August morning in 1945, Captain J. C. Fremont Whitaker, USAF, was one of twenty-three Americans who actually saw the flash at Hiroshima. He was in the weather plane which led the *Enola Gay* to the target.

So when Monty Whitaker returned to the Lunaliho in 1946, he didn't feel that his future was secure. Elegant hotels were gone, along with elegant guests. Waikiki had to adapt itself for the masses. The Lunaliho's four perfectly-situated acres were too valuable for a two-story hotel. Costs were high, and Waikiki had to undergo Vertical Development. Hotels had to tower twelve stories to be "economically feasible," and to fill them, most of the guests had to be coupon people on packaged tours, in a hurry, on a budget, hard to entertain.

Experts in Mass Handling were *en route* to Waikiki: Kaiser and Hilton and Sheraton. They would adapt Waikiki to the Jet Age. The Whitakers could adapt or sell out. Either way they could not avoid being rich, for their forty-nine-year lease on the four best acres at Waikiki was worth a capital gain of two million dollars.

Thinking about Henry Kaiser depressed Monty Whitaker almost as much as thinking about the Bomb. In nightmares he saw unending walls of pre-set concrete, every wall painted shocking pink. He saw concrete monoliths towering higher than the bomb cloud, each monolith honeycombed with tiny concrete cubicles, each cubicle fitted with tight-fit plumbing, aluminium-and-glass windows, standard aluminium furniture, and TV-in-every-cubicle.

When he thought about Conrad Hilton, Monty Whitaker got drunk. He stayed drunk a year. When he sobered up he made a disastrous marriage. He became the third husband of Annalee Johnston.

39

Annalee was a descendant of missionaries. She was rich, little-boned, barren, tormented, beautiful, and sexually overwhelming. Two good men had married her, and each left her within a year. Other men, including Jim Madison before his marriage, had had her. But no husband could impregnate her, no lover could comfort her, and she remained unbearably tense and restless. Monty Whitaker needed to prove something with her : that he could give her what other men couldn't. He married her and ran off with her on his boat to Samoa and Tahiti.

When Jim Madison read about this marriage, he was breakfasting on his *lanai* with his wife, Emily. He shook his head sadly.

"Poor Monty Whitaker!" he thought. "He survived Hiroshima, but he'll never survive Annalee." He looked across the table at Emily and thanked God that he was married to a comfortable Englishwoman who impregnated easily, achieved orgasm readily, spoke softly, moved gracefully, and knew what-the-hell she wanted.

Monty Whitaker, on his boat with Annalee, was searching for an island like the one his grandfather found, but no such island exists any more and he knew it didn't. He learned that with Annalee he couldn't succeed where other men failed: he couldn't relieve her restlessness. He could copulate with her, time and again, as other men had done, but he couldn't reach her. They could achieve orgasm together, but they couldn't achieve union against the dark.

He left her. He signed papers delivering the Lunaliho to the wreckers and the site to the Vertical Experts. He collected his portion of the two million dollars. Then he got drunk again. Mamie Stover sobered him up. He couldn't unite with Mamie either, but he could incorporate with her. Mamie knew how to give him purpose. She showed him plans for a new sort of hotel. She sold him an interest, made him the host.

Monty Whitaker knew Jim Madison. They had never talked, but they knew each other. They belonged to the same country club after the war, but Monty left the club when he took up with Mamie.

While Madison was in the Aphrodisia Room watching Mamie, Monty was upstairs interviewing prospects for the hotel. Jesus telephoned him about the *Vacation* project, and Monty told Jesus to send Madison to him. Madison found him at his desk in his Chinese-modern office with a Japanese secretary. Monty was now thirty-five. He dressed as his father and grandfather dressed: white linen, white shoes, white shirt with French cuffs, soft burgundy necktie. His hair was crew-cut, and he was tanned, inclined to stockiness. His mother, who died when he was five, was sandy-haired, blue-eyed Irish, and he had her hair and eyes. Some people said his face was weaker than his father's and grandfather's. But he pulled an oar on the Stanford crew. He was at Hiroshima. He could fight the sea alone at night in a small sailboat. Madison didn't think his face looked weak. It was the square face of Kentish forebears; in fact, considering his experience and position, Madison thought Monty Whitaker looked curiously confident.

One wall of the office held a floor plan of the hotel. The other walls held color-photographs of the hotel grounds, maps, and an assembly of snapshots: Stanford, the Air Force, Whitakers at the defunct Lunaliho, boats in Samoa and Tahiti. The secretary bowed out as the two men shook hands and sat down.

"Well, Jim," Monty said, "I suppose I must defend myself?"

"Why? I'm not here to attack you."

"You're here to make fun of me. You expect to write that the heir of the 'graceful old Lunaliho' has betrayed his heritage and is now running a funny whorehouse with trash like Mamie and Jesus."

"Well, are you runing a funny whorehouse with trash?"

"No, I'm not."

"You want to show me you're not? You want to co-operate with me on the *Vacation* story?"

Monty Whitaker paused, then answered: "Do we have any

choice? If we refuse, you'll write a story anyway, won't you?"

"Probably. I'd have to use second-hand information."

"Then let's say that we will co-operate with you. We don't want to, but we will. We can't hope much longer to avoid print. In five years we've entertained 43,861 guests, and they've gone home to Canada, Australia, England and the United States and sent their neighbors to us. Some guests have been here three times and now stay a month. Out here, of course, the Press has given us the silent treatment, which is best for everybody. But with Hawaii becoming a state, we're bound to be written about. This puts us in a dilemma. Since we're proud of what we're doing, we'd like to be written about. On the other hand we must fear local landowner reaction. We operate the Luau and the Hotel on short-term leases, so we must fear anything our landlords won't like. Particularly, we must fear satiric appraisal. We don't want to be damaged just to provide a smart-aleck story."

"And you think I'll write a smart-aleck story?"

"I'm afraid so, Jim. I know your books. You laugh or cry at everything."

Madison's eyes narrowed with irony. He said: "But shouldn't I laugh at Hotel Mamie Stover? Or cry? Orderly, hard-working middle-class people spending their savings to follow a rich whore off to a 'remote tropical island' to learn 'secrets of sexual prowess and sexual longevity'? What can anybody do at that except laugh or cry?"

Madison expected Monty to wince, but he didn't. Instead, he smiled compassionately.

"The hotel isn't laughable," Monty explained. "Nor is it a development to cry about. What's wrong with sexual prowess and sexual longevity? Are they good or evil? Are you *for* or against? I'm *for* them. We have fun at the hotel. It may be the last place on earth where mature people can have fun. But it isn't a funny place, or a sad place. It's a good place."

Madison shifted in his chair. He couldn't decide whether Monty annoyed him or amused him.

"One other point, Jim," Monty continued. "You refer

42

callously to Mamie as a rich whore. On reflection you'll realize you're being unfair. Years ago, in a confused time, when she was very young, Mamie *was* a whore. It's true that we've built the nightclub and the hotel on people coming to see Mamie because she *was* a whore, but how long does a woman who was a whore remain a whore? All her life? In the Bible harlots become saints. Mamie's not yet a saint, but she's no whore. She's good, and she's helping many people."

Madison resorted to his perplexed smile.

"Monty," he said, "will I be irreverent if I mention that in this process of helping people, Mamie uses spirit gum to stick her silk *muumuu* to her tail?"

"Of course she uses spirit gum," Monty said. "Do you know a better substance? That's just a dramatic means to an end."

Madison opened and closed his mouth. Then he managed: "You mean, she sticks the *muumuu* to her tail so she can attract more people to the hotel so she can help them?"

"Sure," Monty said. "It sounds anomalous. But that's the way it works. There are strange processes in this world, Jim. Strange causes, strange effects."

Madison surrendered. "Okay, Monty," he said, "let's quit talking about it until after I've seen this anomalous place. Prospective guests are waiting. Suppose you summon one. Introduce me as your assistant. Let me hear what you say."

"I can't let you sit with us, Jim," Monty said. "Prospects expect to talk with me alone. But I'll switch on this inter-com. You go in the next room with my secretary. I want you to hear every word."

Elaine Shelby entered Monty Whitaker's office. She was a compact brunette, five foot two, a hundred and ten pounds. She wore a white sports dress, a pigeon's-blood coral necklace, tan shoes, and carried a tan straw handbag. She wasn't striking, but she'd be judged neat and nice-looking by most street-corner appraisers. Her most attractive features were below her knees: fleshy, curvy calves, delicate ankles and trim, small feet. Her eyes were dark, and she gave an impression of alertness. She was bare-headed, and her short, dark hair framed an intelligent, freshly tanned face. As she sat down she crossed her legs and adjusted her skirt, for she knew where her best features were. She found her cigarettes and accepted a light from Monty before he sat down and scanned a card she had filled in.

"Miss . . . Shelby," Monty said, looking at the application card, "you are single, twenty-eight, from Richmond, Indiana? You are, is this true, a lawyer?"

She expected this. "Yes. I have a law degree from the University of Indiana. I'm employed to do legal research for a law firm in Richmond. You know, the lady wearing the heavy glasses back there among all those books."

"It's been some time since we had a lady lawyer at the hotel," Monty said. He looked back at the card. "You arrived four days ago by ship, you have ten more days before you return to the Mainland via Pan-Am. Why do you think you might like to go to Hotel Mamie Stover?"

"Curiosity, I suppose. I heard talk on the ship. I read your brochure. It sounds completely insane. But . . . well, my trip has been disappointing thus far. So I'd like to hear your particulars."

"I'll be as brief as possible," Monty said. "If or when I mention a condition that's unacceptable to you, stop me so we can save time."

She nodded, pulling on her cigarette. Monty's appearance surprised her. From the brochure and Mamie's past, she had expected the hotel manager to look like Jesus Portales. Instead, Monty looked like the chairman of the entertainment committee of the Richmond, Indiana, Country Club.

"First, money," Monty said. "The shortest visit we permit is one week. One week costs two hundred and eighty dollars for a single guest, five hundred dollars for a couple. Payable in advance, returnable in full if you decide to leave within twenty-four hours after arrival. Returnable in full if, at any time during your stay, we ask you to leave. This covers everything, including round trip transportation from Waikiki. No tips, no extras, in fact, you can't spend money at the hotel."

When she didn't object, Monty continued: "Neither tobacco nor alcoholic beverage in any form is permitted. Is that acceptable to you?"

"Obviously I smoke," Elaine replied. "I like a drink sometimes. But I can take them or leave them."

"The native Hawaiians didn't have tobacco or distilled spirits," Monty replied. "Mamie believes smoking and drinking make people less attractive to one another."

Without commitment, Elaine Shelby nodded.

Monty moved to his wall photographs and floor plans. He used a pointer. "The hotel is on the finest, whitest, cleanest beach on earth. But the hotel is not luxurious. It's colorful, adequate, modern, but not luxurious. The buildings are about as comfortable as first-class Army barracks. In fact, women who served in the WACs tell us that coming to the hotel is, in many ways, like WAC boot training. For women, we are a combination of athletic, beauty, dance and conversation club. Mamie Stover is now devoting her life to: *making people more attractive to one another*. This is her aim, her life purpose—she believes that the survival of modern society depends on it, so this is what the hotel is for. You may sleep in a small, semi-private room, but Mamie hopes you will prefer to sleep in the barracks-like common room. Our plumbing is modern, but there are no private facilities. No TV, no radio, no newspapers, no magazines. For reading, we offer Mamie's own tracts. Actually, you'll have little time to read; most of your time is taken up with the hotel's program. You can't order food. You eat, cafeteria-style, the special diet, and there are tables on the beach with special fruits and juice-mixtures."

Monty paused. "Have I lost you yet?"

"Not completely."

"Then perhaps this will lose you. And please don't be offended. On arrival, every guest enters the Shedding Room. You shed every bit of clothing, every bit of jewelry, every personal item including lipstick and toothbrush. The only item you keep is eye glasses, if you use them. You are examined by the house doctors. Hawaiian nurses give you a prophylactic scrubbing from head to toe. You are steamed, then stretched out on a stone slab and scrubbed with special suds and brushes."

Elaine Shelby laughed. "Good Lord," she said. "I've always been considered overly fastidious. It's shocking to learn that I require all that to become clean."

"I'll explain," Monty said. "You know that Mamie's early training was in a brothel. So the program for the hotel is a marriage of two experiences. First, it's what a remarkable woman learned as a prostitute; and second, it's what the Hawaiian people learned through tragedy. The old Hawaiians were free of venereal infection. Syphilis and gonorrhoea, introduced here by white men, all but exterminated the Hawaiians. So the surviving Hawaiians find it psychologically impossible to relax with white people unless the white people have been cleansed in this drastic manner. The cleansing also helps Mamie relax, and it enables the hotel to *positively guarantee* every guest against infection."

"Well," Elaine Shelby said, "let's see if I get the picture. I've been shorn, medically probed, steamed, scrubbed, and I'm lying on my bunk naked, clutching my reading glasses. What happens next?"

"Nothing . . . for half an hour," Monty said. "You lie there and continue to shed. You shed attitudes, and slowly you begin feeling the spirit of the hotel. Then the masseuses lead you to the massage tables, and for an hour they give you Hawaiian massage with secret oils and lotions and perfumes. The hairdressers arrange your hair and adorn it with flowers. A fresh, colorful, perfumed silk *muumuu* is slipped on you. A fresh *lei* is put around your neck. And there you are! A new, different, more lovely woman, ready for a week of civilized living."

"Am I barefooted?"

"Naturally. You are bare all over except for the flowers and the *muumuu*. For variety you change to the wrap-arounds, the silk squares which the Hawaiian women wrap round your hips and your breasts when you don't wear a *muumuu*. All clothing is supplied by the hotel: fresh and sweet-smelling. You'll begin at once to move more gracefully, with more rhythm. You'll begin to feel more beautiful, relaxed and friendly, so you'll *become* more beautiful, relaxed and friendly."

Elaine Shelby said: "Let's hear about sex. Is there a man, similarly shorn, relaxed and friendly, lying in the bunk next to me?"

"Definitely not," Monty said. He used his pointer. "See . . . here is the women's wing of the hotel. Over here is the men's wing. The sexes are strictly segregated. Moreover, the different wings are guarded. No woman can visit the men's wing, and vice versa. Men and women meet twice a day, on the beach, in the gardens, for conversation and dancing. If they choose, they meet in rendezvous lounges which are in this third, entirely separate, area. These rendezvous lounges are for advanced conversation . . . and how far it advances is at the discretion of the woman. When a woman considers advancement, she is both protected and advised."

"Protected? How?"

"She is protected against fear," Monty replied. He leaned towards her and became fervent. "Miss Shelby, no woman can be really attractive to a man unless she feels protected. She must be protected against the three medieval fears: fear of discovery, infection, pregnancy. Mamie Stover feels that these old fears have no place in civilized society, so we have banished the three fears. If you choose to visit a rendezvous lounge, we have an ingenious arrangement which makes it impossible for any other guest, any other human being except your partner, to know about it. The man can enter the lounge only if you unlock the door. With this arrangement, and with our medical staff, we *absolutely guarantee* every woman guest against discovery, disease and pregnancy. Hotel Mamie Stover is the only institution on earth which does this."

"And advice? You say women are also advised. How?"

Monty Whitaker smiled for the first time. To this point with Elaine Shelby, perhaps because he knew Jim Madison was listening, perhaps because Elaine Shelby was a lawyer, Monty had been unusually serious and fervent. Now he smiled, laid aside his pointer, and sat down.

"Miss Shelby," he said, "advice for women at Hotel Mamie Stover is as plentiful as salt air. Doctors advise you. Hawaiian women advise you. Mamie's tracts advise you. Mamie's tape recordings advise you. Mamie's films advise you. Most helpful of all, you attend Mamie's seminars which have saved hundreds of marriages and helped countless women."

Elaine Shelby snuffed out her cigarette. "No one in Richmond, Indiana, will ever believe this," she said. "What sort of men will I meet?"

Monty replied: "You will meet and practice elementary conversation with a hundred white men and several Hawaiian men. Perhaps a dozen of the white men will be single; the rest married. Most visitors to Hawaii are couples or single women. Mature, single, white men who can spend two hundred and eighty dollars and who are acceptable guests for us are not plentiful. Every white man will be your approximate equal: physically, financially, intellectually, socially. The Hawaiian men, of course, have nothing, financially. They are part of our athletic staff. They teach our men guests boar hunting, war canoeing, wrestling and jungle fighting. Every man, white or Hawaiian, sits down at least once under a palm tree, alone with every woman. Every man and woman will have been instructed by Mamie in elementary conversation. At every *tête-à-tête*, both the man and the woman will strive to be *more attractive to one another*."

Monty Whitaker had presented his particulars. He leaned back in his chair.

"That's a brief summary," he said. "There is more . . . much more. But do you begin to feel what we're trying to do?"

"I think I'm getting the picture. You present it well."

"Would you like to consider it until tomorrow?"

48

"I'm afraid to do that," she said. "I might be sane tomorrow. I'd better pay now and announce that if I'm accepted, I'm ready to be shorn, advised and protected."

"Good," Monty said. "Just three more questions. Are you in good health as far as you know?"

"Yes."

"Any rashes, scars, or unsightly discolorations on your body?"

"No."

"Are you, or have you ever been accused of being, a sexual deviate?"

"No," Elaine Shelby replied. "But that brings me to an embarrassing handicap I have been waiting to reveal, and which may disqualify me. You see . . . I'm a virgin."

Monty Whitaker coughed, swallowed hard.

"Really?" Then, after a silence: "It doesn't disqualify you. It isn't unprecedented for us. But . . . since our minimum age is twenty-eight, well, we don't get many. We don't anticipate it, so we don't cover it in our questionnaire. It's a problem for us. You'll need personal interviews with Mamie. The Hawaiians can't help you: your condition would perplex them, even anger them. They wouldn't get mad at you, but they'd have a very low opinion of the males in Richmond, Indiana."

"I don't want to cause any regional or racial discord," Elaine Shelby said. "But . . . well, that's the way it is. As I told you, I may be overly fastidious. My mother was a fanatic: she was always warning me to postpone sex until after marriage. I postponed . . . and postponed . . . and got too many college degrees . . . and bingo! The calendar announced I was twenty-eight."

Elaine Shelby noticed that Monty Whitaker was gazing intently at her best features. She reached to pull her skirt down. But then . . . well, she didn't tug at the skirt; she only smoothed it and left it where it was.

She said: "Don't let my condition upset you, Mr. Whitaker. It isn't as bad as an unsightly discoloration, is it?"

"Oh, no," Monty said. "It's just . . . well, it's goddam surprising. Maybe it makes me a little mad at somebody. It's another indictment of our outworn society. It's more reason for us to work *harder* at the hotel. After all, you're a very attractive woman . . . as well as a lawyer."

"Well . . ." she said, "do I make the team?"

Monty rose and walked around the desk to her.

"Certainly, you do. My secretary will fill out your papers. Our white station wagon will pick you up at your Waikiki hotel at 2 P.M. tomorrow. Bring *absolutely nothing* except your reading glasses. You'll fly in our plane along with several other guests. As a matter of fact, I'll be piloting the plane tomorrow."

"Splendid," she said. She gave him her hand. "Maybe we can practice a little elementary conversation under a palm tree after I've been shorn and massaged."

As Elaine Shelby left, Jim Madison returned to Monty's office.

"You surprise me, Monty," he said. "After processing thousands of guests, can't you spot a virgin?"

"Apparently not," Monty admitted. He was having trouble dismissing Elaine Shelby. "Do you suppose she's lying?"

"Why should she lie?" Madison answered. "A maidenhead is something a twenty-eight-year-old woman apologizes for now."

"It's a damn shame," Monty said.

"Mamie will help her, of course?"

"Sure, Mamie'll help her," Monty insisted. "Elaine Shelby is an attractive, decent, warm, intelligent, free American woman. Why should she have to live in that condition?"

Madison looked at his watch and decided not to try to answer.

"It's nearly midnight," Madison said. "I'll reserve further comment. I must get some sleep if I'm to do much 'boar hunting, war canoeing, wrestling and jungle fighting.' Not to mention elementary or advanced conversation."

"You want to hear more? There's still time for me to interview a couple for you. Couples have different questions."

"No, thanks," Madison said. "I'll meet your married men and women at the hotel. I can imagine how attractive you are to a bored couple. You give them enforced separate holidays. You exploit one of the disasters of the century: that wives and husbands spend too much time together. You offer them a little blessed freedom-from-one-another. I'll be ready tomorrow. Don't tell any guest what I'm doing. I'll be your hundredth male guest, and for *Vacation's* five million readers I'll take your full program. I'll even study Mamie's tracts and implore her to lead me toward 'sexual prowess' and 'sexual longevity.' "

"I'll send a car for you."

"Thanks."

Madison left the office, then stepped back inside the door and asked: "Monty, do you suppose *you* might find time to do Elaine Shelby some good?"

Monty opened his mouth, but Madison didn't wait for his reply.

CHAPTER FOUR

In which we discover that *en route*
to Hawaii Elaine Shelby, while prospecting for like-sex, suffered "unsightly discolorations" which nearly
disqualified her for Hotel Mamie

IN HER concrete-and-aluminium cubicle on the twelfth floor
of her Waikiki hotel, Elaine Shelby was taking a bath. The
cast iron tub with the baked enamel finish was too small to
lie in, but Elaine was sitting and splashing. She had slept
late because twice during the night she woke up, and was a
long time getting back to sleep. She felt lonely and disturbed,
and was considering cancelling her trip to Hotel Mamie
Stover.

It's just too obvious, she thought. Too vulgar, too indecent.
It pretends to be nothing but a sex resort. One goes there
with nothing but sex in mind.

Elaine knew better than to have nothing but sex in mind.
Her mother taught her better; for her mother was principal
of a high school and knew the folly of sex risk. Elaine's father
and brother taught her better by example : her father was a
salesman who cheated his family by wasting his earnings on
sex "on the road"; her brother, two years younger than she,
knocked up a girl when he was eighteen.

In high school Elaine played kissing games. In college,
where she was known for her sense of humor, she necked
discreetly. But she bridled at risk, and after she was employed
by a law firm she learned how wise she had been. In case after

52

case she encountered the shabby consequences of reckless sex.

Each year since she was fifteen, with her intelligence and will to independence, she had advanced farther ahead of the youths she might have married. Now, at twenty-eight, she had concluded that, having missed marriage in her early twenties, her next hopeful season would arrive in four or five years when she might become the second wife of some middle-aged man. Meanwhile . . .

I just can't visit Mamie Stover, she thought. I can't join a party of hunters at a sexual Happy Hunting Ground. I'll stay here where the hunting is discreet. This hotel is famous, and everything costs only twenty-five dollars a day. I've met pleasant couples and lone women. They want me for beach parties, for sightseeing, for meals, for bridge. Perhaps here I'll meet the man with whom I can attempt some advanced conversation. How about an authentic Chinese dinner tonight, with pleasant, decent people, followed by a few rubbers of bridge?

That "few rubbers of bridge" was a jolting thought. Elaine grimaced as she stepped out of the tub and began towelling herself. Imagine a woman spending her savings to travel to romantic Waikiki to play bridge! She was besieged again by all the impulses which had caused her to travel to Hawaii and which had directed her to Mamie's Luau.

In twelve years she'd be forty. She wanted love-sex. She wanted a lover to want love-sex with her. She had always hoped that when she had love-sex it would be leavened with the prospect of marriage and would therefore be discreet. But back in Indiana she had decided that she was now willing to consider risk. . . .

"In the absence of a lover," she quipped to herself, "I'm at last ready to consider a liker."

But she knew that at home she could not allow herself to be deflowered by a liker. So the honest purpose of her trip to Hawaii was to seek the right liker. In short, although she had never heard the expression, Elaine had travelled to Waikiki as a prospect for like-sex.

She had thought she might meet her man and her moment aboard ship. She had read that women surrender themselves more readily aboard ship than anywhere else, and she had pictured shipboard routine as something like Monty Whitaker described the program at Hotel Mamie Stover. She assumed the swimming pools and bars were places where male and female hunters practiced elementary conversation, and cabins were rendezvous lounges for possible advanced conversation.

But her five-day voyage had been a disaster. In her inexperience she had neglected to pay the extra fare which would have secured a private cabin. On the crowded, cabin-class ship she shared with a schoolteacher named Mabel Albright from Pine Bluff, Arkansas. And to the dismay of Mabel Albright, Elaine was so seasick the first two days she couldn't leave the cabin. By the second day Mabel could no longer contain her frustration.

"My God, Elaine," Mabel said, "I don't want to be a bitch, but can't you see what you're doing to me! I've saved for five years to make this trip. I'm here for one reason : men. I've got men waiting for me. But they've got wives in their cabins, and they can't meet me except in *my* cabin. And I don't want to make love in the upper bunk while you're sick in the lower. Can't you possibly lie in a deck chair? Please, for God's sake !"

Late the second afternoon Elaine fought the horrible dizziness, let Mabel dress her, and struggled to stand. She couldn't.

"I'm sorry, Mabel," she said. "God knows I'm sorry. But I must lie here. I can't possibly reach the deck."

"Then you must get in the upper bunk," Mabel said.

Elaine didn't realize what Mabel meant, but with Mabel's help she struggled into the upper bunk. And that evening was the most humiliating of her life. In misery and shame she lay in the upper bunk while Mabel entertained in the lower. Elaine had never overheard a sexual union, but now she heard unions between a rutting woman and two truant husbands.

The moaning and groaning, the sharp, brutal words, the

urgings and entreaties, the muffled scream, the triumphant slapping of buttocks . . . Elaine heard it all as she wept for the human race. Most shameful to her: even sick and despairing, she felt her own desire mount with each thrust and moan.

Next day Elaine and Mabel didn't look at one another. Mabel made one speech.

"Elaine," she said, "I'm sorry . . . but can't you understand that this is a once-in-a-lifetime excursion for me? That each of these precious days of freedom has a number on it? That I don't have an hour to waste? That in just seventeen more days I'll be Miss Mabel Albright, the English teacher, back in Pine Bluff, Arkansas?"

By the third afternoon Elaine was able to sit on deck, weak and queasy. Mabel told her to examine the keyhole before she attempted to enter the cabin. A small x in lipstick would signify that Mabel was occupied, the door was bolted, and Elaine could not enter, so she was not to insert her key and bother the occupants with "key noise." If the red x was not visible, Mabel was unoccupied or out and the door was not bolted. Elaine spent most of two afternoons and evenings on deck, making periodic trips to her cabin door, waiting for the red x to disappear.

Mabel made one concession: midnight was curfew. She agreed not to be "occupied" a moment after midnight, so that Elaine could sleep.

On the fifth day Elaine came alive. She experienced that blessed return from the grave, that wondrous feeling of well-being, which the gods sometimes grant suddenly to those who have nearly died from seasickness. As she swam in the pool and drank rum cocktails, she regained her sense of humor. She even felt charitable towards Mabel and the studs who had given her what she was looking for.

The ship had entered the sensuous latitudes, and the moon rose for the last-night-out celebration before arrival in Honolulu. Elaine's ego climbed a notch each time a man noticed her and deplored: "Where have *you* been all this voyage,

honey? I should have found you before tonight. But there's
still tonight!"

Mabel became generous.

"Tonight's your night, honey," she said. "You get what
you've been missing. You use the cabin at least half the time.
Just remember to put the x on the keyhole and bolt the door."

Elaine thanked her, then avoided Mabel and the hunters
who, as the evening wore on, concentrated on one side of
the swimming pool. Elaine danced. She drank. But she was
careful to stay with the conservative passengers.

By 11 P.M., however, the conservatives had all gone to their
quarters against the 7 A.M. arrival day breakfast on deck.
Elaine went to her cabin door, noted the red x and assumed
she had another hour to wait. She stood at the rail for a few
minutes, felt the awesome vastness, then came back to the
pool and accepted charily a seat among the hunters. She was
more spectator than joiner, but she wanted to meet people and
she was curious. Illness had cost her four-fifths of her long-
planned first ocean voyage : this was the last of it. She smiled
off the jokes, all of which emphasized that this was last-night-
out, that the ship was near the islands, and that only a female
iceberg could consider sleep without having "been initiated"
and "welcomed a stranger."

Elaine noticed nods exchanged, after which men and
women disappeared. She understood that she was now among
the restless and the reckless, the people who had become
sexually excited at entering romantic seas, the hungry husbands and wives who, with another drink or the right partner,
might risk adultery. Elaine could sense the hunger around her,
but remembering Mabel and her studs, she resolved to resist.

She allowed herself to be dragged up to "dance" with
several men, but each "dance" was no more than a half-
drunken shuffle to semi-privacy, a clutch, a kiss, and a proposition. She submitted to the kiss, but she rejected each probing
tongue, each squeeze of a breast. She shook her head and
moved away at each whispered : "Let's go to your cabin,
baby? What's your number?"

Elaine would never go with any man to *that* cabin. She couldn't take a man to that door, make sure that Mabel's x had been erased, mark an x of her own, then duplicate one of Mabel's performances. And her moment would never come during a drunken revel. She was determined to avoid conduct which could be interpreted, even by a drunken man, as a promise. Once she wondered whether her presence among the hunters, after midnight on last-night-out, was a sexual commitment. She decided it wasn't.

About 1 A.M. Elaine walked along B-deck towards her cabin, which opened on to B-deck forward. She met two or three people, but the deck was almost abandoned, in shadows, with many of the lights out. She stopped at her door, above which a light was burning. Since Mabel's x had been erased she began fumbling in her bag for her key. Suddenly she noticed that a man had come up behind her and was standing perhaps fifteen feet from her. Apparently he had followed her, expected to overtake her as she opened her door and force his way in with her. Luckily, she thought, she had seen him in time. She snapped her bag shut, stepped back to the center of the deck. The man was one she had "danced" with, but she didn't know his name.

"If you don't move on," she said, "I'll just have to go for help."

He sprang at her. He grabbed her wrist, jerked her to her cabin door, turned the knob, opened the door, jerked her inside, and bolted the door. The cabin was in dim light : the reading lamp was burning over her tidy upper bunk. Mabel was gone, her bunk rumpled. Startled and angry, Elaine faced the intruder. How could her door have been unlocked?

"No," she said. "I told you no at the pool. Please get out."

He chuckled. He was tall, in his early thirties. He weighed a great deal more than Elaine. He had been drinking all evening.

"You thought your door was locked, didn't you, baby? I bet it was unlocked. You lost. I won."

57

"Please get out."

He shook his head. "We played a game. I captured you. Surely you know what happens when a man captures a woman in the islands on last-night-out?"

"I didn't play any game with you."

"Oh, yes you did," he insisted, nodding his head vigorously. "Didn't you dance with me in the dark after midnight on last-night-out?"

"Yes, but . . ."

He kept nodding.

"Yes, you danced with me. Except that wasn't dancing and you knew it. That was just feeling-and-propositioning. And while I was feeling for you you let me kiss you, didn't you?"

"You kissed me. But I wouldn't take a sexual kiss. I pulled away from you."

He laughed. "Baby, what sort of kiss after midnight on last-night-out is not a sexual kiss? I kissed you and you took it." He held out his left hand and flexed his fingers. "And while I kissed you, you let me squeeze that pretty right teat of yours with this very hand. Didn't you?"

"I didn't let you. You tried it . . . and I pulled away."

"Pulling away doesn't mean a thing. Just standard operating procedure, as we say in the service. You played with me after midnight on last-night-out. I stalked you. I captured you. Now you're gonna 'welcome a stranger.' "

He grabbed her and pulled her into Mabel's rumpled bunk; good-naturedly he wrestled with her. Only gradually, and with surprise, did he realize that her resistance was determined. He rested, holding her and facing her in the dim light. He wasn't a rapist: he was a captain in the US Air Force.

"What's the matter, baby?" he asked. "Don't you want to welcome this stranger? This is the islands and last-night-out. I'm just going to give you what you need."

Breathing heavily, Elaine glared into his eyes. She hated that smug assertion: "I'm going to give you what you need, baby!" She had heard studs say that to Mabel, and now Elaine could think of nothing else but that she was on Mabel's sex-soiled sheets, with a stud on top of her, perhaps one of Mabel's, saying the same words to her, determined to enact the same scene with the same sound effects.

Elaine lunged against his grasp, twisting and squirming, and they fought silently for a long round, punishing the bed as Elaine had heard Mabel and her studs punish it. His good nature receded and he began to get rough with her. Since his heavy body pinioned her left arm and he held her right wrist in his right hand, his left hand was free. Methodically, piece by piece, he ripped off her dress, her brassière, her pants, until she was naked except for her stockings. He paused again to catch his breath.

"Goddam you!" he gasped. "Don't you know the rules! I've got you naked under me on last-night out. Do you think I'm gonna let you get away without initiating you? I'd be laughed out of the Officers' Club."

She opened her mouth as though she considered screaming.

"Go ahead, scream," he said. "You'll amuse the ship. Everybody who hears you will laugh, and say: 'There's one getting something she really needed!' Everybody's pulling for *me*, not you. How do you think I knew your door was unlocked? Your girl friend helped me capture you."

What he said horrified Elaine. Not even her legal training had prepared her for it. The horror was that he was ninety-nine per cent correct. Under the circumstances her predicament was not tragic, not even provably illegal. Just comic. A situation for leers and jokes. Suddenly she felt inadequate, foolish, ashamed, alone and unprotected. She wanted to cry, and had he assailed her at that instant she would have surrendered. But now, by the chemistry of sex, he hated her, and he delayed his assault to taunt her.

"Now I'm gonna *really* initiate you, you little bitch! When you get through welcoming this stranger . . ."

He plunged at her, trying to assist with his left hand.

He reacted like a runner who learns in mid-race that the prize has been doubled. "You'll never forget me," he gasped. "I'll always be the guy who chopped you!"

Had she been even partially aroused he would have made it. But the maidenhead, in more ways than one, cost him the race. It raised his temperature too high, and he lost ignobly. With a groan of humiliation he spent himself.

He lay cursing. Now he deserved to be laughed out of the Officers' Club! Elaine lay unmoving, sensing he was still dangerous. Victorious, he'd be harmless: he'd slap her across her buttocks triumphantly as she had heard Mabel's victors do. But humiliated? In a different way she feared him more than ever. When he rolled over she saw that now he despised her.

"You still got your goddam cherry," he said. "I missed it, like a clumsy sophomore in a back seat . . . but you got something to remember me by. You'll have a blue tail and blue teats. You can look at yourself in the mirror for days and remember I did it to you."

He was on his feet, partially composed. He started to leave the cabin when he whirled and with his open palm slapped her across the face.

"There's a blue cheek to remember me by, too."

Still towelling herself, Elaine shuddered at the recollection. She examined her body in the mirror, manipulating and feeling each breast, then turning to look at her buttocks. She remembered Monty Whitaker's question whether she bore any "unsightly discolorations." A day earlier she couldn't have answered no, but now only shadows of the bruises remained. She had spent her first four days in Waikiki erasing the bruises of a "romantic" voyage. Nevertheless, last evening she had gone to Mamie's Luau. She had listened to love drums, seen love dances, drunk Passion Punch, then filled out an application card, joked with Monty Whitaker, written a check for almost her last two hundred and eighty dollars, and agreed to go to Hotel Mamie Stover!

She marvelled at her conduct. My Lord, she thought, haven't I had enough? For a twenty-eight-year-old lady lawyer with a maidenhead-by-grace-of-male-failure haven't I

had enough sexual adventure for one trip? First, Mabel
Albright educating me in the sounds of zestful sex? Then an
assailant with a cave-man point of view? What a brutal, unreasoning, obscene force sex is! Why don't I forget it and look
at mountains and play bridge?

As she combed her hair, Elaine examined her face in the
mirror. Would zestful sex add luster to her hair, sparkle to her
eyes, color to her cheeks, warmth to her lips? And was there
a man somewhere who could make her want it? Was there a
man who would persuade her to do the giving, and not claim
that he was giving her "what she needed"?

Couldn't sex be zestful without being obscene? Potent without being cruel? Vigorous and still tender? Healthily animal
without being brutal? Not in shame, but in health and exhilar-
ation and triumph.

It was questions like these which caused Elaine Shelby to
listen with interest as Monty Whitaker described a place where
women have privacy without marking a lipstick x on the keyhole, where doors are unlocked only by women to men of their
choice, where advances are at the woman's discretion . . . and
where there is freedom from medieval fears.

Elaine Shelby had spent much of her adult life among law
books and in a small apartment in a community whose rules
she had to respect. She hadn't come to Hawaii to look at
mountains or play bridge. She had come on a sexual excursion.
Her first nine days had been shameful, but revealing . . .
perhaps maturing.

She had nine more days.

She tossed the wet towel across the rim of the tub. When the
white station wagon from Hotel Mamie Stover came to her
at 2 P.M., she'd be downstairs, waiting.

Nothing so frustrates hotel managements as "premature
check-outs." They cost the hotel money; they are embarrassing; they require explanations to bankers and boards of
directors; and no amount of explanation can dispel the
suspicion that the guest is departing earlier than he expected to

61

either because he is disappointed with the hotel or because he has found something better.

Hotel Mamie Stover causes ten thousand premature check-outs a year from Waikiki hotels! Two hundred a week! Around thirty a day! Ten per cent of the total guest list! A loss of almost three million dollars a year! The managements of each of the five larger hotels each day must face five or six guests who are sorry but "something has come up." Instead of staying on for another week or ten days as they had planned, they are leaving at once. Each departing guest then twists the knife. "And by the way," he adds, "where I'm going I won't be needing any baggage. So will you please store my bags in your check room for me?"

This makes for a high incidence of ulcers among Waikiki hotel managers. It makes for noisy board meetings, and for almost as alarming a turnover in managers as in guests.

Elaine Shelby was a case in point.

She had entered her world-famous Waikiki hotel with a reservation for two weeks. She had paid the required four days in advance. She wasn't bound to stay the other days. But why shouldn't she? She was in the best room of the best hotel? She had a private bath, a private TV set, and a private view of Diamond Head?

After she finished breakfast, Elaine walked straight to the manager's desk. He had noticed her when she checked in, with a bruised cheek from a too-deep dive in the ship's swimming pool. He saw that she was now recovered and looked extra-ordinarily well. She was the sort of guest he enjoyed having : trim, neat, fastidious, nice legs, obviously intelligent . . . the smart, successful, young American professional woman.

"I'm sorry," she said, "but I expect to check out after lunch. You see, well, I've met some people who have invited me to their home. I won't be needing much baggage, so will you please store it? I'll pick it up on my way to the airport."

The manager began counting ten before replying. He clenched and unclenched his fist, laid his open palm on the desk. She was announcing the loss of at least two hundred and eighty dollars to him. "Goddam," he thought, "her, too, huh! Even this one's rutting." He looked deep into her blue eyes which held steady, then dropped.

Looking at Elaine, the manager recalled speeches he had made to distress meetings of the Waikiki Hotel Association.

"Goddam it, gentlemen," he told the association, "I'm tired of smiling and nodding my head while premature checkouts inform me they are taking gold out of my teeth to deliver to Mamie Stover, Monty Whitaker and Jesus Portales. We are losing ten per cent off the top of our gross because we refuse to fight fire with fire. We don't provide enough zest at Waikiki! We got no program except a half-assed effort to teach big-assed women to hula. When men and women travel thousands of miles to the Paradise of the Pacific, goddam it, a percentage of them hope to find . . . well, *something* sexual. Our hotel rooms are *too* private! We must fight Mamie on her own terms!"

Everybody agreed Mamie should be fought, everybody made suggestions, but every suggestion for a program was rejected by the Church crowd as distasteful if not downright indecent. Each year Mamie and Monty and Jesus leached away more gold, and now a virgin was standing before the manager of the most famous Waikiki hotel asking him, please, to mind her baggage while she took her money to Mamie and sought zest.

"Of course, Miss Shelby," the manager said. He yearned to make a crude remark, but he was too disciplined.

"The porter will store your baggage," he said. "Our residents in this Paradise of the Pacific are so hospitable that, of course, we lose many guests to them. Have a pleasant visit."

He gave her a disciplined smile as she departed to prepare for the arrival of the white station wagon.

CHAPTER FIVE

In which we meet Tom and Sally
Rogers, of Eugene, Oregon; Bob and
Mary Ferrell, of Eau Claire, Wiscon-
sin; Doctor Ralph Anderson, of
Sioux Falls, South Dakota; Becky
Sanders, of Bethesda, Maryland; and
fly with them from Honolulu to
Hotel Mamie Stover along with
Elaine Shelby, Jim Madison, Monty
Whitaker, Jesus Portales and Leo
Hirshman.

THE WHITE STATION WAGON, at 1:40 P.M., came first to Jim
Madison's hilltop house. He saw it coming, from his desk
where he had been working since 7 A.M.

James Monroe Madison was a disciplined writer. He wrote
seven mornings a week, 5 A.M. until noon, and he devoted
much of the rest of each day to organizing, reading, research-
ing and corresponding. The first hour after 5 A.M. he worked
in bed, scribbling notes, rearranging his thoughts, focusing
his mind on whatever he was writing. He worked by clock
and by calendar. Last evening he had been at Mamie's Luau.
Today he was going to Hotel Mamie Stover for a week. Seven
days after he returned, he'd air-mail a ten-thousand-word
story to *Vacation* magazine on: Mamie Stover—First Lady
of the Islands. He'd be paid ten thousand dollars by a publisher who could re-sell the story at a profit in a competitive
market.

Jim Madison didn't think of himself as writing for "the ages," or when he "felt inspired." He wrote for people living now, about people living now, and he strove to communicate clearly and rapidly with readers who lived in a rapidly moving world.

Madison was a poor husband by modern standards, an even poorer father. He loved his wife and children, he provided for them well, but he was away from them four or five months a year, and when he was at home he had limited time for them. He was an acceptable husband only to a wife who agrees that home and family are primarily her responsibility; that a husband and father's primary responsibility must be his work. Madison's American first wife rebelled and divorced him. His second wife, whom he met in London while he was in the Navy, accepted him.

While he was a Southerner from generations of Southerners, after college he had forsaken the South. He decided not to write about either old Southerners or new Southerners, but about Americans in the age of the diaspora . . . the airplane years when Americans, through war and its aftermath, occupied the earth.

Here are excerpts from Madison's notes after his visit to Mamie's Luau:

THE QUESTION : Why do 37 per cent of all visitors to Hawaii dine at least once at Mamie's Luau?

PARTIAL ANSWERS : They are curious about Mamie : they want to see her, hear about her, think about her. World has always rewarded erotic female appearance : today's rewards, with mass communications and press agencies, higher than ever. Mamie one of most erotic-looking women on earth. She's in perfect position to exploit "sexual disappointment" at "romantic Waikiki" which has now become crowded, sexless and Un-romantic. Also : Mamie's reputation for being rich whore great financial asset rather than liability. Why? Because an erotic reputation is even more saleable today than an erotic appearance. Middle-class wives, far from boycotting a whore, will pay to look at her IF she has sold it for a fortune.

IMPORTANT : Sexuality far from sole reason for nightclub's

65

success. Probably best eating place in Hawaii. Other food-sellers make racket of "luau." Operate on principle: douse 'em with enough cheap rum and they won't notice cheap fish, cheaper pork. Mamie, Monty and Jesus too smart for this. Top-grade, well-prepared food plus customer-flattering service . . . by Japanese of course . . . Japanese masquerading as Polynesians. Entertainment fast-paced. Idea of drums smart. Hawaiian music saccharine, cloying after three days. Drums and flutes always been erotic instruments. Smart to discard hula. Hula, on a stage, boring after first day.

QUESTION NOW: Why do 10 per cent of visitors transfer from Waikiki hotels to Mamie's hotel?

The white station wagon stopped in Madison's driveway. The driver was a young Japanese woman in white skirt, white blouse, white beret, like an airline stewardess. Madison heard her speaking with his housekeeper in Japanese. He could have bet the driver would be Japanese, because a smart Japanese woman knows how to put white strangers at ease.

Madison was ready to travel, or more accurately, he was unready. He wore sandals, socks, brief underwear, orange-colored linen slacks, a blue silk sports shirt. He put on his sun glasses, no hat or cap, and in one shirt pocket were his reading glasses, in the other was a fold of Kleenex. In his pocket he had not a penny, no wallet, no keys, no credit cards, and he carried nothing, not even a pencil or a toothbrush.

"Very smart business," Madison thought. "Mamie demands that her guests travel without impediment. Starts everybody off on a carefree right foot."

In Japan Madison had stopped at inns where kimonos, razors, new toothbrushes are supplied to guests. Whatever a guest wears during the day is laundered at night, and a man needs only a briefcase to travel. Mamie travelled in Japan after the war, and appropriated the plan.

The driver invited Madison into the front seat and they sped towards Waikiki. He noted that the car was a new Chrysler with red leather upholstery, immaculate inside and out. Nowhere on the car or on the blouse or cap of the driver was there any commercial lettering. At a Waikiki hotel entrance the driver curbed the car. Since it was time for afternoon sightseeing tours to begin, perhaps a hundred tourists were standing there, waiting for buses. But among them the driver spotted the seven she was to pick up. Since she had never seen them, how could she identify them? Because each one, without his knowledge, had been photographed at Mamie's Luau, his photograph had been attached to his application card, and the driver had memorized names and faces. She got out of the car and approached each one, smiled, called him or her by name, and assembled them. She introduced each guest to every other guest, rattling off names as though each one was a celebrity which each of the others was privileged to meet.

The seven consisted of two couples, one lone man, and two lone women. The couples were Tom and Sally Rogers, of Eugene, Oregon, and Bob and Mary Ferrell, of Eau Claire, Wisconsin. The lone man was Ralph Anderson, of Sioux Falls, South Dakota. The remaining women were Becky Sanders, of Bethesda, Maryland, and Elaine Shelby.

These seven, with the driver and Madison, made nine passengers for the fifteen-minute drive to the airport. The car had three seats. The driver seated each one by name. On the back seat: Tom Rogers, Becky Sanders, Bob Ferrell. On the middle seat: Mary Ferrell, Ralph Anderson, Sally Rogers. On the front seat: the driver, Jim Madison, Elaine Shelby.

"More smart management," Madison noted. "Even this first car ride has been planned."

It had the planned effect. Four of these people, like Elaine Shelby, had had second thoughts about going to Hotel Mamie Stover. They had become apprehensive as to associates. Will the crowd be the sort of people one wishes to be seen with? Is this a mischievous house-party-for-broadminded-adults? Or is it indecency with the wrong crowd?

Now apprehension gave way to delight. One needed only look to his right and left to see that he was the beneficiary of smart selection. Everybody looked nice, educated, prosperous, attractive, decent. Everybody smelled good. Everybody smiled and relaxed, enjoyed the smart car, the smart driver, the sweet-smelling ginger flowers along the way, the sensuous air, the prospect of adventure in worthy company.

Elaine Shelby looked at Madison and relaxed. Watching his eyes as he smiled, feeling his thigh against hers, she guessed he was gentle and intelligent. She glanced at the other lone man. *Doctor* Ralph Anderson. Perhaps forty : tall, lean-faced, dark-visaged, somewhat somber, with kind deep-brown eyes and graceful hands. He didn't look tired, travelled and cultured like Madison, he was more the provincial, rough-hewn, self-made country man. But he might be even more interesting. One of Elaine's complaints against life was that most of her male associates, like her father, were inferior to her. Now she was holidaying with two lone men both of whom she guessed were her superiors. She liked this.

The sight of Becky Sanders, the other lone woman, reassured Elaine. Becky, thirty-four, was a government worker, a willowy ash-blonde. Becky was the sort of woman one is surprised to see travelling alone : one expects her to be protected by a strapping, aggressive husband. Becky was not Mabel Albright : she wouldn't be clutching at moments. But she was at ease with men. Elaine noted how easily, with her low voice, she was entertaining Tom Rogers and Bob Ferrell in the back seat.

Tom Rogers, forty-four, was a man's man. He'd had two years at Oregon University, and had captained his National Guard infantry company in the Second War. He was tall, tough, virile. He liked to hunt and fish with men. He was a partner in a road construction company in Eugene, Oregon, and he liked his home, his two tall sons, and his wife Sally . . . who thought she looked like Mary Astor. Instead of flying to Hawaii, Tom would have preferred a trip to the woods, but Sally, thirty-nine, insisted that every woman deserves to visit Waikiki before her fortieth birthday. So he had humored her. But four days at Waikiki had demonstrated what Tom already knew : that a man and woman who have been workers and who've been married twenty years can't holiday together without help. They can't spend two weeks "just looking at things" and trying to entertain one another. They must travel in parties and have programs. So Tom Rogers felt grateful to Mamie for rescuing him. Now he could fish and hunt while Sally flirted around, talked about sex, and got herself tanned, massaged, and perfumed. He knew Sally, what she'd do and what she wouldn't do, and he wanted her to enjoy her excursion and leave him free to capture a fighting fish and shoot a fighting boar. If an Hawaiian girl shook her tail at him the night after he killed the boar . . . well, he'd cross that bridge when he got to it. Sex, he thought, was something a man did on impulse, quickly contemplated, quickly accomplished, quickly forgotten. A man didn't devote time to it.

Bob Ferrell, thirty-four, was not so self-assured. Stocky, light-haired, blue-eyed, he was the only man present who had not gone to college. Yet he was the husband of red-haired, brown-eyed Mary, thirty, who was the only beautiful woman in the car. For a secret reason Bob and Mary Ferrell were indebted to Mamie Stover. Unlike these other travellers, they had visited Mamie before . . . two years ago. Their first visit had been successful, and now Bob and Mary were going back hoping for more success.

From seventeen Bob Ferrell had worked himself to death, up through grocery stores, to part-ownership of a wholesale grocery firm in Eau Claire, Wisconsin. Flat feet excused him from the second war. At twenty-six, when he had one retail store, he became Mary's slave when she consented to drop the idea of college and marry him. A small-grocer's daughter, she had been the prettiest girl in her high-school class.

The first six years of marriage had been proud years for Bob. They had also been undignified years. For Mary wanted babies and she couldn't get pregnant. The doctors, examined her, then him. There was nothing "wrong" with Mary, so Bob was the inadequate partner. He was subjected to all the clinical and social indignities a man must bear if he possesses a beauty whom he cannot get with child.

69

The doctors said to him : "You are working too hard, Bob. You are too tense, too strained, too uneasy. You are too anxious to please your beautiful wife. You obviously get too nervous during love-play. So your sex act is inadequate; you leave your wife unsatisfied, nervous . . . that's why she gets these headaches. You need to go away on a holiday. Forget work. Take it easy. Lie on a beach. Breathe salt air. Make love to your wife when you're relaxed and rested. If you'll just do that for a couple of weeks, maybe you'll hear some good news."

The doctors said to one another : "The poor bastard! The gods cheated him. He's a victim of infantilism. He's half normal size; his ejaculate is weak; his seminal stream has no force. And with all these handicaps he had to marry a beauty who dominates him, who holds him in an inferior position, and he collapses the minute he begins congress with her. The poor sonofabitch!"

In this predicament Bob and Mary came to Hawaii. They went to Mamie's Luau, then to Hotel Mamie Stover. They conferred separately with Mamie, and Mamie wrought the miracle. Whatever she did must have helped, because six weeks after he and Mary returned to Wisconsin everybody was congratulating Bob for "coming through." The baby was a girl in Bob's image.

Then Mary wanted a second child. For a year they had been working at it, but no good news had been heard. Now they were back to see Mamie. For Mamie was the one physician under whose care Bob could accomplish miracles.

By the time the station wagon reached the airport, the eight guests, including Madison, had become a party. Excepting Madison, each guest felt that he had left an impersonal hotel where he was only a guest with a room number, and now he was *en route* to a private estate as a participating member of a party.

The station wagon didn't stop at the air terminal. It proceeded to a white-frame building which served Hotel Mamie Stover as a depot. Two freshly painted, all-white airplanes, without markings, were parked there. As the station wagon halted, two other station wagons, with similar drivers and parties, stopped. Each driver herded her party on to the plane. There were none of the delays of commercial travel.

Madison noted that the plane was a rebuilt Air Force C-46. He remembered that Mamie, during the war, married an Air Force major whose death made Mamie a government pensioner. Madison recalled also that Monty was a lieutenant-colonel in the Air Force Reserve. So Madison didn't doubt that Monty had bought "surplus aircraft" at five per cent of cost.

The C-46, a troop carrier, is the most spacious of two-engined aircraft. Mamie had designed the interior. It was in island colors, and there were no lined-up seats. Instead the interior was divided into three lounges with chairs, semi-circular couches and service tables, where each load of guests could be seated as a party. The car driver became the stewardess, and again she seated her charges by name. Madison sat between Mary Ferrell and Becky Sanders, Elaine between Ralph Anderson and Tom Rogers, and Bob Ferrell was between Becky and Sally Rogers.

The airplane took off at once, flying east, holding a course out in the bay for scenic effect. All of Honolulu from beach to mountains was visible and the parties crowded together at the windows. The plane passed Waikiki, Diamond Head, then Koko Head.

Since this scenery was familiar to him, Madison moved to the right side of the plane and studied members of his party as they looked out of the windows. He wanted to understand each of them. Who was he or she? What did he want or need? What would he find? As Madison regarded each one he made these mental notes :

ELAINE SHELBY. She's prettier than I imagined last night while I listened to her interview with Monty. Neat feet, delicate ankles, curvy legs. She's not sorry for herself; she can make jokes. Women like her are "good sports" but they usually lack a compelling sex urge. Without prospects for love-and-

71

marriage she wants to lose her maidenhead on excursion. She wants to try like-sex. Will she really try it? Or will she carry the burden of virginity back to Indiana?

BOB AND MARY FERRELL. What are they doing here! They say they visited Mamie two years ago. Why! Mary's beautiful in a limited-culture way, but petulant, selfish. Bob's insecure, constantly turning towards Mary to see if she approves what he's saying. Surely he doesn't want like-sex with other women : he beats himself to death in love-sex with her. So why would he risk her, then and now, at Hotel Mamie Stover where he can't watch her? Isn't he afraid that while he's boar hunting Mary is sampling like-sex? Does he want a pair of horns?

BECKY SANDERS. She's not dramatically beautiful like Mary Ferrell but lovely, soft, low-voiced, the girl from the small Southern town who came to Washington. Now sad . . . heavy heart. What was it Aristotle asked in his *Problems*? "Why are those that are melancholy so addicted to venery?" . . . Becky's the libidinous woman in this group : with the right man her back scorches the sheet. But she's had love-sex. So why is she looking for like-sex?

RALPH ANDERSON, M.D. Has wife and children back in South Dakota. Now drives Cadillac. Pillar of community, but gets restless now and then, yearns for something he feels he missed during long fight from penury. Grabbing holiday from routine. Sad-faced, like Lincoln. Which one of these women will he have like-sex with? All of them?

TOM AND SALLY ROGERS. Tom remembers those good old days of war and barracks life. He wants Sally to run and play and leave him alone while he kills something, and wrestles, and rides horseback, and grabs off a piece of some long-haired Hawaiian girl. Tom *knows* Sally is incapable of adultery . . . but he could be wrong. Sally's worked hard to keep herself thin, tried to read books and go to lectures and *develop herself* while raising family. She looks juicy for forty or thereabouts. Her sex with Tom has lost zest, and *just one more time* she'd like to feel that electricity run down the backs of her legs. Will Mamie show her how to find it?

As the island of Oahu receded on the left side of the airplane, the island of Molokai appeared on the right. Molokai is sparsely settled, with cliffs falling off to the sea, and it means one thing to the tourist: spectacular misery. On a peninsula on the north shore of Molokai, walled off from the rest of the island by a cliff, is the leper colony. The aeroplane, at fifteen hundred feet, held just north of the leper colony so the passengers could see the buildings and moving figures. As Madison's party shifted from the left windows to the right, every pair of lips tightened.

"This is a mistake," Madison thought. "Why doesn't Mamie direct the plane to fly south of Molokai so the leper colony can't be seen? The effect here is like passing a funeral procession *en route* to a rendezvous."

"Is that it?" Sally Rogers asked.

"That's it," the stewardess replied.

Madison watched the faces as they clouded. Mary Ferrell pulled back from the window as though she feared fifteen hundred feet might be too close.

"A dramatic contrast," Madison thought. "In this airplane . . . perfumed health . . . not even a discoloration allowed. Down there . . . loathsome mutilation." Then Madison realized why the plane flew this course. "More of Mamie's calculation. She orders the plane over the leper colony. She knows that passing a funeral procession *en route* to a rendezvous doesn't diminish the libido. By saddening and frightening, its heightens licentiousness, makes partners cling to one another."

As proof, Madison noted that the leper colony was aiding the integration of his party. The members instinctively formed tighter groups. Madison felt Mary Ferrell and Becky Sanders pressing closer to him.

"How many are down there?" Elaine asked.

"About the same number you'll see at Hotel Mamie Stover," Madison answered.

"How awful," Becky said.

"Awful, yes," Ralph Anderson said. "But leprosy has served the human race well. From the Bible to Ben-Hur, it's been the spectacular misery which fascinates people. Leprosy

73

has provided purpose for people who must sacrifice themselves to the relief of spectacular misery. Now D.D.S. cures leprosy. Every leper down there is cured or being cured. He suffers no physical pain, he can't infect anybody. In a few years, no more lepers. So perhaps we should shed a tear for all the leper-helpers who'll be robbed of purpose . . . and who'll prostrate themselves on psychiatric couches."

"What a horrible thing to say!" Becky said. "You're a doctor, yet you seem to feel that curing leprosy is not good."

"I welcome the cure," Ralph said. "I'm simply pointing out that the eradication of leprosy may mean more people without purpose. Therefore, more people deranged."

"There'll be new miseries to take leprosy's place," Tom Rogers said.

"I doubt it," Ralph replied. "The new miseries are mental. Mental miseries can't be seen. A mutilated mind is not spectacular like a mutilated body. No leper-helper can find purpose in helping a schizophrenic."

As the leper colony receded, the stewardess deposited a thermos on the table and began passing out cups of juice. Each one tasted it sheepishly. Elaine broke the tension.

"Well, here I go, mother," she sighed. "I'm sure it's reeking with aphrodisiacs."

Everybody laughed, and the stewardess knelt by the table and explained.

"This is your first of Mamie's drinks. The formula is old and secret. It's what we call *mobani*, a friendship drink. Mo-BONN-ie, pronounced slowly and meaningfully. Each of you must use this drink to toast each of your companions. You look directly at him or her, say *mobani*, and then drink. Now let's all do it."

Madison thought of a Rotary Club meeting, with strangers trying to call one another by first names.

"What does *mobani* mean?" Sally asked.

"It's a most important word at our hotel," the stewardess replied. "It means 'my friend,' but it means more. It means 'my friend-whom-I-value-and-who-values-me.' Perhaps it's

74

what the Communists hoped the word 'comrade' would mean. *Mobani* says to the person you speak it to : I think you're important, and I believe you think I'm important, too. Whenever you address a fellow guest at the hotel, you must use it and try to mean it. You must try to value the person you are talking to."

The word was pronounced several times around the table, and the juice made everybody friendlier.

"We *ought* to feel friendlier," Madison thought, "this juice is kava. The Polynesians call it the marriage drink. It's the crushed root of the pepper plant, with ambergris, musk and honey added. They say it makes a man 'demanding,' a woman 'eager.' "

"In about five minutes," the stewardess said, "we will fly over the hotel, then land. At this moment we are at the one spot in Hawaii where four islands are visible from this altitude. We have just flown over Molokai. Ahead is Maui and the hotel. On our near right is Lanai, and to our far right, in the distance, you can see the small island of Kahoolawe. So that you won't be frightened at the hotel, you must understand Kahoolawe. It's a target island, completely uninhabited, the only living things on it are wild goats and some small burrowing animals. Hawaii's biggest business, bigger than tourism or pineapple or sugar cane, is war. We practice war constantly, and while you are at the hotel, almost every day, sometimes at night, you will hear distant bombing, or shelling, or rockets being exploded on Kahoolawe. You need not be frightened, we hope you will not be disturbed. Just remember that no human beings are dying, only a few goats and small, burrowing things. Our business at Hotel Mamie Stover is *mobani* . . . friendship. Kahoolawe accompanies us with the sounds of war."

The party became as silent as when moving over the leper colony. The only one who gazed at Kahoolawe was the citizen-soldier, Tom Rogers.

"Anything ever drop close to the hotel? I'm an old infantryman, I know these fly boys. They can miss by miles."

"We've had no serious misses," the stewardess answered. "A few times we've seen explosions in the water between the hotel and Kahoolawe. Perhaps they were misses. Perhaps they were planned underwater explosions. But the Air Force assures us we are safe."

"This one I didn't anticipate," Madison thought. "But I should have. Who knows better than Mamie the effect of the sounds of war on genitals? In every city that was bombed during the war the birth rate leaped upward. I remember how I used to cling to Emily in England trying to ignore the buzz bombs." Somewhere Madison remembered the line: "The sounds of war double our claims on each other."

The plane approached Maui on a course which would have brought it over the coast two miles north of the hotel. But three hundred yards off the beach, the plane turned, flew parallel to the beach, and brought the hotel in view at an altitude of five hundred feet. Each passenger felt the sensations of remoteness, isolation, apartness. Knowing that her guests' first view of the hotel would be from the air, Mamie had designed it for aerial-view effectiveness.

The "hotel" was forty cultivated acres surrounded by green. Seaward was green water with white beach and white wavecaps. Landward was green trees, green foliage, green sugar cane, rising in terraces from white beach to green mountain. The buildings gave no vertical impression. All lines appeared horizontal. No building was higher than the palm trees around it, and each building appeared molded to the earth. The buildings were of wood, with dark green roofs, Chinese red walls, and yellow lacquered paper screens and windows. Every foot of the area had been gardened: low, manicured hedges, brilliant, tropical flowers, all in Oriental patterns.

Becky said: "It looks just like the travel posters of Tahiti."

"That's what I'd call the real Hawaii," Sally said.

Mary said: "It doesn't look like Waikiki, does it?"

When you look at Waikiki from the ocean or from the air, you see a busy portion of a city. The hotels tower, the lines are vertical. When you look at Hotel Mamie Stover you see an

76

isolated garden, and the horizontal buildings are part of the garden.

Madison thought: "It's Japanese. Mamie must have spent hours flying at a thousand feet over the Inland Sea.

The airplane landed three miles from the hotel, at. an abandoned Marine Corps base. Waiting were a white bus and a white station wagon. Madison was the last guest to leave the plane. As he approached the exit, the door to the pilots' cabin opened and out stepped Monty, Jesus and Leo Hirshman.

"Who's minding the store back at Waikiki?" Madison asked.

"We came along to make sure you see everything, Mr. Madison," Jesus replied. "It isn't every week we're visited by a writer for *Vacation* Magazine."

Madison joined them in the station wagon for the ride to the hotel. The flight from Honolulu had taken twenty-eight minutes, and the time was now 3 P.M. Twenty minutes later, after being briefly examined by a Japanese-American doctor, Madison joined Mamie on the beach.

CHAPTER SIX

In which we hear Mamie explain
how the Rendezvous Lounges are
used for like-sex.

"... FORGIVE ME FOR imposing all this clinical treatment on you. We are the only hotel which requires a woman, the moment she crosses the threshold, to crawl up on a medical examination table. After which you spend hours getting steamed, scrubbed, massaged, rested, perfumed and dressed. But I'm sure you understand why we do it. We not only guarantee that you are clean and healthy, we also guarantee that everybody you touch is as clean and healthy as you are. So we have rigid routines from which no one, no guest, no colonist, not even me, is exempt."

Ten women sat before Mamie. They wore *muumuus* and sandals and they were sipping angel water. It's a mixture of orange flower water, rose water, myrtle water, and spirits of musk and ambergris. The Polynesians use angel water to make women "lusty and compliant." Each woman wore also a *lei* and a flower in her hair. Four of them were Elaine Shelby, Becky Sanders, Mary Ferrell and Sally Rogers. It was now 5 P.M. Mamie had just returned from her swim with Madison. She wore a blue *muumuu*, she was barefooted, and her gold-blonde hair hung loosely on her shoulders. She was standing before her guests in a blue-walled room which looked out on the ocean and which was now lighted by two electric torches. An Hawaiian woman, wearing a *muumuu*, sat near Mamie, facing the guests. Her name was Likelike. She was thirty years old, and she had had two years at the University of Hawaii.

Mamie referred to employees of the hotel as "colonists." They were either the "last surviving Hawaiians" or Japanese-Americans pretending to be Hawaiians, and all of them lived in the hotel grounds. Mamie had designed the "hotel," with its many acres and buildings, as her home and as an Hawaiian colony to be visited by paying guests.

"I won't labor the subject of hygiene," Mamie continued. "But the colonists will force you to consider hygiene every hour you are here. In their stories about the romance of the islands the writers evade such realities as lice, sweat, filth, measles, tuberculosis, and seven varieties of venereal infection. With my background you'll understand that I became a fanatic on hygiene or I wouldn't be alive. So I'll close the subject by stating that I'm still a fanatic, that ours is the cleanest hotel on earth, that we have the cleanest colonists and guests, and that, considering our size, we are the world's largest users of every solution and device that cleans, protects, lubricates, assists, deodorizes and perfumes the human body. Hygiene is not requested of our colonists and guests; it is imposed on them. Anyone who objects is dismissed. Perhaps with your backgrounds you can't appreciate how difficult it is to create a truly healthy colony in the islands. But, believe me, it is very difficult, very expensive, and we are very proud to have achieved it."

As Mamie talked she still felt the unease which had caused her to falter against the undertow. Ordinarily these explanations to arriving guests were made by Likelike. Mamie was making them today because Madison's coming had focused a camera on her. She felt that her life was being added up so, as preparation for her discussions with Madison, she was reviewing her achievements.

"Our hygiene relieves us all of the fear of infection," Mamie went on. "Then comes that greater fear: pregnancy. A poet has called it 'the cruellest fear that shadows the human heart.' It has spread more terror than the fear of death. The scientist who relieves women of this fear will be a greater benefactor than the one who finds the cure for cancer. I'm proud to say that one of our doctors, Dr. Mordecai Ezekiel, uses Hotel Mamie Stover as the laboratory in which he seeks the cheap contraceptive pill the world is praying for. If our hotel has no other achievement, our support of Dr. Ezekiel justifies our existence. Meanwhile, until he finds the pill, we try to protect you and the Hawaiians. Each of you who wanted it has been fitted with a pessary. This, with our other measures, will make you ninety-nine per cent safe. To make you a hundred per cent safe, we practice abortion."

'But isn't abortion illegal here?" Elaine asked.

"At present it is. But Dr. Ezekiel tells us that this is just like Prohibition, that the United States will soon legalize abortion. Abortion is not illegal on the high seas on a vessel not of U.S. registry. So we give you this guarantee. If you follow our instructions as to contraception, if nevertheless you find yourself pregnant, if there is reasonable certainty that you became pregnant here, then you telephone me from your home, and at no expense to you we will fly you back to Maui and give you a legal, professionally performed abortion. We are the only hotel on earth which respects its guests enough to do this."

"How many abortions have you performed?" Elaine asked.

"For guests, about forty. For the Hawaiians, considerably more, since the Hawaiian women are Dr. Ezekiel's guinea pigs. Of twenty thousand women who have visited us in five years, about forty have asked for abortions and we have performed them. Each abortion has cost us about fifteen hundred dollars because where the woman is employed we make up the salary she loses. No woman has suffered any ill effect. And my greatest satisfactions have come from the gratitude of these women. There is no gratitude as sincere as that of woman who has been rescued from a pregnancy disaster."

"But what if a woman, for her own reasons, simply cannot submit to an abortion?" Sally Rogers asked.

"She should discipline herself," Mamie replied. "Perhaps she shouldn't have come here. If she's here, perhaps she should accept our money back offer and leave. If she stays, perhaps she should only observe and not participate. If she participates she'll be disappointing to her partner because she's afraid and can't relax. So for everybody's sake she should abstain if she's single, restrict herself to her husband if she has one. If pregnancy would be a disaster for her, and if she can't manage it if it comes, how can she afford the slightest risk?"

This caused the women to become more reflective.

"Let's understand each other," Mamie said. "You are here on an excursion to observe, perhaps to participate briefly in the life that the Hawaiians and I live. The Hawaiians and I are disciplined and we respect discipline. In sex perhaps we appear undisciplined to some of you because, in addition to love-sex, we engage in like-sex. This like-sex has nothing to do with love or marriage or parenthood: it's no more and no less than a zestful activity of the flesh.

"Many visitors have come to Hawaii since 1820. Very few of them have come offering love and marriage. Virtually all of the men and many of the women have come wanting what we sometimes call excursion-sex. Excursion-sex may be either money-sex or like-sex. There is no more money-sex in Hawaii, but with excursionists the Hawaiians and I still engage in like-sex. I'm personally experienced only in money-sex and like-sex. Thousands of men have wanted money-sex with me. Others have wanted like-sex. None has offered me love-sex. So I now engage in like-sex.

"The Hawaiians and I invite you to participate in like-sex. But we don't urge you. If you have disciplines which restrain you to observation only, we respect them. In fact, we respect your disciplines so much that whether you participate or not, and to what degree, is something that only you need know."

The interest quickened. The women knew Mamie was about to explain the rendezvous lounges.

"At this point," Mamie said, "I hope you are beginning to understand the *design* of Hotel Mamie Stover. Our purpose is to make you sexually free for one week in your life. Whether you are married or single, our plan enables you to hunt men

81

and be hunted in a free, erotic environment. We enable you to consider sexual intercourse with many men, to discuss sex with many men in our garden and on the beach, to discuss sex further with a few men in a private lounge, and, if you so decide, to engage in sexual intercourse with a man or men of your choice completely free from all fear. Our hygiene frees you from the fear of infection. Our contraception and abortion free you from the fear of pregnancy. And our rendezvous lounges are a unique device to free you from the fear of *critical knowledge* ... of anybody learning what you do who might object or criticize you."

The women exhibited noticeable degrees of excitement. Sally Rogers, in a red *muumuu*, was flushed with excitement. Elaine Shelby, also in red, was not flushed but she seemed intensely curious. Becky Sanders, in soft blue with her ash-blonde hair, was quietly interested. Mary Ferrell looked lush, with her dramatic coloring . . . dark red hair, large brown eyes, long lashes, and a yellow *muumuu*. But having heard Mamie before, her face was impassive.

"First," Mamie said, "you will recall what you were told at Waikiki. Our guests are segregated. No male guest *ever* enters the women's area, and vice versa. Women guests never spend nights with men guests or have meals with them. There is no communication *whatsoever* between the men's area and the women's area The men are busy with their program for attractiveness, freedom and potency. You are busy with beauty culture, swimming and sunbathing, dance and exercise routines, massages and hair styling, dressing and perfuming, and instruction in advanced and physical conversation. For thirteen hours each day, from midnight until 1 P.M., no woman guests sees or communicates with a man guest."

"What about messengers?" Sally asked. "Can my husband send me a note to meet him?"

"No," Mamie replied. "That would be restrictive. All communications must be person-to-person during the general meetings: from 1 to 2:30 P.M. and from 7 P.M. until midnight. These meetings are in the garden and the beach. This evening you will all attend your first general meeting. Likelike will escort you to the garden and help you begin conversation."

Likelike held up a chart for Mamie.

"Most of you," Mamie said, "have already noticed the four buildings which house the rendezvous lounges. They are the only two-story buildings on the property. You have noted that there are no windows on the ground floors, this is because the ground floors are given over to the maids and to two secret passageways: the men's and the women's. All lounges are on the second floor. Each lounge has two entrances: one from the women's passageway, one from the men's. There is a stairway to each entrance. Now note this feature. No one can reach a rendezvous building from any general area, so no man and woman can go to a rendezvous together; they must go separately. The only way you can reach the rendezvous buildings is through this enclosed, secret passageway which you enter from the women's barracks. The only way for a man to reach a rendezvous building is through a similar passage from the men's barracks." Mamie pointed out the buildings and passageways.

"I'll take you as an example, Miss Shelby," Mamie said. "This evening you go to the garden with Likelike. She introduces you to a number of men. Some of them you dismiss with a friendly greeting. You decide at sight that you couldn't like them enough to have sex with them. Other men interest you. You walk with them in the garden, converse with them, perhaps dance for them on the beach. With one of them you decide to go to a rendezvous to discuss the possibility of like-sex. Likelike will have given you a lounge number. You whisper the time and the number to your prospective partner, and at some time before the rendezvous you return to the women's sector to make yourself even more attractive. You walk to the Carnival Room, which is in the women's barracks at the entrance to the secret passage. In the Carnival Room you will finds several types of disguise. There are robes to cover your entire body, masks to cover all of your head. If you like, you can dress so that no woman seeing you in the passage can recognize you. You walk to your lounge number and find the door open. You enter, lock your door, arrange the lights.

"Your prospective partner in like-sex arrives at his entrance and rings. You go to his door and use the device which permits you to see him but he can't see you. You recognize him, admit him, then re-bolt the door. The two of you then converse further ... what we call advanced conversation. You decide whether you want like-sex. We also refer to like-sex as physical conversation.

"If you decide you don't want the man, or if he decides he doesn't want you, the two of you drink a *mobani* toast and part as friends. If the decision is mutually favorable, you proceed from advanced conversation to physical conversation. You stay as long as you like, remembering only that all lounges must be vacated by midnight. When he leaves, you bolt his door. Then you put on your disguise, return to the Carnival Room, where you replace the disguise, and no one knows you made the trip except you and the man you met."

"Doesn't Likelike know?" Elaine asked.

"She isn't curious enough to remember. She knows only that she assigned you a lounge and a time. She doesn't know whether you went there, or whom you met, or what you did. And what makes you completely safe is this: Likelike and all the other Hawaiians are your friends. They want you to find delight. As you walk towards a rendezvous always remind yourself that the Hawaiians want you to 'touch Heaven.' No guest at this hotel has even been hurt by an Hawaiian. The Hawaiians are on your side."

Becky Sanders had a question. "But why must we get a number from Likelike? Why don't you handle it like some resorts handle *cabanas*? Why don't you assign a woman a lounge when she arrives and it's hers as long as she's here?"

Mamie shook her head. "That would restrict freedom. If a woman kept one lounge all the time, a man who had been with her could stand in the men's passageway and see whether another man entered. No woman ever uses the same lounge for a successive rendezvous. Every man is told this. And surely,

Miss Sanders, you don't imagine that all our lounges, like *cabanas*, are alike! Like-sex is not always successful but it needn't be monotonous. Your Hawaiian friends know how to keep it from getting monotonous. In order to learn what the Hawaiians know, we study new methods for giving sexual delight. We study this in the women's area where we have tracts, recordings, films and seminars. The lounges are our laboratories where we practice what we've learned. Some lounges are elementary; others are more advanced."

Elaine Shelby laughed aloud. The other women smiled. Mamie smiled, as did Likelike.

"The lounges," Mamie continued, "can be used every day between 1 and 5 P.M. and between 7 and midnight. If you prove attractive enough, we impose no limit on the number of rendezvous you can have. Some women come here and never visit a lounge at all. Our program for attractiveness plus 'just talking about sex' seems enough for them. Our only objection to this is that it saddens the Hawaiians. They feel sad that a woman has travelled to the islands without once 'touching Heaven.' Other women do little else except eat, sleep, sun, drink juices, have massages and occupy the lounges. This disappoints the Hawaiians, who feel that excess dulls the appetite."

Mamie turned to Likelike. "Have I forgotten anything?"

"You might explain conversation a little more fully. Particularly physical conversation."

"Oh, yes. You know from *Lady Chatterley's Lover* that D. H. Lawrence defines sexual intercourse as physical conversation. In our seminars we use Lawrence's term as synonymous with our expression like-sex. When our men and women meet in the garden they speak to each other. They speak one or two sentences or many sentences. Our term elementary conversation covers all the inquiries and observations that pass between them before sex between them is suggested. And note that I say sex *between them*. A discussion of sex can remain elementary as long as it's general. A man and woman can talk for hours without ever advancing beyond elementary conversation.

They talk about sex but they don't propose it to each other. Once sex is proposed, we say the conversation has advanced. And when a man reaches advancement with you, you should do one of two things. If you think you *might* like him enough for sex, you should meet him in a lounge and discuss advancement with him. If you think it's unlikely you can like him enough, then stop the conversation with him and move to another man."

"But if a woman agrees to a rendezvous," Elaine asked, "isn't that agreement a sexual commitment?"

"I was coming to that question," Mamie answered. "And it's very important. Their first rendezvous together at Hotel Mamie Stover is *not* a sexual commitment by either partner. The man and woman agree *only* to meet, to drink friendly juices together, and to explore the possibility of like-sex or physical conversation. Both parties agree in advance to accept a negative decision and part as *mobani*, friends. Every man here understands this, so feel free to go to a first rendezvous with any man you think you might like sex with : you are promising nothing but friendly consideration."

"Suppose the man decides to use force?" Elaine asked.

"We don't often find such a man here. We recognize him at the interview and don't invite him. We want our men to be aggressive, potent, virile and insistent, but not cruel. We take precautions against cruelty. In the lounges assigned for first rendezvous you'll find a cord with a button on the end ... like those cords to summon nurses in hospitals. Just hold the button in your hand and if unpleasantness develops, ring. At once an Hawaiian woman will enter your door with a pass key and the man will be dismissed from the hotel. Or if you feel apprehensive as you go to the rendezvous, tell one of the maids and she"ll stand outside your door until you dismiss her. We tolerate no cruelty. But remember this : the second rendezvous *is* a commitment. If you give a man a first rendezvous and refuse him, then give him a second, you have let him advance to where he has the right to expect physical conversation. And if you refuse him then *you* are being cruel, and the man has the right to summon the Hawaiian woman to help him hold you while he takes it."

Mamie looked at her watch.

"I believe that's all you need for a first general meeting. Now Likelike will walk you through the secret passage and show you how to find and use the lounges. Then you'll have your dinner in the women's cafeteria and be ready to go to the general areas for elementary conversation. Just one more point. With your dinner I hope you will not take coffee or tea. We plan your diet to make you healthy, vibrant, desirable and desirous. Coffee and tea, like alcohol and nicotine, are antiaphrodisiacs. The Hawaiians say they 'dim the fire in a woman's eyes.' So take our jasmine tea or our ginger tea."

"Will you be here tonight?" Elaine asked.

"Later, probably. I have to appear at Waikiki but I'll be back later or tomorrow morning. I'll be here every day to see how attractive you're becoming. I want you to feel more attractive than you have ever felt in your life. You only live once. Most people come to the islands only once. So try to feel attractive. And try to make everybody you converse with feel attractive."

CHAPTER SEVEN

In which we learn how Mamie likes
like-sex. And how Monty likes it.

THERE ONCE WAS a party game for adolescents called progressive conversation. Its purpose was to compel every girl
guest to converse with every boy guest. Chaperones did the
pairing, and pairs would form in the parlor, then venture into
the moonlight for twenty minutes during which they would try
to communicate by talking, then touching to the limit insisted
on by the boy or permitted by the girl. They'd return to the
parlor, change partners as directed, and venture out again.
From all this pairing it was hoped love-sex would in time
develop : that a boy and girl would so attract one another that
they would proceed towards courtship, love, engagement,
marriage and parenthood.

The party game at Hotel Mamie Stover was similar. The
pairing place was not a parlor but ten acres of garden and
beach on an island thousands of miles from the homes of the
visiting players. The garden was sensuous. The trees included
Samoa palms, MacArthur palms with their bamboo-like stalks,
royal palms, mangoes, papayas, and Norfolk pines. Under the
trees were many kinds of flowers and foliage : circular plant-
ings of *ti*, the bushes up to twenty feet high, with lacquered
leaves in green and pink and red; oleanders, white and yellow
ginger, waxy anthuriums, honohono orchids, Singapore plum-
eries (frangipani) and, because they were Mamie's favorite,
many varieties of hibiscus. The most prevalent hibiscus was
Mamie's delight, the Maui Beauty, which has a red bloom
fringed with yellow.

After dark lights added color. Chinese lanterns were strung through the trees. Hawaiian kukui torches, both flame and electric, illuminated many areas, and a fire was lighted on the beach. Clothing was as colorful as lights and flowers. Women wore the *muumuus*, *leis*, sarongs, and "grass" skirts made of green or red or pink *ti* leaves. For the brief afternoon meeting men wore swimming trunks, and during the evenings they wore *aloha* shirts with shorts or duck trousers. Some guests wore sandals : others preferred bare feet.

Music in the afternoon was from records. At night drums were beaten for dancers around the beach fire. Men and women did not dance with each other but for each other, in the island manner.

The absence of liquor made Mamie's parties different from garden parties on the Mainland or from *luaus* at Waikiki. Voices, whether talking or singing, remained soft; sensitivity was sharpened, not dulled, and inhibitions were relaxed, not by harsh stimulants, but by aphrodisiac food and drink, rest, massage, salt air, languor, moonlight and firelight, distance, color, erotic music, the feel of a hand, and the nearness of the incessant sea.

The pairing was done, not by chaperones, but by Likelike and her Hawaiian assistants. They smilingly shuffled men and women, encouraging new pairs to walk in the garden, or sit under the trees, or dance around the fire.

But the chief difference between progressive conversation for adolescents and the pairings at Hotel Mamie Stover was in expectations. Mamie's guests were past adolescence. All but a few, like Elaine Shelby, had already known courtship, love and marriage, and now their expectations were limited to time and place. So as each new pair formed, ventured towards garden or beach, began elementary conversation, then weighed advancement, no one expected to find love-sex. The maximum expectation was like-sex.

Monty Whitaker was feeling good. In his cottage on the hotel grounds he and Mamie and Jesus and Leo Hirshman had dined on crayfish *bisque*, woodcock stuffed with truffles and seasoned with yohimbe, artichokes and onions, honey cakes sprinkled with ambergris, and ginger tea. The Polynesians say such a dinner "strengthens all slackened sinews." Casanova ate truffles to keep himself "exacting," and Du Barry fed honey cake and ambergris to the fading Louis XV to enable him to continue physical conversation.

Monty pushed back his chair from the table and stretched his legs. "Now that I've thought it over," he said, "I doubt that we have much to fear from Madison. All he'll see here is what he probably does himself. He's got a wife and two kids, but when he's in London or Rome or Beverly Hills he probably uses his hotel room as a rendezvous lounge when he gets the urge. Wouldn't you say so, Leo?"

"He's lived around show business for years," Leo said. "He's a writer, and hungry show business women think writers can help them. That's the most potent aphrodisiac in the world ... a woman thinking a man can help her in show business. That sends more women to men's hotel rooms than yohimbe will ever send. So Madison has his chances, and I'd guess he still partakes now and then."

"What do you think, Mamie? You were with him on the beach this afternoon. You think he partakes?"

None of the three men knew that Mamie had met Madison before. "I don't know. He's tired. He's showing his forty-two years. Maybe he partakes, maybe he doesn't."

"Aside from sex," Monty said, "what general impression did he give you? Does he seem antagonistic to the hotel? Or to any of us personally?"

"He's not personally mad at any of us. He spoke well of you, Monty, and of your father. He said he had once met you, Leo, and he was glad you had escaped from 'the rat race.' He mentioned you, Jesus. He said you were an 'honest brothel-keeper.' He said he was glad they decided you are white and let you move to Kahala. So he's friendly with all of us. And I don't think he'll be shocked by anything here. But whether he'll take a woman, or what he'll decide to write, I just don't know."

Jesus, as usual, had been listening and smoking his heavy pipe. "I don't think it makes much difference what Madison does here. When he gets back to Honolulu he'll be visited by friends who'll tell him that writing about us at this time of approaching statehood will not be in the best interest of the islands. His visitors will be his neighbors and the men who control the land his home stands on."

Mamie shook her head. "I think you better go easy on that."

"I think so, too," Monty said. "I don't think it'll be necessary. Madison's staying here a week. He'll rest and swim and ride horseback and get off his work routine. He'll eat nothing and drink nothing but what makes tired men feel young again. Likelike will soap his back and give him special massages. In a day or so, after he has rested, Mamie can take a couple of nights off from the Luau and stay here with him. Then when he goes back to Honolulu how could he write that we're 'reviving paganism' or 'encouraging adultery' or 'threatening the family'? I think it's even money he'll decide we're doing good. At worst he'll write that we're like any other resort hotel, maybe smarter and more honest."

"Maybe," Jesus said. "But what's best for us is for Madison to decide not to write anything. In the Statehood Edition of *Vacation* I don't want him complimenting me as 'an honest brothel-keeper.'"

Monty Whitaker left his cottage and walked through his private garden towards the general garden. It was about 8 P.M., and he could hear the singing and drumming. He enjoyed walking among his guests, speaking with them, seeing them become more zestful. He spent several hours each week teaching the men to row the heavy Hawaiian war canoes. He enjoyed also the hotel's judo wrestling : he was built for wrestling, five feet six, one hundred and eighty-five pounds, all muscle. Now, as he approached the general garden, he pondered a question. Among his guests were two women who interested him, and the question was which one should he converse with first.

Monty's attitude towards sex derived from experience. All his life his home had been a cottage in the grounds of a beach hotel which either his family or he controlled. In 1920 he was born in his father's cottage at the Lunaliho. After his mother died in 1925 he was reared at the Lunaliho, as his father often said, "on the beach, in the water and the trees." When he was adolescent he didn't learn sex from girls his own age, whom he thought he loved. Nor from prostitutes or any loose females socially inferior to him. He learned sex from his superiors, from the Lunaliho's affluent guests, from cultured ladies who were on excursions to romantic Waikiki, who found their rooms lonely and didn't hesitate to invite the stocky, square-faced Monty to help them find rapture in the islands.

From the time he was sixteen until the Lunaliho was sold, from 1936 to 1949, Monty could hardly remember a night when he didn't know the number of a door which would open to him if he knocked. And inside there was a lady, much older than he, who wouldn't give him the clap, whom he didn't have to woo, or pay, or worry about getting pregnant. She was naked when he entered, or soon after, and sometimes she shed a wedding ring before she reached for him. She didn't tell him she loved him, she didn't ask if he loved her, she asked him only, when he was very young, to "wait for" her.

Monty remembered the summer he was eighteen and home on holiday. His father spoke to him at breakfast the day after he got home.

"Monty," his father said, "you are eighteen this summer. So I suppose I should counsel you further about...sex. A doctor once told me that a man reaches his sexual peak at eighteen. He can't do it as well but he can do it more often than he ever can again, so I suppose I should advise you against excess. Of course a man can't kill himself at it. If he could, I would have died right here on this beach the summer I was eighteen."

"That would have been a double tragedy," Monty said. "Then I would never have been born."

His father smiled. "Well, you see what I'm driving at. Just try to ease off a little every now and then. Don't ease off anything superior, but leave the marginal stuff."

With the counsel of the Hawaiian beach boys, Monty learned the beach sex games. By mid-afternoon a hundred ladies and thirty men would be sprawled in the sand, impassive behind their sun glasses, the ladies reading *Forever Amber*. Monty and the beach boys would be fetching drinks, rowing canoes, sailing the catamaran, or teaching some athletic lady surfboard riding.

The first game might begin when a lady who was travelling alone summoned Monty with the wave of a jewelled hand. As he strode towards her he couldn't see her eyes behind the glasses but he could feel them on him. He watched her for one of the signs : a twist of a hip in the sand, a toe stretching and flexing, a hand fluttering towards her neck. "Oh, Monty," she'd say, "please bring me a little...papaya juice." He'd look down at her, smile, nod, and turn slowly away, waiting for the afterthought. "And Monty, I believe I'll have it in the cottage. I'm getting too much sun."

The juice didn't take long to deliver. For Monty learned the tactic of delay...to let her reach the cottage, shed the suit, then become *just impatient enough*! If he timed her right, she required him powerfully but only briefly; and he required her briefly, for his trunks had begun to constrain him before he reached her door.

That was the advantage ladies had who were travelling alone : they could use their cottages. Wives travelling with husbands didn't enjoy this advantage, so the next game might begin at the *cabanas,* the colorful cabins with floor space for two chairs and a table for drinks. Outside the *cabanas* would be wives whose husbands were playing golf. Such wives seldom risked even the quick rendezvous in a cottage or room because : "You never can be sure about golf : he might not have got a game, or he may play only nine holes instead of eighteen."

But a wife would sometimes risk like-sex in a *cabana*, and when she was ready she gave the same signs as the lady travelling alone.

Monty remembered his service trips to *cabanas*. He remembered how the lady's suit came off as he closed the latticed door. He remembered how she exhorted him as he served her powerfully and briefly on the floor.

Monty also remembered the little red-and-yellow beach tents at the Lunaliho. For it was in one of these that the final game of the afternoon was sometimes played. The lady with the tent was usually a wife who had arrived too late to obtain a *cabana* and whose husband lingered at the "19th hole." After soaking up sun all afternoon, reading many chapters of *Forever Amber*, *she* began the game as shadows reached the beach and the bathers thinned out. She asked Monty to move her tent. She didn't suggest where to move it; she let her electricity tell him where. She walked with him to the remote spot, then sat in the sand while he pegged the tent down. The side flaps of the little tent had been rolled up all the afternoon. Now Monty looked in her eyes, dropped the flaps, and she smiled. She said: "Now, Monty, I believe you might bring me a ... manhattan."

As he walked away he added zest to the game. He bet himself that he could divine the instant when she'd rise from the sand to enter the tent. He counted his steps, resisted impulses to turn, until right then he knew she was getting up. He turned abruptly and, almost every time, she was rising. As he stood at the beach bar while the cocktail was mixed he never looked towards the tent. She'd be out of sight, and he thought he could sense when she made each move. He felt her crawling into the tent. (They were four feet high: you couldn't stand up in them.) He felt her spreading the towel on the sand. He felt her slip the straps from her shoulders, free her arms, expose her breasts, her navel, her hips, then free her legs. When he got back to the tent she was naked and excited. As he crawled in, she reached for the drink, and gulped it while he freed himself. Then he took her astride his lap.

94

Most of these ladies breathed words into Monty's ears, but he seldom heard the word love, either as noun or verb, and when he heard it the lady meant it only as a synonym for the word the ladies more often used. This influenced Monty's attitudes, and he was influenced even more by the sentence the ladies most often breathed to him. He remembered the first time he heard the sentence. He was sixteen. "Good God!" the lady moaned. "How I needed this!"

Thereafter Monty noticed how often he heard the same sentence. So he asked himself: how can I be doing anything evil when I'm only giving the lady what she says she needs? If she needs it, it must be good for her. Then I must be doing good.

It was not until years later Monty began to reflect on what the ladies, in their erotic throes, had *not* said to him. They had not said: "Good God, how I needed *you*, Monty Whitaker!" It was a long time before he understood the difference.

These ladies, of course, used Monty only for holiday-sex. Scattered over the mainland today, in Canada, Australia and England, are scores of sedate, fifty- to sixty-year-old ladies who used him, neglected to love him, and forgot his name. Nor did they individually mean anything to him. But their collective effect was to give him attitudes different from those of the average man on the mainland.

The average man on the mainland associates holiday-sex by women with obscenity or immorality. Monty associated it with need. The average man thinks it's done by low-classed women. Monty thought it was done by high-classed women: by talented, cultured, respectable women. Not necessarily the Church crowd, though some of his ladies were diligent church-goers on the mainland.

As for adultery, Monty couldn't associate it with evil. Because the wives, too, in the *cabanas* and tents, told him they "needed this," and how could what was needed be evil?

When Monty finally attempted love-sex he was unlucky. The attempt came after he had seen the flash at Hiroshima, after he had known fear and disarrangement. For a wife he needed a woman who could give him, not more holiday-sex, but love-sex. But Annalee Johnston had nothing but holiday-sex to give. He married her, took her on his boat to Tahiti, and when the holiday was over the marriage was over.

So in 1950 when Monty met Mamie, after his divorce from Annalee and after the sale of the Lunaliho, he and Mamie were more likely partners than would at first appear. True, Mamie was a legendary whore while Monty was respected, and Mamie was six feet tall while Monty was five feet six. But they were the same age : thirty. They each had the same amount of money. Neither of them knew anything about love. The missionaries used to say that the "curse of Hawaii" was that the travelling man wanted, not love, but fornication. The same curse applied to the travelling ladies. Both Mamie and Monty had been influenced by this, and about the only difference was that the travelling men had paid Mamie while the travelling ladies had not paid Monty.

Their first meeting was at the Luau. Monty had gone there with no particular purpose, but after watching Mamie he asked Jesus to take him to her dressing-room.

Monty remembered his first conversation with Mamie.

"Monty," Mamie said, "you and I haven't met before, but we know one another. You know the legend of Mamie Stover. I know who Monty Whitaker is. I know the Lunaliho is coming down. I know you broke up with Annalee Johnston and at present you're a lost ball in high weeds. You say you want to talk to me. What does Monty Whitaker want to talk to Mamie Stover about?"

"Maybe about me. Maybe about you."

"That interests me if it's true. I'd like to know about you, but you understand why I ask. Many men come in here at midnight just like you are now. They know the Mamie legend. They've watched Mamie's legendary rump sway-and-swivel, and they've decided they want some of it. But they know that Mamie is rich and doesn't sell it any more, so they come here to play a game. They want to take Mamie to a couch, feed

96

her whisky, and try to persuade her to give them what so many good men have paid for."

"Sure. I can understand that."

"Then you understand why it can't work. In the first place I don't drink, not even coffee. In the second place I know the game so well it bores me. And in the third place I don't know how to give it away. After you've sold it for years you feel awkward trying to give it away. So if you want to talk about you and me, I'm interested, but I'm not interested in either selling it to you or trying to give it."

"That's fair enough."

"Okay. We'll go over to my apartment."

When they reached the apartment Monty noted what didn't happen. Mamie didn't grab him : she invited him to sit down. Her servant brought coffee. Mamie took off her clothes, but not in front of him. She went into her bedroom and changed into a pair of doeskin slacks and a pink blouse. He took off his clothes, but not in front of her. She handed him a pair of blue silk pajamas and told him to go into her bedroom and put them on so that he could talk comfortably. When he came back to the living room she was in a chair with her long legs stretched out, her feet propped on an ottoman. He had never seen such a relaxed woman. She wasn't tense or nervous. So he sat opposite her, put his feet on the same ottoman, drank coffee, and talked.

The irony of it struck him! Monty Whitaker and Mamie Stover, in a room together, at romantic Waikiki, at 2 A.M., doing nothing but talking!

At dawn they were still talking, and Mamie knew more about Monty than anyone had ever known. He had never talked so much in his life. The next night, and the next night, he was still talking. Except that now Mamie began talking.

"You know, Monty, things are changing out here. The whorehouses are closed, the Lunaliho is coming down, big hotels are going up. Crowds of people are coming, new kinds of people. But one thing won't change. Some of the men and some of the women are going to want holiday-sex when they

97

reach romantic Waikiki. When they rest and swim and get massaged and soak up sun and breathe salt air they'll begin to feel restless and reckless. But the men can't go to whorehouses, and there won't be enough beach-boys for the ladies. The beaches will be too crowded for *cabanas* and tents. So what are these sex-hungry visitors going to do at romantic Waikiki?"

"God knows," Monty said.

"God may not care," Mamie said, "but I know. You and I are going to build a hotel. We're going to build it on a lonely beach on one of the Outer Islands. The *real* Hawaii. The hotel will be the home of the last *real* Hawaiians, and from all these men and women who arrive here, you and I will select the ones who are sex-hungry. We'll fly them to our hotel and introduce them to one another."

Monty hadn't laughed heartily since the war. When Mamie said that he roared. He walked around the room, still laughing. Like all good and logical ideas it was so simple, so sound, financially, socially, sexually.

"You and I will rid Waikiki of sin," Mamie continued. "We'll do more to clean up Waikiki than the missionaries could ever do. We'll make Waikiki the most decent, most sexless beach on earth, because we'll take the sex-hunters with us. Then all these good, respectable, hard-working, middle-class people can fly here, coach class. They can start bringing children here, even church conventions can be held here. Waikiki can be crowded and decent. There'll be no more fornication in hotel rooms, no more adultery on *cabana* floors or on beach towels behind windbreakers. The wickedest thing that can happen at Waikiki will be a *luau* in the hotel grounds where some good woman from Omaha strips off a brassière and leaves it in the ladies' room. And our hotel will make things hygienic and safe for the hungry ones."

Monty roared again. "Mamie, I started learning when I was sixteen how much the lady needs it!"

"Then you and I should be capable selectors. With your experience you ought to be able to look a prospective lady guest in the eye and tell whether she's hungry. And surely

I should know something about detecting hunger in men."

The more Monty thought about it the more he realized how good it was. "You know, Mamie, this idea is really good for Hawaii. I think it would be good for the whole world."

"I don't know whether it would be good for the whole world, or not," Mamie said. "When people travel to other places maybe not as many of them get as sex-hungry as when they come to the islands. But the idea is good for Hawaii."

When Mamie explained her plan for the rendezvous lounges, Monty doubled up in laughter again.

"Let me design the lounges, Mamie. I want to dedicate the lounges to the memory of all those wives who had to get it in sixty seconds on a *cabana* floor or astride my lap in a tent. Now the hungry wife can come to our hotel and get it in a bed just as comfortably as the lady who is travelling alone. She can relax and get what she needs and not have to worry about whether her husband is playing nine holes or eighteen, I want Monty Whitaker to be remembered as the man who took wives off the floor in Hawaii and put them in beds!"

Mamie laughed with him, then became serious again. "Two things we'll have to remember, Monty. The ladies who'll be our guests will be different from the ones you knew at the Lunaliho. The lady you knew in 1938 was either richer or bolder or both. When she lay in the sand and read *Forever Amber*, and decided she wanted it with you, she was brazen enough to summon you, then walk off to her room with everybody looking and knowing what she was doing. Even the wife in the *cabana* or in the tent didn't much care if strangers suspected what she was calling you for. The women who'll be our guests won't be as rich or as bold, and they'll be more afraid of what other women think. So we'll have to arrange that they can have excuses for disappearing. We'll have to manage it so that they can disguise themselves and other women can't recognize them while they're walking to rendezvous. They'll go to the rendezvous just as often, but our women will want to tell themselves nobody knows about it. So we'll have to pretend more. Even our men will want to pretend. They won't be the same men who used to line up in the street in broad daylight and wait for me and didn't give a damn who saw them."

"I guess that's true," Monty said. "What's the second thing we'll have to remember?"

"We mustn't call attention to what we're doing. We can't allow any publicity, because the Church crowd will want us to do this and pay them high rent at the same time, but they won't want to be reminded of it. They won't want to have to defend 'what Mamie's doing,' or have to defend themselves for 'making money out of Mamie.' So to do the maximum amount of good, and to make the maximum amount of money, we must keep quiet, let our prospects find us at the Luau, and at the hotel we must pretend we're doing nothing more than 'preserving Hawaiian culture.' Everybody will want it this way . . . guests, landowners, bankers, everybody."

That's how Hotel Mamie Stover was born. Monty took up with Mamie because she had shown him how to do something absorbing and profitable. Since they worked day and night he rented an apartment near hers. He lost himself in planning, building, organizing. Jesus was brought into the partnership because he and Mamie were already partners in the Luau, which was to become part of the hotel, and Jesus knew how to deal with landowners and bankers. Monty and Mamie spent days in a Piper Cub plane looking at beaches in the Outer Islands. They flew and walked over miles of Kauai, Molokai, Maui, and Hawaii. The hotel needed to be near Waikiki, yet remote, so the beach near Lahaina was selected. Two million dollars went into clearing, draining, designing building, furnishing, gardening.

Then one evening it was finished and the hotel was within a week of opening. Monty and Mamie dined at her cottage, and that evening she didn't appear at the Luau. She had dressed for dinner in a white shantung sheath, jewels, nylons, high heels, her gold-blonde hair low on her neck in a chignon.

Monty looked at her across the table and marvelled. With all their experience together he had never touched her! He had been astonished to learn that the legendary Mamie Stover had no man. He had been more astonished that he hadn't insisted on becoming her man. At first he had wanted her. He often jokingly asked when was she going to "break down" and attempt the "awkward business" of trying to give it to him. He had gradually dropped the subject, and now he had no desire for her.

But how could Monty Whitaker not desire Mamie Stover! He liked her, and here they were alone together, in a sex-setting, a remote resort which they had created for like-sex, with Mamie so erotic-looking, Monty so virile, and both of them experienced. Why couldn't they have like-sex with one another?

Monty wasn't sure of the answers. He thought it might be their difference in height. Maybe when day after day a man associates with a woman who looks down at him, maybe he loses desire for her, and how can a man desire a strong woman who drives him, tells him what to do?

"Mamie," Monty said, "let's not talk business tonight. Let's talk sex. Yours and mine. How have you and I, of all people, built a hotel together without once getting on a bed together? It seems unbelievable. Nobody believes it but us."

Mamie became pensive. "You really want to talk about it?"

"Yes. I'm curious. It seems so strange that we can build this hotel for sex-hungry travellers but we don't try to satisfy each other's hunger."

"It's my fault, Monty," Mamie said. "After we had talked three or four nights, you wanted sex with me. But what I wanted was for us to become friends and business partners, so I began worrying about what I'd do if you insisted. We're lucky you didn't insist, because I would have tried, and whatever I did would have driven us apart."

"What do you mean by 'whatever you did'?"

"I mean this. If you had insisted, you would have forced me to one of two choices. I would have probably decided to give you the professional Mamie as the lesser risk. You would have expected the legendary Mamie. The professional Mamie knows every position described in *The Perfumed Garden*. She can fake every moan, every spasm that makes a man feel like he's conquering a woman and the world. What if you had got that from me, Monty, a week after we began conversation? Would we have built this hotel together?"

"I don't know. Maybe. Why not?"

"Had I given you that, this hotel would not have been built. That sort of sex doesn't make a man want any kind of permanent relationship with a woman."

"Why couldn't you have just given me yourself? Like you are when you aren't being professional?"

"I considered that, too. After the first month with you I decided that if you pressed me I wouldn't give you the professional Mamie. Instead I'd try to give you the real Mamie, but I'm inexperienced in giving the real Mamie. I never tried it only once, and the real Mamie would have driven us apart, too."

"What's wrong with the real Mamie?"

"The real Mamie would have disappointed you. She would have been poor competition for your memories of Annalee Johnston. She would have been no competition at all for your memories of those travelling ladies on the *cabana* floor. The real Mamie would have left you deflated, probably resentful."

After a moment she added: "You and I have been lucky, Monty. We are now good friends, permanent partners, and we'll make money together. We trust one another. But if we had ever tried sex with one another . . . well, if you'll pardon the language, we'd have done nothing but loused up a good friendship and a good business."

They moved to the lanai and watched the moon rise through the palm trees. Mamie didn't want to talk about herself but she knew Monty was still curious.

"Mamie," he said, "you're right about sex between us, we'll never mention it again. But I'd like to know more about the real Mamie. You know everything about me, but you've never talked about yourself. You don't mind me asking questions, do you?"

"No, I don't mind. But remember there's a difference in us. You don't have much to forget. I do."

"I know. But tell me this. You said that if you had given me your professional performance you would have faked satisfaction. And if you had given me your real self I couldn't have satisfied you. Does that mean . . . ?"

She interrupted him.

"It means that sexual satisfaction is something I sacrificed to business. I got off a freighter at a fruit dock in Honolulu on a May morning in 1939. Eleven years ago. That night I started whoring in a house in Iwilei. I put my mind on money, not on sexual satisfaction."

"But you were married for several months during the war?"

"It wasn't a marriage for my sexual satisfaction. The satisfaction he ·wanted was my servants, my Cadillac, my black-market comforts, my professional sex performance. The satisfaction I wanted was a wedding ring from an Air Force major while I kept right on whoring."

"But didn't you have some man you . . . ?"

"Didn't I have a man I turned to each week to give me some sexual satisfaction? Every whore must have such a man, mustn't she? Well let me remind you of something. There were two hundred and one licensed whores in Honolulu in 1939, and a lot of people got rich on whoring here during the war. Jesus Portales got rich. Landowners got rich. Madams got rich. Cops got rich. Shyster lawyers got rich. But two hundred of those whores didn't get rich. They made money but they didn't keep it or multiply it. You know why? Because they were lonely, they wanted to feel they belonged to somebody, they needed a friendly man to turn to and each week they gave their money to their friendly man . . . who ran off with it. That's how two hundred whores wound up broke after the war, and that's how one whore got rich. I didn't buy anybody. I did without a man to give myself and my money to."

"But you must have had some help with your money? You couldn't keep much money in a whorehouse?"

Mamie hesitated. She didn't like this conversation, but Monty was her business partner. He was asking her a business question.

"Yes," Mamie said, "I did have some help. There was one man I could turn to. He kept my money the first year, but he didn't run away with it. He gave it back to me so I could start doubling it. He didn't want any of my money, and he didn't want me."

"And after the first year?"

"Well, he helped me some more. He helped me feel protected. He got me a lawyer who wasn't a shyster and who'd help me make black-market deals and who wouldn't steal from me. He was always friendly to me. He let me turn to him. But he wouldn't take anything from me, or let me give him anything."

"What happened to him?"

Mamie paused. "He went off to the war . . . and never came back."

"And what happened to you after the war?"

"You know most of it. I quit whoring. I travelled some. I read a lot. I tried to educate myself. Jesus and I started the Luau. No man has touched me since 1945. After a whore gets rich and quits whoring, if she respects herself there's not much way she can have a man. Your experience with me shows you some of the problems."

Monty reflected a moment, then said: "Mamie, do you know what you're saying? You're telling me that in eleven years in Hawaii Mamie Stover has never had sexual satisfaction from any man. Is that the truth?"

"Before you ask me to repeat it," Mamie said, "we'd better remind ourselves that this is a dangerous conversation. If we ever let it get round that Mamie Stover has never had an orgasm in Hawaii we could lose a million dollars. Right now we're spending money on a publicity agent to spread the impression that Mamie is so hot she sometimes has orgasms while she walks at the Luau."

Monty chuckled. Almost everything Mamie said surprised

him, that was why he liked to be with her. "It just seems so unbelievable, Mamie. How can a woman who looks like you do, with a body like yours . . ."

"Well, first," Mamie said, "I didn't say I have never had one. I said I have never had one in Hawaii. You learned about women's orgasms from ladies who were having holiday-sex. Travelling is a sex stimulant, travelling to Hawaii is a powerful stimulant. One of your ladies can sprawl in Waikiki sand, soak up sun, read *Forever Amber*, watch you play in your trunks, and she's almost ready to pop by the time she decides to offer it to you. Then if you'll let her wait five minutes in her room, thinking about how near she is to it, you can make her come in seconds. I used to use that delay trick on young sailors and Marines. My maids would line them up on the Bull Ring. Each one stood in a little stall, alone, with his pants off, while he listened through a tissue-paper partition to what I was saying and doing to his buddy. He could see our shadows on that partition : I had fixed the lights so he could.

"When I walked into his stall on high heels, naked, looking down at him, with this yellow hair on my shoulders, and these big teats at about eye-level, his teeth were chattering. He was so nervous, and looked so insignificant I felt sorry for the little bastard. His sex dream had suddenly materialized : what was he going to do about it! He often went off the instant I touched it with my hand, if he got any further he was finished in seconds. I could knock off a hundred of them almost without effort, and without the slightest feeling of participation. Now do you understand?"

For a long time Monty and Mamie sat there, looking out over their beach. The Air Force began practice-bombing Kahoolawe, and every few minutes the target was illuminated by flares. Mamie's story had depressed Monty. He wished he hadn't insisted on talking about it. But he had one more question.

"Mamie, you said that once you tried to give a man your real self, and that once you experienced satisfaction. Was it the same man . . . the same time?"

"Yes. It was on the freighter I came to Hawaii on. I was broke and beaten up and scared. I was a beauty contest winner at seventeen, and I had learned sex in Hollywood. Well, on this freighter there was one other passenger . . . just this man and me. He was the same man who later let me turn to him out here. He was twenty-six, I was nineteen. He was lonely and drinking. The weather was bad, raining and blowing. And he was the only man I ever tried to give my real self to."

"What was unusual about him?"

"Nothing, physically. Except he was the only man I never felt tall with. He wasn't but five-nine, so I was three inches taller than he was. But I felt he was taller than I was. And what made me feel so close to him was one little thing that happened with us."

"What was that?"

"In his cabin there were two bunks. When we were together we were in the lower bunk, then he'd sleep in the upper bunk and I'd sleep in the lower. We slept like that for six nights. And each night, far in the night, maybe three or four o'clock, for some reason he'd wake up, not for sex. The sea would be rough and the cabin pitch dark. He'd turn over on his stomach and he'd reach his left hand down to me. And maybe you won't believe this, but I'd be awake at the same time, and for some reason I'd reach my hand up to him at the exact instant he was reaching down. For some reason I'd *know* when he was reaching down. And in that pitch darkness, in the middle of the Pacific Ocean, with the ship rolling, my hand would slip into his just like it was broad daylight and we were both looking at each other. He never said or did anything: he just squeezed my hand, then turned it loose and we went back to sleep. At least once each night I reached up like that, and every time, without waiting an instant, his hand closed over mine. He told me that he never once reached down that my hand wasn't there. Wasn't that strange? I couldn't explain it, he couldn't either."

"Do you suppose he loved you?" Monty asked this question

offhand. He couldn't believe that any man could really *love* Mamie. A man could want sex with Mamie, a man could like her, but a man couldn't *love* Mamie. She was too tall, too strong, too determined.

"No, he didn't love me," Mamie said. "He never said he loved me, but he cared about me. I wasn't just another woman to him. He cared about me as a person. He liked to talk with me. He asked me a lot about myself . . . and not just about sex. He wanted to know about me, and he wanted to help me. He urged me not to become a whore and offered me money to go back to San Francisco. And I'll never forget how our hands met there so easily in the dark, and how safe he made me feel, and how quickly I went back to sleep after he squeezed my hand."

"Why didn't you go with him? Did he have a wife?"

"No, he didn't have a wife. I pleaded with him to let me go with him. He wouldn't take me. He said he had been married once and it didn't work because he didn't have enough time for a woman. He said he was a driving man who worked and travelled all the time, and he couldn't sleep much at night, and any woman who tried to stay with him would soon give up. When he wouldn't let me go with him, I started whoring.

"He wouldn't take me sexually after I started whoring. He tried once or twice, for my sake, but he gave up. He said he couldn't have sex with a whore because he felt too sorry for her. He said a woman can give sex to a man because she feels sorry for him, but a man can't give sex to a woman once he feels too sorry for her. But he continued to help me, and he's responsible for Mamie Stover being rich. Without him I'd have wound up the war just as broke as the other two hundred."

"What was his name?"

Mamie shook her head. "His name means nothing. He'll never turn up again."

Monty Whitaker was entering the general garden. Five successful years had passed since that conversation with Mamie.

She had proved loyal and capable. She didn't pretend with Monty, she pretended only with the guests. She told the women that she engaged in like-sex. As proof, on one afternoon each week, she donned a disguise in the Carnival Room and walked through the women's passage to the rendezvous lounges, knowing that every woman who saw her would notice her height and pass the word that Mamie was enjoying like-sex.

But Monty didn't pretend: he still liked like-sex. He could do it better. So he kept his practiced eye on his guests, still willing to help the lady who needed him. He avoided tall ladies: they never looked like they needed him. The ladies he thought needed him were compact little ladies, no taller than five-two-or-three, no heavier than a hundred and ten . . . with delicate ankles, trim feet, and curvy calves. When the right one like this came along, Monty believed he had what she needed.

Tonight he knew of two such compact ladies. They were Elaine Shelby and Mary Ferrell.

CHAPTER EIGHT

In which we hear Elaine receive
detailed instructions in like-sex.

THE HAWAIIAN woman, Likelike, was a humanitarian. She
had known bitterness. She left the University of Hawaii to
marry a junior grade lieutenant in the United States Navy.
Later, with her husband and their two children, she travelled
to Wells River, Vermont, there to be rejected, first by her
husband's parents, then by him. Neither an Hawaiian wife
nor her half-Hawaiian children belonged in Vermont. Her
children were now in school in Honolulu, and Likelike, thirty,
was Mamie's valued assistant.

Likelike's body resembled that of the early Dorothy
Lamour. She wore her hair in a bun low on one side of her
neck as Miss Lamour had in several South Seas films. Likelike
had appeared in one film made in Hawaii: that is, her body
had appeared. When the white star danced the hula, it was
Likelike dancing. It was Likelike in the long shots as well as in
the close body shots. But when the face of the dancing image
was seen in close-up, it was the face of the star.

When Likelike was asked how she liked being the body of a
movie star she replied philosophically. "The bodies of
Hawaiian women have always been available to mainlanders
. . . one way or another."

Each morning, by airplane from Honolulu, Likelike
received the photographs and application cards of the guests
who would arrive that afternoon. From this she made the first
draft of a "Pair Sheet," using her judgment as to which man
would most likely be attracted to which woman. When the

guests arrived, while they were being medically examined, the chauffeur-stewardesses reported to Likelike the results of the initial pairings in the station wagon and on the airplane.

While the guests were being scrubbed and massaged, the doctors rushed their reports to Likelike. By this process she was informed as to each man and woman's possible erotic experience: in effect, medical judgment as to which partners could be paired most hopefully. Likelike then met the arriving women. She usually made the welcoming explanation, noting questions asked and other individual reactions. She walked the women through the secret passage and the rendezvous lounges, noting degrees of excitation. From this wealth of information and observation Likelike was prepared to advise each woman as to the man or men she might like.

This evening Likelike was concerned with Elaine Shelby, Becky Sanders, Mary Ferrell and Sally Rogers. She had watched them closely, studied their records, reflected on them. As they returned from inspecting the lounges, Likelike invited Elaine to her office. Likelike called Elaine by her first name because after new arrivals had inspected the lounges together they were supposed to begin using first names.

"Elaine," Likelike said, "I'm aware that you are a most unusual guest. I've studied your medical report. Would you like some personal advice before we go to the general meeting?"

Elaine felt annoyed. She had taken tongue-in-cheek all the talk about "advice" from Hawaiian women. Now Likelike was presuming to offer "personal" advice from a "personal" medical report. Elaine thought this was becoming too personal. She started to say no, but Likelike seemed so friendly that Elaine softened and replied: "Sure. As a lawyer I.appreciate the value of informed advice."

"I hoped you'd feel that way," Likelike said. "When we reach the garden I advise you to begin elementary conversation with Madison. I think you'll like him."

"Why do you think so?"

"He's our only guest who's listed in *Who's Who in America*.

A woman usually finds it easier to like a man who is considered important. I've read Madison's books. He seems a likeable man."

Elaine felt more annoyed: she had not read Madison's books. She felt inclined to resist advice.

"He's married, isn't he?"

"Yes. He has a home in Honolulu. He has an attractive English wife and two children by her. She's his second wife. She's thirty-three, he's forty-two."

"Then why is he here?"

"His wife and children are in England. He's tired from travelling, wants to rest and relax. And since he's a novelist I imagine he's curious about how we operate the hotel."

"Why should he want me?"

"He'll want you only if he discovers he likes you. He's on a holiday in the most erotic environment on earth. He can be with you. He can walk with you in a garden, talk with you, have you dance for him, touch you . . ."

"Why shouldn't he prefer Mary Ferrell? Or Becky Sanders? Or Sally Rogers? They all have advantages over me."

"And you may have advantages over them . . . with Madison. You're his type of woman, sensitive, intelligent, with a sense of humor, and here you'll be prettier than you ever thought you were. Encourage Madison and I think he'll like you. I think you'll like him."

Elaine began to feel better. "But shouldn't I try first with one of the single men?"

"That's a mainland or Puritan question," Likelike said. "I can only give you an island answer. We have twelve single guests, each one is selfish or he wouldn't be single. None is capable of really liking anyone but himself. You are an educated, mature woman from a Puritan society, and you are going to attempt a first sexual experience without love. So you need a man you can *really like*. He must be capable of being unselfish with you. He must be self-assured and self-restrained. Yours is a complex problem, so you need either a very complex man or a very simple man."

Elaine wondered how this conversation would sound in Indiana. She also wondered how Likelike had learned so much.

"You must understand," Likelike continued, "that your virginity is a real problem. In a woman your age it's no slight obstacle: the doctor verifies this. So you need a man who knows how to overcome it with the minimum amount of pain and shock to you. And you can provide no protection for yourself against pregnancy in your first intercourse. The doctor explained this to you, so your man must be capable of protecting you."

Elaine reflected. Not only was sex brutal, unreasoning and obscene: it was also complicated. For a moment she wondered again why she hadn't been content to stay at Waikiki and play bridge and look at mountains.

"This may sound like another Puritan question," Elaine said. "You keep emphasizing that I *need* Madison. That irritates me. On the ship coming to Hawaii a man tried to rape me. I might not have resisted so much if he hadn't kept telling me that he was going to give me what I needed. When you tell me I *need* Madison, I see myself in an inferior position, with him condescending to give me something I need. If I find I like Madison, and if he likes me enough to want me, is there any way I can feel that he also needs me?"

Likelike hesitated, then answered: "Well, first, you might accept this. Whatever man takes you, physically you'll be in the inferior position. You'll be in approximately the same position as when the man tried to rape you. That's natural. As a lawyer perhaps you resent that. As a woman you'll have to accept it. Then think of it this way. Madison is not a man who 'needs a woman.' He's had many attractive women. If Madison likes you enough to want sex with you, it won't be because he just wants sex: it'll be because he wants *you*. And if he wants you, he needs you. Isn't that enough?"

They sat looking at each other. Elaine sighed. "Suppose Madison doesn't appear this evening? Or is he already committed? How about the doctor for me?"

Likelike picked up the doctor's application card and medical report. "Doctor Ralph Anderson," she read. "Sioux Falls, South Dakota. He still has his first wife. She's thirty-nine, he's forty."

"I noticed him in the car and on the plane. He looks sad."

"Perhaps that's because of his specialty. He's a gynecologist."

That restored Elaine's sense of humor. "He's here on a sort of busman's holiday, I suppose."

Likelike's black eyes twinkled. "Yes. He wants to spend a few days approaching things from a different angle.

"Seriously," Likelike went on, "we get many doctors. Their knowledge sends them here. Doctor Anderson looks like a superior, likeable man. He needs an attractive erotic woman."

Elaine's interest quickened. "You say the doctor needs a woman. Madison doesn't. Do you suppose the doctor might need *me*?"

"Well, does the shoe fit?" Likelike asked. "Are you a skilful, erotic woman?"

"I don't know. Maybe I am. Maybe I can become one in a few hours."

"Maybe you can," Likelike said. "But the indications are that you can't. Twenty-eight-year-old virgin lawyers don't usually have hot, compelling sex urges. If they did they wouldn't be virgins. You need time to develop erotic skill and desire. That's why I recommend Madison. He can afford a virgin. He can spend several days teaching sex to a woman who needs time to become erotic and skilful. The doctor can't. He needs sex in a hurry. He needs to reassure himself *now* that his sex drive is still powerful, so he needs Becky Sanders. She's perfect for him if she'll take him."

Elaine squirmed in her chair. "And you don't think the doctor would give me enough time?"

Likelike sighed. She wondered why virgins always think they can learn in a few minutes what other women have spent years learning.

"In one way," Likelike conceded, "I suppose you might

like the doctor better than Madison. The doctor would be much more aggressive with you. Madison will be so thoughtful of you, so anxious not to persuade you against your better judgment, that he'll force you, not to acquiesce but to consent. With the doctor, once you reached the lounge, you could be passive. He wouldn't force you to consent. He'd go right ahead while you quietly pleaded with him to stop or wait. He'd allow you the decency of a little maidenly protest. Madison won't. He'll be so decent that he won't proceed until he has forced you to the indecency of consenting."

"That word indecency is tricky, isn't it?" Elaine said. "Intercourse with the doctor sounds more decent than it does with Madison."

"If you are so concerned about decency, why didn't you submit to the rape? That would have been the most decent way of all."

Elaine nodded. "I thought of that. But the bastard kept infuriating me by telling me he was going to give me what I needed."

She stood up to go. It was time for dinner in the women's cafeteria, but with some effort she turned back to Likelike and asked: "What about Monty Whitaker? Why haven't you suggested him for me?"

Likelike looked appalled.

"Monty is the last man on Maui I'd recommend to you."

"What's wrong with him?"

"Everything, for you. Among the many obstacles in life Monty has never encountered is a maidenhead. He's God's gift to the thirty-year-old wife who has had children and who now needs much more than her husband can offer."

Likelike shuddered: the thought of Monty with Elaine really appalled her. She added: "We'd have to send a stretcher to the lounges, carry you to the clinic, and treat you for multiple lacerations and shock! And you'd be pregnant as a goat!"

Elaine knitted her brows but she didn't shudder. "That sounds obscene and painful," she said. "But it leaves me wondering if Monty isn't the one man of the three who needs me most. And I wonder if he'd be quite so unrestrained if he *really liked* me?"

Likelike felt perplexed. She usually understood mainland women, but Elaine confused her.

"Elaine," she said, "you've now set me wondering if I haven't misjudged you completely. A moment ago I said you needed either a very complex man or a very simple man. I assumed you'd want the complex man and recommended Madison. Now it appears you might prefer the simple man. So I'm going to reveal something to you that we don't ordinarily reveal to arriving women until their second day. You heard Mamie explain sex between men guests and women guests . . . complicated sex which must be preceded by hours or days of elementary and advanced conversation. But what Mamie delayed mentioning is that we also offer like-at-sight-sex."

"Like-at-sight-sex?"

"Yes. You've heard of love-at-first-sight. This is like-at-first-sight. Here's how it works. This evening in the general area you'll converse only with white men. The only Hawaiian men you'll see will be ancient, white-haired drummers. But tomorrow afternoon as you lie in the sun on the women's private beach, you'll see the Hawaiian men. No white man can visit that beach.

"The Hawaiian men are all carefully selected, eighteen-year-old beach boys. They'll be playing on the women's beach in their swim trunks, fetching drinks, paddling canoes, sailing the catamaran, and teaching a few ladies surfboard riding. You'll be sprawled in the sand, completely relaxed by massage, and reading *Lady Chatterley's Lover* or one of Mamie's tracts on how to give more sexual delight to your partner. The beach boys are wonderful. They smile all the time, and they regard sex with the white ladies as wholesome sport . . . like mainland boys think of football and baseball. If you sight a beach boy you like, you wave your hand. Like-at-sight, see! As he approaches, you employ your towel discreetly, and ask him to please bring you some *mobani* juice. He'll nod, smile, and turn away. But he'll hesitate for ten seconds, waiting for your possible after-thought. Then you add : 'And, Joe—they are all named Joe—will you please bring it to lounge seventeen. I'm getting too much sun.' You walk to the lounge, lie naked across the couch, look at the aphrodisiac pictures, wait four minutes in delightful contemplation, and Joe will arrive smiling and zestfully relieve you of your virginity . . . like *that*!"

Likelike snapped her fingers.

"Sounds wonderfully efficient," Elaine said. "And Joe would have me pregnant . . . like *that*!"

Elaine snapped her fingers.

"Not necessarily," Likelike said. "Joe won't like it, but I'll see that he's equipped to protect you. I'll promise him that when you honor him next day you'll do the protecting."

Elaine held up a protesting hand. "There's one flaw in the story," she said. "You say I wait four minutes for Joe. But men can reach the lounges only from the men's barracks. How can Joe leave the women's area, cross the general area, enter the men's area, reach the men's barracks, and traverse the men's secret passage all in so brief a time? Is Joe an angel with wings?"

Likelike's eyes twinkled again. "Your trained, analytical mind knows better than that, Elaine. The beach boys *never* enter the men's area. They stay in the Hawaiian colony and in the white women's area, and they go to the lounges through the women's secret passage. The men guests never know beach boys exist at Hotel Mamie Stover. In fact, they *don't* exist . . . officially."

"Lord Save Us!" Elaine said.

"As a matter of fact," Likelike continued, "in our like-at-sight-sex, which we also call no-conversation-sex, if you don't want to take the time to reach the lounges, and if you don't mind the other ladies knowing what you are doing, we have a few colorful little *cabanas* on the women's private beach. Each *cabana* has a comfortable couch inside."

Elaine nodded. "And my trained, analytical mind sees the

other side of the coin. In the men's area are the Hawaiian women . . . sixteen years old, fetching drinks, scrubbing backs in sensuous, relaxing baths, and reaching the lounges through the men's secret passage. Or using similar *cabanas*."

"Officially I must deny that," Likelike maintained. "Unofficially, you've made two mistakes. The girls are not sixteen but fifteen, and they are not Hawaiians. They are Melanesians from the island of Woola Woola. Their Woola Woola husbands don't want them until they have become sexually skilled, so the girls are sent here as virgins by their husbands and fathers to train for a year."

"No wonder Mamie is a millionaire!"

"Mamie is rich because she deserves to be rich. She knows how to do good. On Woola Woola she is regarded as a saint. She goes there once each year to return the trained girls and select the new ones. The Woola Woolans worship her in a week-long festival. Why shouldn't they? Woola Woola has no juvenile delinquency, Mamie has wiped it out. Woola Woolans are free of tuberculosis and venereal disease, because three years ago Mamie built them a modern medical clinic and staffed it with doctors. The Woola Woolans send their daughters to Hotel Mamie Stover like people in Vermont send their daughters to finishing schools. If you want to realize how good this all is, visit Woola Woola and then visit Samoa. The United States has converted Samoa into a pesthole. Mamie has converted Woola Woola into a Paradise. If the President of the United States could only persuade Mamie to advise him. . . ."

Elaine felt overwhelmed. There was so much in the world that she hadn't learned at the University of Indiana. "That answers questions I've had in my mind," she said. "I wondered how you entertained the less attractive men and women guests."

"Well," Likelike said, "now you know most of it. There'll still be little sexual surprises for you . . . that's part of our program. Everybody who comes here finds what he or she wants. Sally Rogers, for instance, might be miserable here except for the beach boys. Sally couldn't compete with you and Mary Ferrell and Becky Sanders for the more attractive men. And she'd be further handicapped by worrying about adultery if she went to a lounge with a white man. But with a beach boy it's not adultery for her . . . he doesn't count."

"And her husband?"

"Sure. He'll think he's an infantry captain back in Italy in 1944. He'll shoot boars and wrestle and ride horseback and enjoy the Woola Woola girls. And both Tom and Sally will return to Eugene, Oregon, looking ten years younger. Each one will wonder just what the other did, but they'll decide not to mention it . . . they'll be too busy planning to come back next year."

"One more question," Elaine said. "What effect do the beach boys and the Woola Woola girls have on the meetings in the general garden between men and women guests? I suppose these meetings are not as active as I had assumed they would be?"

"That surprises every arriving man and woman," Likelike answered. "On their first evening they go to the general meeting expecting to see furious sex-hunting. They look at the guests who have been here a day or so, and what do they see? Men and women so relaxed they are almost lethargic."

"And how does this affect a man like . . ."

"Like Madison?" Likelike's eyes twinkled again. "It doesn't affect him at all. He doesn't want to shoot any boars or take any fifteen-year-old girls. He doesn't want no-conversation sex. He doesn't want a woman who'd be interested in Joe the Beachboy. He needs a complex woman, educated, sensitive, understanding . . . a woman who'll hold his hand, walk in the garden with him, and tell him about herself. He needs a woman he can really like. If he finds her, he's capable of telling her he needs her, then meeting her in a lounge and being erotic and strong and aggressive with her. He's also capable of being tender and restrained."

Elaine looked deep into Likelike's eyes. Then they both smiled.

CHAPTER NINE

The first evening, continued: in
which we learn how Mary Ferrell
acquired what she wanted at Hotel
Mamie Stover.

MONTY WHITAKER had reached the general garden. After
greeting several guests he spoke with Likelike.

"How's Elaine Shelby coming along?"

"Fine. She attracted whistles and yells when I introduced
her on the platform. A dozen men came milling around her.
All of them want conversation with her as soon as they can
get it. She's in the garden now with Madison."

"You think they'll make it?"

"They were laughing as they went off together. They can
amuse one another. The question is whether or not he's going
to be aggressive enough."

Monty frowned. "He won't be. He's a cynic . . . and he's
tired. He's not what she needs. How about Mary Ferrell?"

"With her looks! She brought down the house! She's out
doing a duty walk with Tom Rogers. Bob Ferrell is with Sally
Rogers."

"Who's next for Elaine?"

"Doctor Anderson. He's with Becky Sanders now."

"Let me break in and talk with Elaine a couple of minutes
before she goes out with Anderson."

Likelike nodded. She watched Monty's broad back as he
sauntered away. She felt sure he didn't really want Elaine.
He liked experienced, erotic women. Elaine didn't excite his
libido: only his curiosity. But then, Likelike asked herself, if

a woman can make a man curious about her, isn't that one way to begin making him want her.

As Monty sauntered and waited for Elaine to return to Likelike's "pairing post," he found himself wondering why he, at thirty-five, had never had a virgin. "It's really strange," he thought. "How is it that I have taken so many women, over so many years, and yet I've never had *one* virgin!"

He decided that the answer lay in the island attitude towards virgins. After all, he was more islander than mainlander. He was more Hawaiian than white. And islanders don't value virgins as mainlanders do. Islanders send virgins off to learn sex just as mainlanders send virgins off to learn manners.

Then why, Monty demanded of himself, was he thinking about Elaine Shelby? How did a man act with a virgin? What preliminaries were advisable? He decided that before he went to a lounge with Elaine he'd discuss the problem with the doctor who had examined her.

But that decision brought another thought. Suppose after he went to all the trouble of discussing it with the doctor he should discover that Elaine had ceased to be a virgin? Would he be disappointed? He decided he would be. And this led Monty to a strange sort of feeling he had never experienced before : he suddenly felt *concerned* about a woman! This concern was almost an emotion. He couldn't ignore it : he had suddenly become *concerned* about what happened to Elaine Shelby!

As Monty reflected on this concern, he kept looking towards Likelike, waiting impatiently for her signal. When it came he rushed back, nodded to Madison and Doctor Anderson, and hurried Elaine over to a palm tree.

"Elaine, I just have a couple of minutes," he said. "I've been thinking . . . about your situation. Is everything all right?"

"Wonderful," Elaine said. "Everything is exactly as you said it would be. I'm ready for real civilized living. Do I look civilized?"

She turned around for him. She pulled up the *muumuu* to

show him her sandals . . . with her trim feet and delicate ankles.

"Just as I predicted," he said. "You're prettier than you've ever been." Then, for the first time in his life, Monty experienced difficulty with words. "Elaine," he stammered, "the point is . . . well, I don't have time to walk in the garden, and being the manager I'd have to stop and speak to everybody, and I was wondering if we couldn't meet in a lounge . . . say in half an hour or so?"

"Oh, I'm sorry," she said sadly. "I really am." She took him by the hand and suddenly he smelled her perfume. He thought he knew every perfume at the hotel, but this was a new one : the most exciting he had ever encountered! "It's impossible. I'm dated up until ten . . . and since I've had such an exciting day I must turn in at ten and then try to sleep. But I very much want a nice, *long* conversation with you. How about tomorrow at one . . . here in the garden?"

Monty searched her eyes, trying to see if she was laughing at him. He wasn't sure whether she was or not. All he knew was that he had her by the hand and for some sudden and compelling reason he didn't want to let her go.

"Elaine," he persisted, "I'm sorry to appear persistent, but let's make it tonight. Please."

That was the first time Monty ever said *please* to a woman in his life. He didn't know why he said it. Elaine shook her head. "It's impossible, Monty. If you wanted conversation with me tonight why weren't you here an hour ago, when I was introduced?"

"I intended to be. I got tied up."

"Then we'll just have to wait until tomorrow."

She pulled her hand, for Doctor Anderson was waiting for her, but Monty held on.

"Just one more minute," he said. "Elaine . . . well, goddamit, you haven't agreed to meet Madison in a lounge, have you?"

Elaine's eyes widened in surprise. "Monty, that question is heresy. It's a violation of everything Hotel Mamie Stover stands for. This hotel is designed to protect a woman from questions like that. Remember?"

Monty couldn't remember when he had been this uncomfortable. "I'm sorry," he said. "I'm just concerned about you. You're an unusual guest, I want to protect you. So don't let anybody rush you into anything. Take your time. And . . . well . . . dammit, Madison is not what you need."

"Why not? Suppose he likes me? Suppose I like him? Those are the only requirements for like-sex, aren't they?"

"Not necessarily. Madison is a cynic. He laughs or cries at everything. A girl like you shouldn't associate with a cynic."

"And you're not a cynic?"

"Not like Madison. He thinks people are crazy. He laughs at everybody. And didn't he tell you? Madison is *married*."

Elaine looked startled. "You're not yourself tonight, Monty. Three hours ago Mamie told me that like-sex has nothing to do with marriage. It's no more than a festivity of the flesh . . . a little physical conversation. And two hours ago Likelike warned me against a single man. She urged me to prefer a married man and gave me convincing reasons for doing so."

Monty now remembered that Elaine was a lawyer, and his shoulders sagged. "Don't make fun of me, Elaine," he said. "I'm trying to be your friend. Madison is not who you need, and this Doctor Anderson is not who you need."

"Then who do I need?"

Monty didn't realize it but Elaine would have given him the rendezvous had he made the correct reply to that question. After forty minutes with Madison she had agreed to a first rendezvous with him at ten-thirty. But she would have cancelled this, and would have gone with Monty, if he had only made this reply: "Elaine, I don't know which of us you need most. But this I'm sure of. *I* need *you* much more than Madison does, or Doctor Anderson does." But nothing in Monty's experience had taught him to make that reply. Instead he answered: "I don't know whether you need me or not. But I'd like you to promise me that . . . that you won't make any final decision, or take any action, until after you've conversed with me tomorrow." •

That wasn't quite what Elaine wanted to hear. So she stiffened and said: "As we say in courtrooms, Monty, a promise like that in this free, erotic environment would be entirely out of order. However, you meet me here at one sharp tomorrow afternoon, and I'll probably be in approximately the same condition as I am now. I'm not promising . . . I'm just giving you an offhand opinion." She pulled away from him and joined Doctor Anderson.

Monty watched her until she disappeared behind some foliage. He wasn't accustomed to disappointment with women. Then Mary Ferrell returned to the pairing post. Madison was waiting to walk with her, but again Monty asked for the two-minute interruption. He led Mary to the palm tree and suggested a rendezvous at nine-thirty. She agreed, whispered the lounge number, then walked in the garden with Madison.

At nine-twenty-five Mary entered the Carnival Room. She selected the Cleopatra disguise and put it on. It was a plastic head representing the Queen of the Nile, large enough to slip over Mary's head and rest on her shoulders. She also draped an Egyptian shawl over her body, down to her ankles, then she stepped into the lighted secret passage and began the walk to her lounge. She walked determinedly, as though she knew exactly what she was doing.

In acquisitive societies there are two pivotal moments in every human life. The first is the moment when the individual defines for himself what he wants to acquire; the second is the moment when he loses his nerve and gives up. And the wonder is not that so many millions want so little and give up so quickly, but that so many hundreds want so much and persist so long.

Mary's story was a variation of the ancient story of the poor-but-pretty girl who decides what she wants, then strives to get it. By the time she was fifteen she knew several things about herself. She knew she belonged to the lower middle classes. She knew that she was prettier than most girls. And what was unusual in one so young, she understood clearly that poor and pretty girls either get pregnant young, and have trouble for the rest of their lives, or resist boys and use their looks to get what they want. Mary intended to get what she wanted. She wanted a husband who was either prosperous or going to be. She wanted a Cadillac. She wanted a one-carat diamond ring. She wanted two children. Not one, not three, but two. She wanted a mink coat. She wanted a substantial home, and she wanted it on Country Club Road. She wanted to go to Chicago twice a year and buy her clothes at fashionable stores.

Usually in this sort of story the mother pushes the daughter, urges her to trap the rich husband so that she may escape the drudgery the mother has suffered. Mary's mother didn't push her much, she only gave her this vulgar advice.

"Mary," her mother said. "There may be nicer ways to say it, but this is the clearest way. You are pretty. You can better yourself. The way to do it is not to let boys touch you. Look for the boy who is going to be something and have something. If you like him, let him touch you, but not much, and when you are alone with him and he's touching you, cross your legs. Keep them crossed. Don't let any force in the world uncross your legs until you've stood before a preacher and have a ring on your finger. Then you can have something, you can move up in the world. But just make one mistake, and you can lose every advantage you were born with."

When Mary was in her teens every boy in high school knew this about her : she was pretty, but she wasn't hot. You could look at her, but you couldn't touch her. You could grab her and kiss her at the price of a clout across the ear.

She tried to attract two boys from prosperous families, but she didn't make it with either of them. They went off to college and she couldn't follow. Then she noticed Bob Ferrell. He hadn't gone to college, but he was going to have money. She investigated everything about him, and saw that he was her best bet to get what she wanted. Then she married him . . . and uncrossed her legs.

But sex had not been included in her investigation. She had seen Bob's financial report but she had not seen his medical report. So she had not learned that he was sexually "sub-normal." And since Mary was a virgin she didn't realize Bob was sub-normal until they had been married two years and had begun to consult doctors.

One doctor advised them to adopt children, but Mary rejected this advice on two grounds. It was not according to her plan, and it might damage Bob's ego. She didn't intend to damage Bob's ego, she intended to feed it. For a man needs ego to go somewhere, and to accumulate something.

It was not until she reached Hotel Mamie Stover, on her first visit in 1953, that Mary faced the whole truth. She faced it in a conference with Mamie.

"Mary," Mamie said, "you're twenty-eight years old. You've been married six years. You've had a disappointment. Nobody has faced the truth with you. Let's you and I face it and see if I can help."

"I'd like that," Mary said. "What is the truth? Is my husband hopelessly inadequate?"

Mamie handed her the medical report. "The doctors here say he is. He'd probably have been inadequate with any woman. He's hopeless with you because he feels inferior to you."

"Can you help him to feel stronger?"

"Yes. We can help his ego. We can give him a girl he thinks he's superior to . . . a girl who'll be lascivious with him, and feed his ego. This will make him stronger with you."

"But not strong enough?"

"Probably not. The doctors say there isn't one chance in a hundred that he can ever get you pregnant."

Mamie and Mary were silent for a moment, then Mary asked: "Does this happen often, or is this a rare case?"

"It isn't as rare as most people think," Mamie replied. "It could be avoided if medical examinations were required before every marriage. Why don't you divorce him and get a normal man? You've got the looks to do it."

"Impossible," Mary said. "He's the only man I want. He worships me. He's getting me all the things I want. I love him. I intend to keep him . . . and I intend to build up his ego."

"Then here's how to do it," Mamie said. "We can professionally inform him that the fault is *yours*, that it's *you* who can't have children. Then go to Chicago and adopt two children."

Mary rejected this advice. "No. I didn't plan it that way. I want to *have* two children. He wants me to have them."

"Then why not try artificial insemination? We don't do it here, but you can get it done in Chicago."

"I've considered that. It won't work. The husband has to be told about it. He has to agree. Such a step would damage my husband's ego."

That stopped the conversation again. Mamie measured her closely. "We're running out of choices, I'm afraid. If we aren't careful you'll have only one left. And that isn't considered nice in Wisconsin."

Mary returned Mamie's close gaze. Her jaw firmed. "Why do you think I came here?"

When Mamie didn't reply at once, Mary continued: "Do I surprise you? It's been done before here, hasn't it?"

"The answer is yes to both questions," Mamie said. "Yes, it's been done before. And yes, you surprise me. That double operation takes the nerve of a government mule. Have you got it?"

"I think I have."

"You know what to look for in a man?"

"I think so. Same general build. Same general facial structure. Same eye and hair color."

Mamie nodded. Then: "The hardest part is with your husband. You must keep feeding his ego. As he gets stronger you must encourage him, compliment him. But if you take on a normal man here, and sandwich your husband in between, you're going to notice quite a contrast. With your

126

looks, and with the added excitement of stealing something, a virile man is going to enjoy you. And you may enjoy him. After those normal sessions you think you can hide your contempt for your husband's feeble efforts? You think you can react successfully and make him think he's finding new strength at Hotel Mamie Stover?"

"Couldn't you do it?"

"Yes, I could do it," Mamie said. "But I'm supposed to be a hardened professional, not a respectable little Wisconsin housewife. You're practically a virgin. You've had one subnormal man. And you're not even lusty. If you were, you couldn't have tolerated your husband for six years. Yet all at once you think you can take on a lusty man and keep him coming back, then an hour or so later you take on your husband and make him feel that he's finding zest in the islands. That's quite an order."

"That's why I came to you, Mamie," Mary said. "You say you can teach me sexual prowess. You can give my husband his lascivious Hawaiian girl who can teach him how to dominate. Do you really help people? Well, help us and we can go back to Eau Claire, Wisconsin, with everything we came here looking for."

As that conference was ending, Mamie said: "Mary, until today I thought I was the only woman on earth who could do *anything* to get what she wanted. In you I may have met my match."

After that, no huntress at Hotel Mamie Stover ever hunted more determinedly than Mary Ferrell. She hurried through the general areas, appraising men. She watched men walk, estimated heights and weights, noticed hair color, and peered deep into eyes. And she found her man: Monty Whitaker.

At first glance few persons would note any resemblance between Monty and Bob Ferrell, but a closer look would reveal the vital resemblances. Bob was a stocky five-eight, Monty was a stockier five-six. Monty's face was so broad it was almost square, Bob's face was only full. Monty's hair was so light it was almost sandy, Bob's hair was only light. Both had blue Irish eyes.

Mary remembered her first rendezvous with Monty. She agreed to it at a noon meeting in the garden, and they set the time for 3 P.M. because he had to fly to Honolulu at five. She didn't tell Mamie whom she had selected. She came back to the women's area and tried to prepare herself. The Hawaiian women gave her their strongest aphrodisiac potion. They soaked her in a hot mustard hip-bath. They rubbed her body with myrrh and coconut oil. They anointed her with exotic, erotic perfume. They left her breasts bare and tied a blazing red sarong around her hips. In the Carnival Room she selected the Cleopatra disguise. Then she began the long walk.

She felt faint and nervous. Her legs trembled as she mounted the stairs to the lounge, and when she opened the door she felt startled and horribly alone. From her looks and marriage record Likelike had assumed that she was experienced and erotic, so Likelike had assigned her an advanced lounge. On the ceiling and on three sides the couch was surrounded by "black" mirrors, with recessed lighting which made tanned bodies stand out in relief.

When the bell rang she jumped nervously. She almost failed to open the door, and when she did open it she was still clutching the Egyptian shawl around her shoulders. Since Monty knew she was married, he assumed she was the hot wife sampling her first holiday-sex, and he treated her as he thought she wanted to be treated . . . and needed to be treated. He grabbed her. He wore only his swim trunks, and as he pulled the shawl from her he rubbed her breasts hard with his broad chest and kissed her hungrily. He paused, shed his trunks . . . and she almost fainted. Because she had not discussed Monty with Likelike she had had no warning that she'd be leaping from one extreme to the other : from a sub-normal man to a super-normal man.

Monty laughed at her surprise, and at what he assumed was her delight. Then he proceeded with the zest of a playful grizzly bear.

"You can't take this big stranger with clothes on, baby!" He jerked off the silk sarong.

He stood enjoying the sight of her. He let her enjoy the sight of him. She had turned the lights low. He turned them up to half-light.

"God, you're pretty!" he exulted. "I want to *see* you, baby! I want to *see* what I'm doing to you! And I know you'll want to see."

He tossed her on the couch, among all the smoky mirrors, and leaped on her. His hands and lips were all over her. His body so dominated hers that she felt she was being drowned in a torrent of hot, clasping, surging, sinewy flesh. He was not being brutal with her, just aggressive and dominant as he thought she wanted him to be. Her scream was from both fright and acute pain, but she held on passively and desperately, counting seconds, expecting the hurricane to end. But it didn't end, it only abated temporarily.

"Get comfortable, baby," he said. "It'll be an hour by the clock before I turn you loose. You're the best piece I've had in a year."

That's how Mary Ferrell learned zestful sex, and that's how she proved she had the nerve of a government mule. For five days she did nothing else but sleep, eat, and study sexual prowess. She ate only amatory food. She drank kava and angel water. She lay on massage tables and took a variety of massages. She experimented with perfumes.

When she left Hotel Mamie Stover she was pregnant as a goat.

Now, after two years, as Mary walked towards another rendezvous with Monty, she had acquired almost everything she wanted. She had the prosperous husband, the substantial home on Country Club Road, the Cadillac, diamonds, mink coats, the shopping trips to Chicago, and one beautiful, fifteen-months-old daughter. She was only one child short. Three or four more sessions with Monty, one more pregnancy, and by her thirty-first birthday she'd have it all.

So far she hadn't lost her nerve, but she had strained some nerves. An autopsy on her would have revealed nerves tight as banjo strings. The first trip to Hawaii had given her and Bob the child, but not without changing both of them. After all that arousal and education, Mary was far less capable of tolerating a sexual cripple. She had grown more petulant and contemptuous of her husband.

Even more disturbing had been the change in Bob. Mary had got the child to satisfy herself and to feed his ego, but the child fed his ego too much, for she was visible evidence that Bob was not sexually deficient: he never had been. All he had needed to impregnate the beautiful Mary was a holiday . . . plus a little diversion with an Hawaiian girl. This assurance had emboldened Bob to defy Mary in ways he had never been capable of before.

Bob couldn't easily forget how he had "dominated" that Hawaiian girl, and since he was now rich and important, and was again trying to impregnate his wife, he decided to repeat that helpful arrangement. He got a girl in Wisconsin he thought he was superior to: a nineteen-year-old "high yellow" Negro secretary. Two afternoons a week, on a couch in his office, she told him how strong and dominant he was. And he raised her salary every month.

Despite all this now-found assurance, however, Bob was still a cripple with Mary. Months went by and she didn't get pregnant. Sometimes he thought he did fairly well with her, but most times he got a humiliating feeling of weakness in his loins and he came to blame her for it.

All his frustration and hate boiled up one Saturday night when he sat on the side of the bed, humiliated, resentful, miserable.

"Goddam you, Mary," he said, "you've always done this to me. You've always thought you were better than I am. You've always made me think you were a little too rich for my blood. Well, I proved you weren't, didn't I? I took you to Hawaii and got you pregnant, didn't I? And I'll tell you something else. While I was getting you pregnant I had an Hawaiian

130

girl you couldn't hold a candle to. And here's something else : I'm still doing just that. I got me a nigger girl right here in Eau Claire. I'm strong as a bull with her. I lay her and then I come home and lay you. How do you like that? I'm not the weakling you think I am. And I'm still able to take you back to Hawaii, rest up, breathe some salt air, and punch your clock again !"

Mary let Bob finish that speech only because she had the nerve of a government mule. She didn't intend to jeopardize what she had. She knew she held the whip : all she had to do was lay it across his back. A few sentences of truth . . . and how strong would he feel !

But the truth was hers alone. They patched up such quarrels because they had too much invested in the partnership. They were both capable of maintaining a marriage for purposes of pride, ambition, convenience, habit, and community property. They needed one another. And strangely, though for different reasons, they both needed Mary to be pregnant again. So they returned to Hotel Mamie Stover where Bob was confident he could find strength.

As Mary walked she was aware that she didn't feel the same towards Monty as she had felt two years ago. Then he had been only the stud she had selected. But now . . . well, he had not only awakened her when she was with him, but in her two years away from him he had been the beneficiary of illusions she built around him. He was a real man, not a cripple. Above all, he was the father of her daughter. Each day for fifteen months she had looked into her child's face and seen Monty Whitaker.

Two years ago she had gone to meet him in fear and unease, she had wanted only his seed. Now she was going to meet him as a starved, erotic, experienced woman. She wanted not only his seed but also many hours of ecstasy with him . . . hours in which she could give and receive all the delights she had learned to give and receive.

"After what I've had to put up with," she said to herself,

"I deserve a week of real sex with a real man, a man who dominates me, a man who can handle a real woman."

As Monty walked towards his rendezvous with Mary, he didn't feel as he had felt two years ago either. Then he had been unconcerned, his mind had been on nothing but that beautiful, erotic, little woman waiting for him. But in the years since then he hadn't known of any child, he had had nothing to remind him of her, and he hadn't built any illusions around her. He hadn't remembered her name, he didn't recognize it on the application card. He remembered her only after he saw her at the Luau.

Tonight she was his second choice. His mind wasn't even on her as he walked. His mind was on Elaine. He was concerned about Elaine. He might even be worried about her. He felt bothered by the possibility that Madison might be succeeding with Elaine at the very moment when he (Monty) was wasting time in a repeat performance of an old routine.

Monty shook his head as he realized that something unusual and confusing was happening to him. This was the first time in his life that he had ever walked towards a numbered door, behind which an attractive woman was waiting, when his mind was on another woman. How could this be! Hell, Mary Ferrell was a sexual jackpot! There was no ecstasy she couldn't give a man! And Elaine? Christ, Elaine couldn't compare with Mary in anything! Not in looks, not in experience, not in prowess ... Christ, she wasn't even erotic. She'd be awkward, cold as a cucumber.

Then, Monty asked himself, why the hell wasn't he walking faster? Why wasn't his desire mounting? He didn't know the answer. All he knew was that, as he walked up the stairs towards that numbered door, he actually felt *tired*!

The rendezvous differed from the first one. When Mary opened the door she wasn't clutching the shawl around her. She had only the silk sarong at her hips. She retreated skilfully, enticing him to grab her, but when he didn't grab fast enough she returned and lifted her arms to him. His kiss wasn't hungry enough, so she employed skill to make it hungrier. It was she, more than he, who rubbed her breasts hard against his chest.

As he shed his duck pants she stepped back and let him look at her while she looked at him. His ego began to feed. He still liked to be reminded that women didn't forget, that they came back for more, especially compact little women as pretty as Mary.

She smiled and said: "He won't be a stranger this time, Monty."

That was a very skillful remark. It caused Monty to jerk off the silk sarong. But this time he didn't toss her quite so boisterously on the couch, among the mirrors. He used more restraint. And her hands and lips were more active than his.

From this point, however, no one could fault the mutual performance. The only difference from before was that Monty operated with a little less zest ... and he was finished twenty minutes short of the hour he had once demanded.

She wasn't exactly disappointed. It was just that she had thought about it so much, and surrounded the first encounter with so many illusions, that she found herself wishing that he had wanted to hold her a little longer. She lay quietly beside him.

"Are you glad I'm back, Monty?"

"After that! Of course I am. You're prettier than ever, and more wonderful."

"I've thought about you a lot since I was here. Have you ever thought once about me?"

"No man could have you and forget you."

What Mary wanted was to hear Monty say he intended to have her every day she was at the hotel. She had expected him to say it while he was enjoying her. Now that he hadn't said it, she felt uneasy. And this uneasiness caused her to make a mistake. Over and over she had heard Mamie say in seminars, "Every man, immediately after an act of possession, feels depressed, lonely, and distrustful. The smart woman *never* asks him for anything at this time. The smart woman *always* waits until she has aroused him again." Now Mary ignored this advice. She took Monty's face in her hands and kissed him tenderly. It was a gesture he wasn't accustomed to, so he smiled distrustfully and asked: "What was that for?"

"Just an expression," she said. "I'm glad to be back where I am at this moment. The kiss was an expression of my . . . my regard for you. I might even say affection, but I suppose affection is out of bounds at Hotel Mamie Stover."

To keep from meeting her eyes, Monty pulled her face down on his chest and held her for a moment. When he let her look at him again he saw tears.

"I'm sorry," she said. "I'm just happy. I feel very close to you, Monty . . . very tender towards you. Will I see you again tomorrow?"

She hoped his answer wouldn't be defensive, but she knew it would be. Every man's answer is defensive at this moment.

"I don't know, Mary. I'm awfully busy. I run a big business, you know. And we're in the middle of a tax audit. Of course I'll see you before you leave, but it may be a couple of days."

That almost forced her into another error. She suddenly felt an overwhelming urge to tell him about his daughter, to explain why she felt so tender towards him now, and why she needed him every day. But she tightened those already taut nerves and said: "I understand. Just remember that I've travelled five thousand miles for only one purpose: to see you. I have nothing else to do here except wait for you."

Mary walked less determinedly back towards the women's barracks. She felt uneasy and lonely. She kept telling herself that she had expected too much . . . that Monty had given her everything she had any right to expect. And she kept telling herself that he'd want to see her again, not one more time but several more times. All she needed was patience. What woman at the hotel had her looks? Her sexual prowess?

Since it was about 10:30, time for the last rendezvous before the midnight curfew, Mary met several women walking excitedly and determinedly forward. All wore disguises similar to her own Cleopatra disguise. The enlarged plastic heads were the women of song and story who had enlivened their days with sexual adventure: Pompadour, Delilah, Helen of Troy, Lady Chatterley, Du Barry, Salome, Moll Flanders, Bethsheba, Jezebel, Sister Carrie, Amber, Madame Bovary. No woman spoke to any other woman, this was the rule, and the huge, painted, erotic heads moved silently through the passage, to and fro.

Then Mary met one compact little woman who wore no disguise at all. She walked brazenly and determinedly, in nothing more than her sandals and red *muumuu*, with a hibiscus bloom in her hair.

She was Elaine Shelby.

As Monty walked back towards the men's barracks he felt tired, and for the first time he wondered if perhaps he wasn't getting old. His session with Mary had been technically perfect, but, dammit, he had been walking away from numbered doors in this manner for twenty years!

"From fifteen to thirty-five!" he thought. "God, that's a lot of years to enjoy travelling women . . . a lot of beds to crawl out of . . . a lot of doors to walk away from."

He met several men hurrying towards the lounges. Each one grinned at him and passed some variation of the standard joke, the one always used when men met in the passage, the one about the fast walk forward and the slow drag back. The joke didn't seem funny to Monty tonight.

Then Monty met Jim Madison, and they both knew they had to pause and exchange some pleasantry.

"You been inspecting the lounges, Monty?" Madison inquired. "Everything shipshape?"

"Everything's fine, Jim," Monty replied. "You doing some research?"

"Yeah, a little. Research is everything in my business. I must get these women to tell me why they come here, what they are seeking, what they are finding."

135

"Yeah, I guess so. But I heard you were tired. I thought you'd be asleep by now."

"Well, that's a funny thing, Monty," Madison grinned. "I was dead-tired when I got here this afternoon. But you've created a remarkable place here. I don't feel a bit tired now. In fact, at this moment I can't remember when I ever felt more vigorous in my life."

Madison walked rapidly forward. Monty continued his disconsolate walk back.

CHAPTER TEN

The first evening, continued: in
which we watch Elaine Shelby and
Jim Madison consider like-sex.

ELAINE SHELBY AND Jim Madison walked together in the
general garden. It was 7:30 P.M. For five-and-a-half hours
Elaine had known that Madison existed. Madison had known
for twenty hours that Elaine existed, ever since he had overheard her conversation with Monty at the Luau. After their
introduction at 2 P.M., they had sat touching one another for
fifteen minutes during the ride from the hotel to the airplane.
They had sat directly across from one another during the
twenty-eight-minute plane ride. Each had looked into the
other's eyes, had heard the other's voice, had seen the other's
smile. About her Madison knew what she had told Monty.
About him Elaine knew what Likelike had told her.

As they walked they looked like an attractive, still-athletic,
but graying forty-two-year-old man with either his second wife
or his mistress. The fourteen years difference in their ages was
apparent, yet Madison didn't look old. And Elaine, walking
beside him in her red *muumuu*, her head reaching his chin,
looked youthful and excited. She looked twenty-eight, but with
her alertness and curiosity, she still gave the impression that
much could yet happen to her for the first time.

"Jim," she said, "you and I are suddenly together in this
strange place thousands of miles from where I live. We are
holding hands and calling one another by our first names. Do
you feel you know me? Or do I seem like a hopeless stranger
to you?"

Madison smiled. "Most of us feel like strangers most of our lives," he replied. "We spend our lives trying to feel close to somebody. I already know something about you, because I was waiting in Monty's other office and heard your voices on his intercom. So whatever you said to him I know. I've thought about you since then. I was conscious of touching you in the car. I noticed your perfume. I watched you on the plane. I know how your eyes light up with curiosity, how you enjoy making humorous remarks. So your hand in mine doesn't feel like a hopeless stranger's."

She walked closer to him. "I know something about you, too. Likelike talked to me about you. She seemed quite well informed. I'm sorry I haven't read your books so that I could have known you even better at this point."

"The books are only about people like you and me . . . what we do in various situations."

"Have you written about what we do in a situation like ours tonight?"

"Not exactly. But approximately."

After a moment she looked up at him and asked: "Do you know why you were paired with me first?"

"Of course. Likelike recommended me to you. She told you that you might like me . . . enough. And that I might like you enough."

"And what do you think of her judgment?"

"I think she was wrong, for you. As for me, I feel grateful to her. You give me a lift walking beside me. But she could have done much better for you. She recommended me to you because, like all island women, Likelike distrusts young white men. She probably has been betrayed by at least one young white man, so she over-values forty-year-old white men. She oversells experience. She should have recommended for you a man eight or ten years younger than I am, and much less experienced. And you need a single man. You rebel at the thought of being used by a married man. Likelike doesn't, but you do. With a single man you can have more illusions, pretend more, hope for more than you ever can with me."

"That's a strange speech."

"Strange only because it's honest," Madison said. "Honesty is one of the luxuries I can afford."

They walked on through the trees and flowers. She said: "I'd like to hear more about how you think, Jim. So much has happened to me during the last twenty-four hours. I feel like Alice in Wonderland. Always before in my life I've felt I knew what I was doing. Now I'm not sure. I wonder if I should have come here? Do you think I should have come?"

"No," he answered. "If I had met you last night at the Luau, and if you had asked me, I would have advised you not to come."

"Why?"

"Because you are different from the rest of us here. You are still happy, the rest of us are resigned. An ideal is still attainable for you. The mainland ideal is love, one man and one woman loving one another from adolescence to death. But there is no love at Hotel Mamie Stover. People here like one another, respect one another, cling to one another, tolerate one another, even have sex with one another, but they don't love one another. All of us here except you have lost the ideal. Something has gone wrong for us, but nothing has gone wrong for you yet, so you don't belong among us. You shouldn't have come."

"But something has gone wrong for me," she insisted. "Virginity at twenty-eight is wrong, isn't it? Unnatural? That's why I decided to come."

"Don't confuse your words," Madison warned. "Wrong and unnatural are not the same. Virginity at twenty-eight is unnatural but not wrong. Turning the other cheek is unnatural but not wrong. One man and one woman is unnatural but not wrong. If you want to understand, stick to right and wrong, good and evil. Don't inject natural and unnatural."

They halted to admire the Maui Beauty hibiscus, and for Elaine to tilt her head far back and look at the tops of the royal palms. Madison would have preferred to simplify the conversation, to hear Elaine talk about her life in Indiana. But

139

he understood why she wanted to weigh big questions. She was educated, so her sexual problem was first an intellectual problem. Only later could it become an emotional problem.

"All right," Elaine continued, "I'll stick to right and wrong, and I'll be specific. Is it wrong to eat amatory food as I did tonight? Is it wrong to drink *mobani* juice and angel water? Is it wrong to allow oneself to be massaged in ways which heighten sensuousness? Is it wrong to select perfumes for the sole purpose of stimulating male desire? Is it wrong to dress sensuously, as I am now dressed, naked except for this silk *muumuu*? Is it wrong to try to learn to move rhythmically, to dance erotically, for the sole purpose of enticing a man? Is it wrong to listen to advice on how to become more skilful sexually, and how to derive delight from the sex act?"

When Madison chuckled Elaine said: "Please don't laugh. That's the easy way...for us to laugh it off. Give me an honest answer."

"Well, first," Madison answered, "sensuousness in itself is not evil or wrong. It becomes evil only if it hurts somebody, if it results in misery, shame or remorse. I remember a quotation ...something like this:

> Sensuousness is no sin, but is, on the contrary, an adornment of life, a gift of God, like the sweet winds of spring. We should enjoy it, with clear conscience. . . .

"The man who said that," Madison went on, "is not a Polynesian but a Scandinavian. I think he's right. I ate an amatory dinner, took amatory massage. I listened to an Hawaiian woman named Sayee instruct the men how to use the lounges, how to increase our potency and desire, how to become more dominant, and tomorrow I expect to engage in the most amatory of all exercises for men: riding. Aristotle asked in his *Problems*: 'Why do those men who ride horseback become steadily more libidinous?' Napoleon found that his cavalrymen needed women more often than his infantrymen. I've always been an enthusiastic rider."

Madison chuckled, looked steadily at Elaine, and added:

"Sensuousness is something to welcome and encourage. Not something to deplore and suppress."

"But mustn't sensuousness wait on love?" Elaine demanded. "If a woman becomes sensuous before she finds love, isn't the result fornication? And fornication is illegal. It isn't a felony like rape, but it's a crime against the community."

"So it is," Madison agreed. "Fornication is a crime, and as a lawyer you resent crime. Crime is wrong, but you also said that virginity at twenty-eight is wrong. Since you haven't found love, which is more wrong for you—continuing virginity or fornication? That's the question you came here to answer, and that's why I said you shouldn't have come. The rest of us here have engaged in fornication, except that here it's called like-sex. It fills a compelling desire for like-sex?"

She evaded the last question. "Let me become more specific," she said. "Let me consider individuals. The people who travelled here with us, are they evil? Will their conduct here be wrong?"

Madison replied: "Before I start judging individuals, let me warn you that I may not be right. I always feel pretentious sitting in judgment on people. And I'm not a religious man, so I don't follow any of the old advice, injunctions or commandments. I try to decide matters for myself. I don't think people or places are evil, and conduct only becomes evil when it hurts somebody. So when you ask me if a person's conduct is evil, I'll ask you if that conduct will hurt anybody."

"Let's take Sally Rogers and her husband, Tom," Elaine said. "You say they have gone wrong, they've lost the ideal. Are they evil?"

Madison replied: "I had dinner with Tom. We exchanged war stories. He and Sally lost the one-man-one-woman ideal through his conduct. He took other women . . . in the war, up in the Oregon woods. In all his life he has known but two kinds of sex: with women he feels superior to, and with his wife. Here he'll take only a girl he feels far superior to. But what he does with a Woola Woola girl isn't likely to hurt him, the girl, or his wife. He tells himself that Sally will only 'play around.' He's probably wrong, for Sally and Tom have suffered boredom. Their sex together after twenty years has become too tame, too matter-of-fact. Yet Sally is still an ardent woman, so she'll take all the sensuous massages. And she'll take a man, but I doubt that it hurts her, or Tom. So I don't consider them evil. Their conduct may even be helpful."

Elaine sighed heavily. "That's going a long way, isn't it? No wonder I feel like a stranger here. You're a civilized, educated, decent American, yet you not only call the crime of fornication *good*, you even suspect adultery may be helpful."

Madison paused, then said: "I'm sorry, Elaine. Laws and rules are expressions of ideals. Some people manage to cling to the ideals throughout their lives. Others of us do the best we can."

Elaine felt some resentment towards Madison for his harsh answers. She wanted to change the subject, but she had more questions.

"What about Mary Ferrell and her husband, Bob? Are they evil? Will their conduct be wrong?"

Madison replied: "My guess is that they have already hurt one another deeply. A petulant beauty can cause misery to herself and others. Bob and Mary both have egos which need feeding, and they can't feed one another, so theirs is a morbid match. Their conduct is likely to be hurtful and evil."

"And Becky Sanders?"

"I don't know. Things have gone wrong for her. She's sensuous. Certainly she'll take a man or men. Whether she'll hurt them, or they her, I have no judgment."

"And Doctor Anderson? Will his conduct be evil?"

"He and I talked a while," Madison said. "He's an honest man beset by an old problem. Sex with his wife has grown too domesticated. He says he needs exciting, licentious sex. If he's honest he isn't likely to hurt anybody. If he makes dishonest representations in order to induce some woman, such as promising to divorce his wife and marry her when he has no such intention, then he can hurt and become evil."

142

"What about his wife?" Elaine asked. "Won't she be hurt?"

"Probably not. She may have been hurt already by the realization that she can no longer give her husband what he thinks he needs. That's a harsh reality, but an ordinary one because monogamy is unnatural. But that hurt has already been done, so what the doctor does here shouldn't affect her. She won't even have knowledge of it. For centuries Chinese wives have known that many men need a new woman at forty. They continue living in the households and find purpose in holding families together."

Elaine stopped, turned to Madison, and smiled. "We've run out of people to be objective about. Now I want to get personal. How about Elaine's conduct? Would it hurt anybody? And Jim Madison? Is he good or evil?"

They stood for a moment looking into each other's eyes.

"If I understood Sayee correctly," Madison said, "our conversation until now has been elementary because we've discussed sex only generally. But now you've advanced it. And all advanced conversation at Hotel Mamie Stover *must* be conducted in a lounge. To conduct advanced conversation in the garden is indecent."

He felt her hands moistening, saw the color rising in her cheeks. She asked slowly: "Did your Hawaiian woman make very clear that the first rendezvous is *not* a sexual commitment?"

"She particularly emphasized it."

Her voice softened. "When would you like to meet?"

He pulled her closer. "It's about 8 now," he said. "My impulse is to suggest 8:30, but this is your first evening, and you shouldn't ignore the other men who are so anxious to converse with you. How about 10:30?"

Elaine, now that she had put her mind to it, would have preferred not to wait so long. But she said: "All right. The lounge number is twenty-four."

He nodded. "That's an easy number to remember. And you are even easier to remember."

They walked back to the pairing post. Doctor Anderson was waiting for Elaine, and Monty was waiting to make his hurried proposition. Elaine walked with Doctor Anderson.

At 9.15 Elaine left the general garden and went back to the women's barracks, where the Hawaiian experts gave her the virgin preparation. She drank the most dependable of ancient marriage potions, and sat in a scalding hot mustard hip-bath. They massaged her with myrrh and coconut oil, and perfumed her with a rare essence once employed by a notorious Hawaiian queen to seduce a missionary.

They wanted to drape a silk sarong around her hips and leave her nubile breasts bare, but she insisted on the *muumuu*. At 10:15 she entered the Carnival Room and considered several disguises. She put on the Lady Chatterley head and wrapper and was about to enter the secret passage when, with a brazen gesture, she tossed Lady Chatterley aside and strode into the passage wearing no disguise at all.

She was flushed and excited. Several disguised women were in the passage, on their way to rendezvous, and Elaine met several others who were returning. She noticed the woman in the Cleopatra disguise whose steps appeared to drag.

As Elaine mounted the stairs she felt her legs quiver. The lounge was elementary, as befitted a virgin. There were no mirrors. The couch was covered with a fresh, yellow sheet and adorned with red pillows. The only decoration was a palm tree, painted on the wall beside the couch, so that partners could remark that at last they were on "a tropical island, lying together under a palm tree." And since this was the most elementary of lounges, arranged for women who might require further conversation, there were two chairs, and a table on which sat two glasses and a pitcher of *mobani* juice.

The bell startled Elaine. She went to the door, recognized Madison, let him in. Silently he took her in his arms, held her for a moment, then kissed her. They stood holding one another, then she backed off.

"Before you become aggressive and dominant," she said, "I

144

have one more question to discuss. And I want to discuss it sitting up, not lying down."

They sat in the chairs, and Madison poured the *mobani* juice.

"It's about this matter of who gets hurt," Elaine said. "Suppose I accept your reasoning that what hurts is evil, and what doesn't hurt is not evil : all right, I accept that. Then the question becomes, if we advance here to . . . to physical conversation, will anybody be hurt ?"

Madison sipped his juice and replied : "Let's use a process of elimination. I won't be hurt."

"Of course you won't," Elaine said. "But what about your wife? Will she be hurt ?"

Madison reflected, then answered : "Let's just say no and let it go at that. A man in this situation makes himself ridiculous when he talks about his wife, and why should you want to talk about her ?"

"Because I don't want to hurt her, and I don't want to encourage you to hurt her. So tell me : will what we *may* do tonight hurt her ?"

"No."

"Why? I really want to know why. I'm new at this, so I want the answers."

Madison sighed and shook his head. "Yes, I see you do. But you won't like this answer."

"Try me."

Madison spoke reluctantly. "Since I must," he said, "I'll begin by explaining that she is an Englishwoman. And wellborn Englishwomen are strange, for in this matter of sexual prowess they are convinced they are without peers."

"Really? I never heard that. I thought French women were supposed to be the best."

"Englishwomen grunt disdainfully at that supposition. In their frosty, self-assured way they think they can give a man more to remember than any French woman. And they refuse to take seriously any American woman as a competitor. My wife is like that. And, you see, when I met her in 1944, I had already had one wife and ... several women. Then I slept with her in lumpy beds in tired hotels along the Channel Coast, and after the war I married her. That made her more self-assured than ever. She figured I married her because I had found her the most attractive woman on earth, that I really loved her and needed her.

"She came to Hawaii, and now she has a daughter of nine and a son of seven . . . and while I am away from them too much, she never doubts that I love both her and them. And finally, as Mamie reminded me this afternoon, the self-assured hussy owns the insurance policies, the home, the stocks and bonds, the book contracts ... every damn thing I've got. At this moment she's in a cottage at Sevenoaks, in Kent. It's 8:45 A.M. She's up with the kids, probably preparing to go picnicking. What do you think? What's your lawyer's opinion? Is she likely to be hurt by the 'little festivity of the flesh' you and I are contemplating?"

Elaine felt lonely, as if she was in a ship's cabin at the end of the world with a stranger. She asked: "Since you have her why do you want me?"

"She could tell you why," Madison said. "She knows that I have a normal amount of self-assurance. She knows there are nights when I wake up in cold sweats, worrying whether my novel is any good. I worry about my hair falling out, about losing my sex drive, about just plain dying and not answering present any more. She knows that with all that I have, including her and my children, I still feel desperately alone sometimes . . . just me and four walls in the dark. She also knows that I still have a little of the Old Adam left in me, that I'm only a man and not a god . . . and that if an attractive little woman who worries about hurting people crosses my path, at just the right moment, and in just the right circumstances, I *might* get in her bed and let her reassure me that I'm not yet dead. . . ."

They sat looking at one another and Elaine felt better. She didn't feel so lonely any more. The man who sat across the table from her didn't look so much like a stranger. Then Madison said: "There's only one question left. Will it hurt the little lawyer who worries about hurting other people?"

Elaine thought for a moment, then decided there was nothing further to say. She got up, went to Madison, took him by the hand and led him to the couch. They lay down together and he kissed her tenderly.

Then he surprised her again.

He pulled away from her and said: "Now you can relax. You can let your blood pressure go down."

She was startled. "What do you mean?"

"I mean that the only thing I'm going to impose on you now is a proposition. I met you here with limited intentions. I don't have to apologize because I wasn't sexually committed. Remember? You made a point of it. I came here only to decide whether you liked me enough, and whether I liked you enough. I do, and I think you do. But the place isn't right."

"You're turning me down?"

"No. I'm accepting the girl, but I'm rejecting the place. Can you tolerate the explanation?"

She sighed and propped herself against a pillow. She felt disappointment: like preparing for a surgical operation, reaching the operating table, then having the surgeon decline to perform. She felt resentment: like tendering your dearest possession and having it rejected. She remembered Likelike warning her that Madison might not be aggressive enough.

"You see, Elaine," he began, "I don't do this often any more, and when I do, I don't do it in whorehouses or assignation lounges. I do it only with a woman I really like, and for her sake as well as mine I surround it with what illusions I can. I spoke of loneliness a moment ago. There is one form of acute loneliness I don't impose on myself any more, and I don't impose it on a woman I really like. You know what it is? It's the loneliness a man like me feels when at night he takes a woman he really likes, then leaves her bed, dresses, and goes wandering off through corridors and streets. If I took you now, then left you and went dragging back through that passage, I'd feel so goddamned lonely and depressed and lost

147

. . . and I'd feel so goddamned sorry for you, making the same walk, that I might just keep walking and walk right on out through the surf and surrender to the undertow. So if I take Elaine Shelby in Hawaii, it'll be in a bed I don't have to leave until next day. Mamie's lounges are ingenious. They fill some human needs, but they don't fill my need, and they won't fill yours."

"But you are here," she said. "I'm here. Time is short. What else can we do?"

"All I can do is make you a proposition, an indecent proposition, perhaps a very selfish proposition. One that I can't recommend to you; I can only offer it."

"What is it?"

"You'll have to wait three days. There are things I must do here. I expected to stay a week. If you accept the proposition, I'll rush and leave in three days. I'll take you to Honolulu. I'll put you in a suite at Waikiki. I'll take you to my home. You can swim in my pool, look at my flowers, listen to my music. We'll have dinner and drink a bottle of champagne. Then we'll go back to the hotel. You won't need any aphrodisiacs. You won't need any Hawaiian women to massage you, or give you aromatic hip baths, or perfume you with Queen Kaahumanu's essence with which she seduced missionaries. You'll just take a plain bath, with plain soap, and use one of the perfumes you brought with you . . . something that reminds me of an apple tree blooming in Indiana. You'll put on a plain nightdress and get into a plain bed. I'll get in with you and stay until the sun wakes us up next morning, by which time I guarantee you will have been aggressively, dominantly, tenderly, and thoroughly deflowered. I'll take you back to my house, and while I work you can lie around the pool, read, talk with my servants, listen to music, and have lunch with me. Later we'll go riding, have dinner, dance, then return to the hotel and do exactly what we did the first night. Only more so."

"And how long does this continue?"

"Four days and four nights. All the time I have. I'll make

some decent speeches, like how I wish I had met you twenty years ago, before I got tired, and before my life became complicated . . . how this interlude with you will be a golden thread in the fabric of my life, how you deserve the best, and how I'll always be pulling for you. Maybe they'll be lies, but they won't be damn lies, they'll be decent lies. In short, since we must be indecent, we'll be as decent about it as possible. Then you can go back to Indiana with my best wishes, and with your mission accomplished. You can go with all the financial and medical insurance that Mamie offers."

Elaine sat up, took Madison's hand and looked down at him. She sighed and shook her head. She wanted to either laugh or cry: she couldn't decide which. "You know, Jim," she said, "I thought this trip to Hawaii would be simple. I thought I'd meet a man. I thought that without too much complexity and embarrassment I'd lose my virginity. Thereafter I thought I'd enjoy what we call back in Indiana 'simple sexual relations' a few times. Then I'd go back home. I really thought it'd be simple. But what happens! I spend five days aboard ship. I get seasick. The only man I'm alone with tries to rape me. I spend four days at Waikiki recovering from bruises, and I don't meet one man I like who's aggressive enough to come to my room.

"I then go to all the trouble and expense of transferring here. And here, at least, I think I'll find things simple. But I meet you and start asking you questions. When I agree to a rendezvous with you, I think the die has been cast, I've crossed the Rubicon. I take the virgin preparation, come to this lounge, ask more questions, offer myself to you, and for reasons of complexity you turn me down. Now you want me to wait three more days after which you'll take me back to Waikiki. You offer me four days which sound zestful, but they may later prove painful. You may arouse me so thoroughly that back in Richmond, Indiana, I may be more nervous than I was before I left."

She looked so forlorn that Madison shook with laughter. She began laughing with him.

"Who'd have thought," she laughed, "that I'd have *so* much trouble just getting simply and plainly and decently *laid*!"

They continued laughing, and the sexual chemistry of this shared laughter, with Elaine looking so winsome and forlorn, so little like a lawyer and so much like a perplexed girl, was so much that Madison suddenly changed his mind. In quick-hot desire for her he forgot the loneliness of the long drag back. He jerked her down, and would have been physically conversing with her in about two more heart-beats, but Elaine had reacted agilely.

"Oh, no you don't!" she said. "A virgin can't shift gears that fast. You should have made your move when I was ready. I've just accepted your proposition. I'm not taking an impulsive rape now. I've opted for the bed at Waikiki . . . with my Indiana perfume reminding you of apple blossoms. So let your blood pressure go down. You're now hooked for the full four-night performance."

After a few more heavy breaths Madison managed a grin. "All right," he said. "Maybe I can finish over here in two days."

Elaine felt better. Madison's impulsive move had restored her self-assurance, and his proposition had given her certitude. She said: "Maybe now you can tell me how I can amuse myself while I'm waiting for you. I gather you'll expect me to avoid the lounges?"

"Naturally. I've contracted for merchandise. I don't want it damaged before delivery."

"That'll disappoint one gentleman."

"Who?"

"Mr. Whitaker."

"I saw him talking to you. He seemed insistent."

"He was most insistent that I rush to a lounge with him. I promised him elementary conversation tomorrow at one. He expressed great concern for me."

A thought occurred to Madison.

"Well, there's how you can amuse yourself," he said. "Play

an old game with Monty, a game at which women once were skilled. See just how concerned you can make him become."

"The game won't last long," Elaine said. "He'll insist on a rendezvous. He'll tell me that since he is the host he can't converse very satisfactorily in the general areas."

"Sure he'll tell you that, but you refuse. Since he suspects it anyway, tell him that you visited a lounge with me and that, being a virgin, you suffered psychic shock from the obscene atmosphere. Tell him you were even more shocked by my abrupt insistence on physical conversation . . . that physical conversation is out of the question for you until you have had time to really know and really like a man."

"But of course he won't believe that," she said. "Since I came here with you tonight, tomorrow he won't believe I'm a virgin."

"Certainly he won't. But since you are a lawyer, surely you can guess how you can flabbergast him."

"How?"

"Well, tomorrow morning, early, you go back to that Japanese doctor who examined you today. Use some pretense and have him examine you again."

"Why?"

"Because Monty will be certain you are no longer a virgin. The doctor will know that you are. Then you maneuver Monty into talking with the doctor, and what the doctor tells Monty will so flabbergast him that he'll be more concerned about you than ever."

The game had begun to appeal to Elaine's legal mind. "But we can't keep conversing in the general garden for three days. Either I come to a lounge with him or he loses his concern."

"The hell he does!" Madison said. "He has a cottage on the grounds. Make him converse with you there. He has a Piper Cub, make him show you the volcanoes. Don't talk much, just tell him it's necessary for you to know a lot about him. Make him talk about the war, about the old Lunaliho, about Hiroshima, about what he reads, about the music he listens to . . . everything. Tell him he's the most interesting man you've ever met. You keep him talking, and keep saying no. A century ago that was the most effective of all female maneuvers. Maybe you can revive it effectively here."

Elaine's lawyer's mind suddenly suspected Madison. Was he trying to weasel out of a signed-and-sealed deal with her?

"Just a minute," she said. "Why are you suggesting all this? You're supposed to want contracted-for-merchandise delivered intact to a bed in Waikiki three days from now. Aren't you suggesting that said merchandise be subjected to considerable risk? I'm told that Monty, alone with a woman, is about as restrained as a grizzly bear."

"Doesn't worry me at all," Madison grinned. "In the first place, if you handle Monty cleverly he's going to be so flabbergasted he won't know what to do. And in the second place, from temporary personal frustration I happen to know that the guardian of the merchandise has the reflexes of a black panther. No mere grizzly bear is a threat to her."

Elaine laughed, and felt so relaxed with Madison that she bent down and kissed him. Then her thoughts returned to the game. "You really think I can make Monty all that concerned about me?"

"I think it's a fair bet. If any woman ever makes Monty feel concerned about her it'll be a woman like you. He's really a nice guy. He comes from good people. He's worth a million dollars. The only thing wrong with him is that he's had too much sex from too many experienced, erotic women. I know the woman he married. Nothing but sex. Most every woman in Monty's life has been at least partially stripped when she opened the door. The only feminine qualities the poor guy has never encountered are innocence, tenderness and elusiveness."

"That sounds sad," Elaine said.

"Hell, it is sad. Monty learned sex at the Lunaliho just before the war. The flash at Hiroshima frightened him, and every frightened man wants to fornicate. He returned here to disruption . . . more travelling-woman sex, and a nervous sexpot for a wife. I met him in the passage as I came here. He looked old, tired and sad."

"Who had he been with?"

"I can't be positive, but I tried to converse with her after he had rushed up and propositioned her. She was too preoccupied to notice much I said, so I'd guess it was Mary Ferrell."

Elaine's countenance fell. "Then he won't be concerned about me tomorrow. If he has a beautiful woman like her, how can he be concerned about me?"

"Oh, hell, Elaine!" Madison exclaimed. "Didn't they teach you anything but Blackstone at the University of Indiana? What can Mary Ferrell give Monty that he hasn't had a thousand times? She's just another beautiful, petulant, selfish woman committing adultery. Don't you know your own strength?"

Elaine reflected a moment. She said: "Jim, do you really believe that my qualities . . . innocence, tenderness and elusiveness, that I might employ them effectively out here with Monty? After all, these qualities have not proved advantageous for me in Indiana."

"Well, I don't know," Madison said. "Maybe that's because there is more innocence and elusiveness in Indiana than there is in Hawaii. You have competition back there, but you have no competition here. There is no innocence, tenderness or elusiveness at Hotel Mamie Stover. So use your lawyer's mind and your innocent body and make the most of both assets."

Elaine laid her cheek against Madison's and asked him: "Are you attracted to me because of my innocence?"

Madison reflected. "As a matter of fact," he said, "it's not impossible that I am. You see . . . well, not even *I* know much about innocence. I've married two women, but now that I think of it, I found neither of them chaste. Yet neither of them had been married before. I don't know just what had happened to them before I encountered them, and none of the others have been chaste. So, hell, I'm almost like Monty. Maybe chastity doesn't concern men any more. But as a student of history I recall that for about two centuries in

153

Europe a great many doctors worked like hell trying to perfect a surgical technique for restoring maidenheads. So I suppose chastity must have had some value once."

The wall clock showed a quarter to twelve. Elaine sat on the side of the couch and straightened her hair.

"All right, Jim," she said. "It gets crazier and crazier. If Monty comes around tomorrow I'll play the game with him. I'll see how long he lasts . . . and whether the game is amusing or not. But I'm still a little disturbed by your willingness to subject to such risks merchandise you say you value and want. Perhaps you had better reassure me again before I leave."

"That's easy to do," Madison said. "If you'll reflect on it, you'll see that I'm not taking much risk. I'm cleverly safeguarding the merchandise. What better way can I keep you out of the lounges while I work than by suggesting this game for you to play outside? I have already made the top like-sex bid for you. The only way Monty can raise my bid is by offering you love-sex, and the odds are against that. So while I work, you play at flabbergasting Monty, and three days from now I get the girl intact. I carry her back to Waikiki and enjoy innocence, tenderness, elusiveness . . . and the scent of apple blossoms in Indiana."

Elaine smiled. She was still smiling as she walked determinedly back through the secret passage. She had never felt so self-assured in her whole life.

CHAPTER ELEVEN

The second day: in which we sit
with Jim Madison and Mamie Stover
and watch Madison trying to decide
whether Mamie is good or evil.

AT 11.30 A.M. ON the second day Jim Madison was walking
towards Mamie's cottage. He was going there to lunch and to
spend the afternoon with Mamie. She had returned from
Waikiki at 10 A.M. and had sent a messenger with the
invitation.

As Madison walked in the sun he felt relaxed and strong.
He had slept well. He had risen at seven. He had fought the
surf and the undertow for twenty minutes. He had breakfasted
with Dr. Ralph Anderson. After breakfast he and the doctor
had gone riding for more than an hour On spirited horses
they had ridden briskly, up the slope of the volcano, along
paths through fields of sugar cane, and they had halted
several times to talk. On his return Madison had soaked in a
bath prepared by one of the Woola Woola girls, and the girl
had scrubbed his back sensuously. Then he had lain on the
massage table for half an hour while the Hawaiian masseur,
with iron fingers, probed for every lump in his viscera, every
ganglion in his muscles. Now Madison, well-rested, well-fed,
well-exercised, well-scrubbed, and well-massaged was walking
easily through the trees and flowers. He wore Japanese-type
sandals, blue swimming trunks, a yellow cotton *aloha* shirt, sun
glasses, and a straw cap shaped like a French marshal's.

As Madison walked he reflected on what Doctor Anderson
had said to him earlier.

"You know, Madison," the doctor said, "this is the first morning in years I've felt like a real man. You know why? Because last night for the first time in years I got what I needed from a woman. God, I was lucky to find her here!"

"Becky Sanders?" Madison asked.

"Yes. She's a real woman. A real man's woman. She knows how to act with a man, what to say, to do. Never in my life have I been as strong with a woman as I am with her."

Later he continued:

"You know, Madison, I'm a gynecologist. I deal with sex. Some of us call ourselves 'sexologists' now. And like most doctors and all sexologists, I now have to spend half my time trying to help my patients psychiatrically. That means I have to talk to the husbands as well as the wives. What a goddam mess we've made of our society!"

"How have we done it?"

"We've done it with our insistence that sex for a man must be only an expression of love. What unnatural nonsense! We've allowed sick sentimentalists to spread the belief that male sexual activity should be confined to marriage. We've allowed wives to be taught that if their husbands take sex outside of marriage then the husbands are 'untrue,' the wives have 'failed' and the whole experience is shameful. Why haven't we taught wives to expect ambitious men to be sexually adventurous? Show me a man who has ever excelled at anything, and nine times out of ten I'll show you a man who was sexually adventurous. Show me a man who has written a great poem, or built a bridge or a railroad, or made a fortune, or composed a great symphony, or discovered some boon to mankind, and I'll show you a man who *needed* and took several women. Sex for a man can be an expression of love with his wife; it can also be a licentious adventure which fuels his ambition, fires his confidence, and trims his lamp."

"You feel strongly about it, don't you?" Madison said.

"I ought to," the doctor went on. "I've experienced it in my own life. And I've struggled with it in my practice. I've seen many homes broken up because a husband needed the sexual assurance that his wife couldn't give him. I love my own wife, to whom I've been married for years. But my wife can't make me feel like Becky Sanders can make me feel."

"What about Miss Sanders?" Madison asked. "You say she's good for you. Are you equally good for her?"

"Yes," Doctor Anderson answered. "The experience is good for her. Her story is sad but not unusual. She's thirty-four. She's had only two men before me, both of them she loved deeply. She married her childhood sweetheart and was a virgin at marriage. He was killed in the war. Then, because she is a superior woman sexually, she became the mistress of a superior man in Washington . . . a prominent man. She was his mistress for ten years. But he either couldn't or wouldn't break up his home and marry her. Now she has reached the age when she feels she must make a marriage-for-security. She can't live an unprotected life any longer. She has found her man. She expects to marry him three weeks from now, have children, be a faithful wife. But she doesn't love the man. She likes him, respects him, can tolerate his hand on her, but she'll never be able to love him. So she needs reassurance.

"She needs to know that she can have sex successfully with a man she doesn't love. That's why she came here. Before I left her last night she quite prettily and decently told me: 'Doctor, you seem to have used me successfully. So I should tell you that I have used you successfully. I've known since I was eighteen that I could give a man what he needs if I loved him. I wasn't sure I could do it if I only liked him. I'm marrying a man I don't love, but I *must* make the marriage successful. I've been fearful that I might spoil it, that I might cringe at his touch, or let him notice that I regarded him coldly. So I came to Hotel Mamie Stover to practice for that marriage, to have my first sexual experience with a man who feels like an intruder to me. Did you feel me cringe from you? I believe I brought it off successfully, didn't I? You've reassured me. Would you like to further reassure me tomorrow night?' "

157

"And what did that do for your ego?" Madison asked. "Didn't that let the air out of your tires?"

"Didn't bother me a goddam bit," the doctor laughed. "Just makes me want her more. I'm going to take her every time I can get her while I'm here. I don't need love from her, I need only licentious sex from her."

"And from that experience, I gather, your professional opinion is that Hotel Mamie Stover is a beneficial institution?"

The doctor was emphatic.

"Madison," he said, "Hotel Mamie Stover makes more sense than any institution I've seen in twenty years. Mamie Stover is a remarkable woman with remarkable insights into human needs. I'm going to urge her to establish a branch hotel in the Black Hills of South Dakota so I can get there often."

As Mamie waited for Madison she was aware that she wasn't herself. Something unusual was happening to her. Her unease had not disappeared, it had grown more acute. She kept trying to understand her strange feelings and actions.

Normally, during the morning Mamie was "all business." She wore linen slacks made for her in Hongkong, with business-like blouses, and with her hair in a net or turban. She worked briskly in her office at the cottage, receiving reports from her assistants, often striding with them about the grounds and giving orders as she went.

But this morning everything had been abnormal. The moment she returned from Waikiki she sent the messenger for Madison. She ordered lunch for 1 P.M. She decided to wear her normal business clothes, so she put on light blue slacks and a severe white blouse, and her maid wrapped her hair in a turban. She would show Madison her business self, for he was here on business. She'd be brisk and business-like with him.

But standing before her mirror Mamie realized that she couldn't be business-like with Madison because he happened to be an unusual man for her. As the one man who had ever come close to showing affection for her, Madison had been the beneficiary of Mamie's illusions. In moments of despair in her hard, obscene, driving life, she had always looked back to those days and nights at sea she had spent with this compassionate man . . . nights when one word, one concession from him would have changed the course of her life. So no visit of Madison's to Mamie's home could be a business visit. For he was the man who had let her turn to him when she was threatened, the only man who had ever evidenced concern for her, the only man she had ever successfully given herself to, the only man who had ever needed to reach for her hand in the dark.

Hastily Mamie had taken off her business clothes. She tried a *muumuu*, but it looked too shapeless. She tried silk lounging pajamas, but so early in the day they made her look like a whore. She tried a slit Chinese dress, then shorts-and-bra. Finally she chose blue "toreador" pants with a frilly pink blouse, and she summoned her maid to remove her turban and fluff out and comb her hair to make her face look softer. For shoes she chose doeskin Italian "flats" to minimize her height.

As Madison approached Mamie's cottage he had no idea that his coming had excited her. He didn't know that he held any place of distinction in her memories. How could he know that the little he had once given her on the freighter, plus the few friendly gestures thereafter, had become a bright thread in the fabric of her life?

One reason that Madison was innocent of such knowledge was that he had little feeling of self-importance. Despite his being listed in *Who's Who*, he knew he wasn't an important writer, he was only a good writer who worked hard. He thought more about his shortcomings than he did about his accomplishments. For every hour in his life when he had felt confident, there had been another when he felt doubtful. And since what he remembered clearest were the sadnesses and absurdities of life, he didn't think of himself as being a man who deeply affected the women he knew for a night or a week.

So while Madison assumed that Mamie remembered something about their days and nights together, and that perhaps she felt some gratitude for his friendliness, he did not suspect that she felt anything more. If she was disturbed about his coming to the hotel, he assumed she was only apprehensive over the possible effects of what he might write.

Madison's first surprise was Mamie's "cottage". It wasn't just a sleeping-and-working place in motel-modern; it was the home of a woman who was struggling to live gracefully. It was a multi-level wooden house of about five rooms with a modest swimming pool.

The furnishings were Chinese, the dominant colors were black, yellow and Chinese red; and almost everything had been found in Hongkong and Tokyo by Mamie. The largest sculpture was a copy of Rodin's *The Kiss*. Then there was Rodin's *Eternal Idol*, with its overpowering sensualism, Matisse's *Reclining Nude*, Maillol's *Torso*, and Henry Moore's *Family Group*. The other sculptures and art objects were Oriental. Many of the books were about Grecian, Islamic and Oriental love rites and orgies. There was also the Kinsey Report, Havelock Ellis, *Lady Chatterley*, and many books about social problems on the mainland. Madison noticed his own books . . . and that they appeared to have been read. There was expensive hi-fi equipment, housed in black lacquer, and a collection of semi-classical records.

Mamie led Madison to the *lanai*, and they sat where they could see the beach and the ocean through the palms.

"You look much better today, Jimmy," Mamie said. "I see that sly, disbelieving twinkle in your eyes. You must have slept well."

"Wonderfully well."

"And the food, the service? Any complaints?"

"Can't think of one. I've been riding, and generally surrendering to sensuousness."

Mamie nodded. "That's just what you need after all your chasing about the earth. Do you think I've created a genuinely sensuous atmosphere for men here?"

Madison smiled. "I'd say you've made a fair start."

"I hope so," Mamie said. "I believe you'll agree it comes none too soon. Mainland men are about to become extinct."

"Really?"

"Don't tell me you don't know about it," Mamie said. "Mainland life is now destroying men, they are losing all their natural aggressiveness. Instead of being dominant they are being dominated, and everything decently masculine is being ground out of men. Half the men who come here look pitiful. We are doing whatever we can to help."

"I'd say your girl bath attendants are your biggest help," Madison said.

Mamie said: "I'm glad to hear you say that. When I began designing the hotel I knew I had to devise a program to make men more sensuous and more aggressive. Otherwise I couldn't help them. I read all I could about Greek and Roman baths, then I went to Japan and studied baths. Public, sensuous bathing is enormously important to human society. And I found that masculinity has always been aided by female bath attendants. I doubt that a man can ever feel like a real man unless he has a girl to assist him in his bath. I think that having a girl to help him with his bath, and help him put his pajamas or his nightshirt on, I think that helps a man, don't you?"

"Definitely," Madison said. "But here's my first question for you. What about the girls, the ones you have here? Does it help them to attend men in their baths, help men into their pajamas, and help some of your men become sexually more dominant?"

Mamie laughed and folded her long legs under her. "Here come the missionary questions," she said. "You are asking that question for your Puritan readers, because *you* know better. You've lived here, and you've travelled in the South Pacific. The forty girls I bring here each year from Woola Woola and other islands are the luckiest girls in the South Seas. With their parents' aid and consent they compete for the privilege of coming here. Their year here is wonderful for them. We teach them hygiene, how to care for themselves and their families.

We teach them how to make men feel important, how to keep from getting pregnant, how to improve their looks, how to dance and move gracefully. We teach them how to work hard and effectively, how to cook, how to clean and adorn their homes, how to care for the babies they will have. Each year when I take the forty graduates back to their homes and select forty more, we celebrate from island to island. Our graduates are the most sought after girls for wives. They marry the superior men, they live the fullest lives, they bear the healthiest children."

"Let's clarify that point, Mamie," Madison said. "You go down there every year and select forty girls who have passed their fifteenth birthdays? Now aren't these girls really just whores? Don't you transport them for immoral purposes? Don't they make Hotel Mamie Stover, really, just a new kind of whorehouse?"

"None of that is true," Mamie answered. "You are using mainland words for evils which don't exist in the islands. The girls can't be whores because I don't pay them. They come here primarily to work and learn and develop. Incidentally, they have sex with decent, mature, middle-class white husbands from the mainland. On each of about three hundred days of the year she spends here, the average girl has intercourse two or three times, so the average girl has intercourse perhaps seven hundred times. Is it your contention, Jimmy, that when a forty-four-year-old white husband from Eugene, Oregon, has intercourse here with a sixteen-year-old girl from Woola Woola, that sin is being committed? That harm is being done? That somebody is being hurt?"

"Yes, as a writer that's my contention," Madison replied. "My readers will regard such intercourse as obscene. They'll say that the husband from Eugene, Oregon, is fornicating and committing adultery and violating his marriage vow. Many of my readers will say the man is being hurt. Most of my readers will say the girl is being hurt."

Mamie shook her head. "Completely untrue," she said. "The white husband is helped enormously . . . both physically

162

and psychologically, my doctors will tell you that he is. The girl would be hurt only if she had been taught that she would be hurt, and she hasn't been so taught. The truth is that the girl is helped, the healthy, natural release is good for her. The feeling that she is learning to give joy is good for her. It adds to her self-assurance and understanding of life. It isn't harmful and evil; it's helpful and good. And because we make such physical conversation possible under hygienic and pregnancy-free conditions, Hotel Mamie Stover is good."

Madison looked closely at Mamie and reflected. On this point she had no doubts.

"Tell me, Jimmy," Mamie continued, "haven't the people on the mainland learned *anything* from the Kinsey Report? The people on the mainland are afflicted by a blind, pitiful yearning to believe that the sex act by mature people must always be an act of love. Many women who come here keep referring to what they do in the lounges, even with a beach boy, as 'making love.' They appear embarrassed when I ask them what love has to do with it. Every once in a while I become exasperated and I say : 'My God, lady, can't you go to a lounge and screw decently without claiming you are "making love"? Have you lost all respect for love?'

"Doctor Kinsey showed the American people something honest, important and true : he showed them that there is an enormous amount of sexual activity by mature, middle-class adults which has nothing whatever to do with love. These sex acts are not acts of love. But they *are* acts of need. They are acts of physical adventure, possession, conquest, acts in response to compelling atavistic yearnings, of revolt against fear, doubt, boredom, decay and destruction. After Doctor Kinsey, can't the mainland people concede that there is a decent place for loveless sex in human society?"

Madison replied : "I suppose most people know that there has always been loveless sex. But on the mainland it is also called paganism."

"Of course," Mamie said. "That's what the missionaries called it in Hawaii a century ago. The missionaries destroyed paganism, and destroyed all but a handful of the Hawaiians. I wonder if paganism didn't come closer to meeting some of the needs of human beings than whatever the missionaries have imposed?"

When they sat down to lunch beside the pool Madison said: "Later I want to come back to your program for men, Mamie. But during lunch let's talk about you. Do you enjoy what you are doing?"

"I enjoy it immensely," she replied. "The Luau and the Hotel now take in five million dollars a year. This is a big business. Five hundred people and their families depend on me for a living. Ten thousand good, middle-class people a year depend on me to help make their visits to Hawaii exciting. That's a lot of people I must think about. It doesn't give me much time to think about myself."

"You stay busy, I assume?"

"I stay completely busy. The Luau is my drawing room. Normally I spend six evenings a week there . . . appearing, signing autographs and talking with people. Three nights a week I sleep at my apartment near the Luau and fly back here in the morning. Three nights I fly back here after midnight. The Luau is closed on Monday nights. I never have time to get bored or to worry about what might have been for me. I take my life as it is and do the best I can. And I like most of my life. I like being rich, both for myself and so I can help other people. I like flying in my own plane, and living in a home like this, and having efficient, faithful servants, and so many people interested in the Mamie Stover image."

"Do you travel much?"

"My big trip each year is to Hongkong and Tokyo. All the fabrics we use at the hotel, clothing, towels, sheets, everything, are made for us in Hongkong. My own clothes are made there. So I fly there each year. Then, of course, I fly South once a year with the girls, to Woola Woola, Bora Bora, Samoa, Tahiti. Sometimes I spend a few days in Australia. I like the Australians."

"Have you ever been back to the mainland?"

"Not once. I don't want to go back. The mainland comes to me."

"You mean a portion of the mainland comes to you?"

Madison thought the implication of that question might irritate Mamie, but she only shrugged and smiled.

"That's right, Jimmy," she said. "I get that portion of the people who are looking for what Mamie Stover stands for."

"And that's my question," Madison said. "What do you think Mamie Stover stands for?"

Mamie knitted her long, wide-set, neatly plucked brows and replied : "I know what Mamie Stover stands for, Jimmy, and so do you. You've known for sixteen years. You know that when I was in high school I didn't have any sweethearts. Whatever I stood for even at that early age, it didn't attract sweethearts. I attracted men, men from eighteen to fifty years old, who wanted only one thing : to get me on my back. None of them wanted to *make love* to me. When I reached Hollywood no man wanted to be my suitor or lover. Powerful men ordered their lackeys to deliver me to beach cottages at 4 P.M. and those powerful men didn't want love or tenderness with me. They only wanted to use me to reassure themselves that they were powerful. They wanted to ravish a new girl who had what I've got and who was taller than they were.

"When I met you on the freighter you were a lonely and compassionate man. You were not lecherous. You didn't ravish me to prove your own dominance or power, you used me to help you against loneliness and despair. You treated me kinder than any man has ever treated me, and you got from me the best I have to give. But you wanted only what you got from me during that voyage. Look at me, Jimmy! You see an erotic-looking woman. But I'm no love-goddess. I'm only a loveless-sex-goddess. I'm too tall, too blonde, my face is too coarsely sensual, my eyes are set too wide apart, my teeth are too white and strong, my lips too thick, my breasts too big. . . . Most people on the mainland find some sort of love and make it last the course. They devote themselves to homes and families and suppress their desires for sexual adventure. But others don't, and when these others reach Hawaii on their once-in-a-lifetime trip, they come to see Mamie. Or they come to see their image of Mamie. These are people who think they want to relieve boredom with sexual adventure. To make their dream trip to the 'islands' complete they think they *need* sexual adventure, and whether you or the missionaries like it or not, these people *do* need sexual adventure. These are my kind of people in the world, the human beings who come to me for help. I try to help them."

After lunch Mamie changed into shorts, and she and Madison sat in lounge chairs in the shade near the pool.

"That's exactly what I'm doing, Jimmy," Mamie said. "I, of course, have made use of what I learned during the war. I read somewhere that if war is ever abolished something will have to be invented to take its place. All I have done here is try to invent that something. The average forty-odd-year-old man *needs* war. He desperately needs an excuse to leave his family and community and go adventuring again. I designed this hotel to help him. He can come here, and even though he must bring his wife with him, he can still find many of the thrills of going off to war."

Madison chuckled. "Mamie," he asked, "do you think you might be working here to prevent war?"

"That's exactly what I'm doing, Jimmy," Mamie said. "And if you'd stop laughing at people and start liking them more you'd understand. One of the differences between me and you is that I like people as they are and you don't. You want to laugh at people. You even stand aside and laugh at yourself. Well, if war is ever abolished societies will have to figure out a way to give every forty-odd-year-old man about one year's vacation from the rat-race of acquiring and supporting. I can't give a man a year's vacation from responsibility, but I can give him a week's vacation."

"Let's take your program step by step," Madison said. "Tell me what you think each step does for a man."

Mamie sat up straight and looked at Madison intently. "First," she said, "the moment a man enters Hotel Mamie Stover he strips. Just like entering the Army. Every bit of clothing he takes off is stored for him : he won't use it while he's here. A man likes to strip with other men. It gives him a feeling of predatory masculinity and of shedding boredom. Then we examine him physically, with accent on his genitals and prostate, just like the Army. But notice this, Jimmy! Here's where I differ with the Army. My doctor doesn't just look at a man and nod an okay. My doctor has a strict routine to follow : I rehearse him in it every week. He examines each man privately, then shakes his head in disbelief and says with great conviction : 'Mr. Smith, you amaze me! You are the strongest, healthiest, forty-two-year-old man I have ever been privileged to examine! You have the sexual equipment of a man fifteen years younger than you are! I have never seen such sexual strength in a man your age!' Didn't the doctor who examined you tell you that, Jimmy?"

"He surely did," Madison laughed.

"And didn't it make you feel good?"

"Wonderful."

"If any doctor I hire ever fails to tell a man that," Mamie said, "he knows to start packing his bag because I'll chase him off the property as soon as I hear about it."

"My God, Mamie," Madison said, "you are hard on doctors!"

"I have to be. A lot of doctors are stupid. They have the power either to depress or elate. When I hire a doctor I lecture him. I say : 'Doctor, your principal job here is to *elate* men and women. When you examine a man for me and find him sound, at that moment you cease being a scientist and become an actor. You send that man out of your office *elated*. You don't just tell him he's sound : you *convince* him that he's youthful . . . that he's strong as a young Jersey bull!' "

Mamie paused to smile as Madison laughed again.

"Okay, Mamie," he said. "We've got your man stripped and medically elated. Now what do you do to him?"

"Just like the Army again," she said. "We issue him new clothes. Then he enters the barracks and is assigned a bunk. A barracks atmosphere makes a man feel wonderfully free. He smiles and sucks up his guts and realizes that his wife has been taken off his hands, that for a whole, grand, delicious week he can be a free man among men and take any woman he's able to take. Even the meetings with his wife will be exciting, just like when she came and met him at a motel when he was in training in 1942. The once or twice he'll have sex with his wife while he's here . . . suddenly she can excite him again because he'll meet her for an assignation in a lounge. Jimmy, do you know we save hundreds of marriages here every year just by encouraging tired husbands to be men again, and by creating the conditions under which a husband can have an exciting rendezvous with a wife he had become bored with?"

"I understand that," Madison said. "But don't rush ahead. Come back to the barracks and the program."

"Well in the barracks," Mamie went on, "our man sees the girls. They are smiling, unblushing, uncomplicated, and their sole desire is to assist him in feeling like a *man*. He has only to look at one of these girls to feel proud of himself. Whether he wants the girl or not, the simple fact that she is there causes him to suck up his guts tighter and brace his shoulders. Then our massage is good for him. Don't you think a mature man ought to have massage regularly, Jimmy?"

"It helps."

"Of course it helps. Then comes our amatory food which is wonderful for a man, nourishing and stimulating. I have never understood why mainland wives aren't trained in the preparation of amatory diets. I seem to be the only American woman who cares about feeding men for maximum sexual vigor. Why aren't girls taught this in high school? How can any society call a woman ready for marriage until she knows amatory cookery? Answer me this, Jimmy: don't you believe that mature men should always try to eat sexually nourishing food?"

168

"As a matter of fact I do," Madison answered.

"Don't you try to eat such food?"

"Sure. I learned about amatory cookery here in the islands. I'm all for it."

"Of course you are," Mamie said. "Every humanitarian is for it. Well, next comes our sports program for men. We have the best deep-sea fishing in the world, wonderful fighting fish. Boats go out every morning with the men who want to fish. We also send a couple of the girls along on each boat, just to make the day pleasanter for the fishermen. There are inevitable periods when the fish aren't biting, or when a man needs to go below for a nap. A girl can help, wouldn't you think?"

"A girl could help me under such circumstances," Madison agreed. "I get bored with fishing after the first hour or so, but whether I'd help the girl is a question I asked before."

"And the answer is the same," Mamie insisted. "The girl likes to feel that she's being of use. And after fishing comes hunting, and here's a fact about many men: they need to kill something. I don't like to see anything killed. But when I was designing the hotel I accepted the reality that if I was to provide a substitute for war I'd have to provide animals for some of the men guests to kill. So we have these wild pigs. Of course we call all pigs *wild boars*, and our hunts are *boar* hunts, for sexual reasons men like the idea of killing *boars*. We have five boar hunts a week. We mount parties of men on horses, give them carbines, and our Hawaiian guides take them up on the wooded side of the volcano and let them fire away, killing *boars*. We have three thousand acres leased, and we keep it stocked with boars. The Hawaiian guides play an elaborate game, exaggerating how dangerous these boars are, they tell stories about how men are always getting 'ripped to pieces' by wounded and enraged boars. A few boars do have long, curling tusks which make them look ugly, but of course they aren't really dangerous. A pig is a pig, no threat at all to a mounted man with a carbine."

"Aren't those hunts expensive?" Madison asked.

"Oh no," Mamie said. "Monty bought thirty surplus carbines for ten dollars apiece, and the National Guard gives us the ammunition, as part of the Defense Program. Twenty men up there on the mountainside firing carbines at wild pigs is about the cheapest entertainment we can provide. We give the pig carcasses to the Hawaiian colonists for food, and the noise of the gunfire is good for the hotel. It sounds exciting."

"Don't you ever run out of pigs?"

"There are thousands of them in the islands. The Hawaiians always raised them, but as the Hawaiians disappeared, the pigs survived, became wild, and multiplied. And just to make sure we never run short, we import a shipment each year."

"Where do you import them from?"

Mamie hesitated, then smiled. "That's one of our top secrets, Jimmy," she said. "But I'll trust you with it. We get pigs every year from Arkansas. Many of the exotic *wild boars* that our guests kill are nothing but poor old razorback pigs rounded up in the Ozark Mountains."

While Mamie and Madison laughed about the pigs, a maid brought some *mobani* juice.

"What percentage of your men want to go boar hunting?" Madison asked.

"About thirty-five out of every hundred. Some of the others shoot skeet with shotguns, but only about half of the men want to shoot. And only about half want to ride, although we try to persuade all the men to go riding every day. We have such wonderful horses. Every real man should ride, there is nothing more sexually stimulating. But these men from the mainland are soft and weak, and at least half of them never get on a horse while they are here."

"I suppose most of your men just want to stay on the beach?"

"That's true. They are satisfied with our Beach Program and our Sex Program. Our program on the men's private beach begins every day at 9 A.M. and continues until 5 P.M. There is judo wrestling, with Hawaiian instructors. The men are taught to paddle the war canoes, and there is canoe racing. They are taught to dance by Hawaiian women, and girls are always on the beach. Sex instruction goes on all day. The doctors lecture on sexual satisfaction, sexual prowess, sexual longevity. The men lie on the beach, look at the girls, examine sex-instruction photographs, and read sex tracts and sex novels."

"How are the girls and the Hawaiian women dressed on the men's private beach?"

"They all wear bikinis, but no brassières, and every afternoon at three, there is a sex seminar conducted by Hawaiian women. Advice is given, and sex-instruction films are shown. You see, all Christian men are sexual ignoramuses compared to Oriental and Polynesian men. The Hawaiian women try to correct this deficiency."

Madison said, "How about you personally, Mamie? Do you give the men any attention?"

"Yes," she replied. "I visit each Thursday afternoon. I make an appearance on the men's private beach at 2:30 P.M. and re-enact the old Beach Walk. Some of them remember seeing me during the war days at Waikiki. They all sit down along the beach, then they begin chanting 'One...Two... Three... Four,' and I walk between them and the water wearing the *muumuu*. When I reach the end of the beach they all begin yelling 'Take it off, take it off.' So I take off the big hat and the *muumuu* and walk back between them and the water wearing nothing but my high heels, the sun glasses and the G-string. I give the men a private, unobstructed view of the Million-Dollar Walk . . . and that makes for a high point of the week. Then I put the *muumuu* back on, and I personally conduct that afternoon's sex seminar. By that time most of them have had a considerable amount of instruction, and I clear up any remaining doubts or questions or problems. It's like a graduation exercise. It rounds off our Sex Program."

"I understand," Madison said. "But what I'm asking is: do any of the men guests ever receive any private, individual attention from you?"

Mamie laughed and shook her head. "Oh no," she said. "None of that any more. I tell them all that they can look at the boss but they can't touch her. If they want to do any touching, they can touch the girls. Or they can go to the general area and try to converse a white woman into a lounge."

"I was wondering about those white women," Madison said. "After all that sex programming in the men's private area, how can you be sure that enough aggressive men will go to the general area and converse with your women guests?"

"We know how to handle that," Mamie said. "The girls in the men's area do nothing but work after 5 P.M. There is no sex available in the men's area from 5 P.M. until next day. So after 5 P.M. most of the men guests have their baths, massage and dinner, and then move to the garden and the general beach for the evening. This makes for a balanced program. It makes for relaxation and quiet conversation in the general area. Perhaps it makes for less nervous insistence in the lounges, but it makes for a higher degree of prowess and satisfaction."

About 4 P.M. Mamie walked with Madison to her front gate. It was time for her to begin preparations for her trip to Waikiki.

"Really, Jimmy," she said, "after you've reflected on it, I think you'll agree that there is nothing extraordinary here. Remember how in ancient Greece *all* the hotels were brothels? There has always been loveless sex in hotels. Why? Because travel provides the freedom for it, and travel in itself is a sex stimulant. Travel to Hawaii is the most powerful of all sex stimulants for Americans. And in every hotel on the face of the earth tonight there will be a loveless sex act. There will be sex acts like that tonight in our lounges, just men and women trying to forget their hurts, trying to feel ecstasy in their loins before they dry up and die. Can't you be tolerant of them? The only way Hotel Mamie Stover differs from any other hotel is that we drop the hypocrisy. You don't like hypocrisy,

172

you don't like pretense. You appreciate freedom, knowledge and honesty, in fact you approve everything that doesn't hurt anybody. So you think about it and you'll like it here, and you'll decide we're doing good here."

Madison smiled his disbelieving, perplexed smile. "All right, Mamie," he said, "I'll think about it."

Mamie stood there, returning his look, and added: "And by the way, Jimmy, in honor of our reunion after sixteen years, I think I'll do something unusual tomorrow night. If you'd like me to, I'll take the night off from the Luau and stay here with you."

Madison continued smiling. "That's generous of you, Mamie," he said. "I'd like that. I'll look forward to it."

CHAPTER TWELVE

The second evening : in which we watch Madison as he listens and questions, feels and reflects, acts and reacts, trying to decide whether Hotel Mamie Stover is good or evil.

AT 5.30 P.M. on the second day, after his long talk with Mamie, Madison was lying on a massage table when a Woola Woola girl handed him a note. Jesus Portales invited him to dine at his cottage at 6:30. Madison nodded to the girl, finished taking his massage, showered, slipped into duck pants and a red *aloha* shirt, and, barefooted, walked over to Jesus's cottage. It was the smallest and most remote of the three executive cottages, and Madison noted with interest that the dinner was to be head-to-head . . . no one but Jesus and himself.

"You aren't following me, are you, Jesus ?" Madison asked. "Do you usually come over here every day ?"

"No, Mr. Madison, I'm not following you," Jesus replied. "I usually come over here maybe once a week. Sometimes I stay overnight. This afternoon I had to come over with the tax auditor. I'm flying back with Mamie at 8. I thought if we dined quietly together maybe I could answer some questions."

Jesus was sipping vermouth. He didn't respect the hotel's no-alcohol rule. Madison took a gin-and-vermouth from the Japanese butler.

Madison asked : "How are the Luau and the hotel owned ? What's your corporate set-up ?"

"Very simple," Jesus said. "One corporation owns both the Luau and the hotel. There are one hundred shares of no-par stock. Mamie is president and owns forty shares. Monty is vice-president and owns thirty shares. I'm treasurer and own thirty shares. We three are the board of directors. Our business is simple and modest and clean and legal."

"And you ... I suppose you stay in the back rooms and count the money?"

Jesus nodded. "Yes. I deal with the Anglo bankers. The customers at the Luau, the guests here at the hotel, none of them ever see me. As you noticed yesterday, when I fly on our big airplane, I hide in the crew's compartment."

"Why do you hide . . . if the business is so clean and legal?"

Jesus smiled his gypsy-horse-trader smile. "You know why I hide, Mr. Madison. I'm a swarthy Latin. Our customers and guests are middle-class Anglos. To them I'd look like Sin. Or Evil. I'd remind them of Al Capone, or Lucky Luciano, or Bugsy Siegel. They'd resent thinking I was taking their money. That would be very bad for business. So I stay in the back rooms and let Mamie and Monty take the money."

"But doesn't Mamie look like Sin?"

"Yes, but Mamie is a woman. Men don't object to giving money to sinful-looking women. That's why whorehouses are run by madams and not by men. And Mamie looks like healthy, clean, blonde, Anglo Sin. Not like swarthy Latin Sin. Or crafty Jewish Sin. And Monty is perfect. He looks like an usher in a Congregationalist church in Boston."

Madison said: "The Nevada gambling houses are following the same course. They are discharging all dealers and croupiers who have swarthy countenances, and replacing them with men and women who look like pie *à la mode*."

"Very smart," Jesus said. "Absolutely necessary today wherever you're entertaining Anglos."

Madison emptied his glass. He wondered what Jesus really wanted to say to him.

"You know, Mr. Madison," Jesus went on, "I'm a lonely man out here. Hawaii is an Anglo creation. Anglos destroyed the Polynesians and acquired the land. They brought in

Portuguese only to work in the fields. I'm the only Portuguese who ever got rich in Hawaii."

"Why did the landowners allow you to get rich?"

Jesus smiled craftily again. "They didn't *allow* me to get rich. I got rich while they were temporarily out of power. For four years during the war the Army controlled these islands. With the Army's help I got rich . . . selling entertainment."

Madison shrugged. "Entertainment? You mean you sold sex and whisky."

"What else do you sell soldiers and sailors?"

"And that's what you're still doing," Madison said. "Still selling whisky at the Luau and sex at the hotel. All you've done is revise your sales plan."

The two men looked at one another for a moment. Then Jesus said: "Let's sit down to dinner, Mr. Madison."

At the table Jesus said: "Mr. Madison, sex and whisky are sold everywhere every day. The only difference is in how they are sold. Nobody understands that better than you. Mamie and Monty are worried about what you might write about us. But I'm not worried. And you know why? Because you are an honest man. When you look at Hotel Mamie Stover you have to compare it with what you've seen in London and Paris and Madrid and Lisbon and Rome and Las Vegas and Miami Beach. You've sat in strip joints in London and watched Members of Parliament watch a girl undress and pretend she's screwing on the stage. She even screams as she pretends she's reaching climax. You've seen big-time selling of sex and whisky, therefore you know that Hotel Mamie Stover is small-time.

"What happens here? Each afternoon at two o'clock we fly about twenty-five people here from Honolulu, then fly about twenty-five others back to Honolulu. And who are these people? Are they juvenile delinquents? Are they Bohemians? Are they the idle, sinful rich? They are only bored, mature, middle-class, small-town, small-city, Anglo Americans. No Latins. No Jews. No Negroes. Just good, average, ordinary Americans with enough money to make one trip to 'romantic islands' in a lifetime. And what do these people do over here? All they do is try to feel 'romantic' or adventurous. And all we do is provide them the facilities to help them try to feel these things. We even protect them so they can't hurt themselves or one another. So you can only smile when you consider Hotel Mamie Stover. You could stay here a year and never see anything evil."

Madison said: "I may surprise you, Jesus. You admit that you provide the facilities for sexual adventure. Such adventure, despite your measures to protect the adventurers physically, sometimes results in people harming themselves or one another. If a man provides facilities for adventures in which people sometimes do harm, isn't he guilty of evil?"

Jesus objected: "You can't trap me with that question, Mr. Madison. I read one of your books last night. You don't believe that facilities can be evil. Or that providers of facilities can be evil. The only evil for you is the individual action which results in harm. Is a bed evil when a man enjoys another man's wife in it? Is the provider of the bed evil? Half the motels in the United States would go broke if they quit providing beds for such purposes. Are those motel keepers evil? Well, that's all we do here. We provide rendezvous lounges for mature adults. If any evil is committed in those lounges it isn't our evil. And you are the last man on earth who would say it is. You believe in individual freedom, individual responsibility for individual action."

Madison stroked his chin and reflected. He said: "Are you quite sure I can't find anything evil here, Jesus?"

Jesus spread his hands. "You may find an evil individual action, but from that you can't conclude that the hotel is evil. Your honesty prevents any such conclusion. You honestly don't believe that like-sex in itself is evil. In your travels you've had like-sex many times with no feeling of doing evil. If a mature man, married or single, meets a mature woman, married or single, and they decide to have adventurous sex together, you don't believe that evil necessarily has been committed. You are too honest to apply a general judgment. You say the act

177

may be evil, depending on whether anybody gets hurt. You also concede that the act may be good. Don't you?"

Madison replied: "If it relieves boredom, loneliness or despair, if it satisfies longings and nobody gets hurt, I think it may be good."

Jesus nodded. "And that means, Mr. Madison," he said, "that here you will find at least as much good as you find evil. Won't that make it difficult for you to write *anything* about Hotel Mamie Stover?"

"Why should it? I can report what you are doing, can't I?"

"I don't know," Jesus said. "I'm not a writer. I'm only a lonely Portuguese trying to survive in an Anglo world. But here, it seems to me, is your problem. If you report what we are doing at Hotel Mamie Stover you may hurt what you found to be good. I'll illustrate. You approve of abortion. But if you report that we practice abortion you may destroy us. You approve of contraception. We provide our guests contraceptive advice and devices. We support a doctor-scientist who is seeking the cheap contraceptive pill. If you report that we provide contraceptive devices, you may destroy our ability to support the scientist. You concede that sexual adventure may be good, but if you write in a big magazine that Hotel Mamie Stover encourages sexual adventure, you will embarrass the landowners and they may feel compelled to cancel our lease."

Madison now understood why Jesus had asked him to dinner.

"So you think I'm helpless?" Madison said. "You've got rich selling sex and whisky. I'm a writer who tries to be honest. But if I report your activities I will hurt you and thereby I will become guilty of evil. You're good and I'm evil. Is that what you're telling me, Jesus?"

Jesus spoke deliberately: "I wouldn't presume to tell you anything, Mr. Madison. Certainly I don't claim that I am good and you are evil. I'm only reminding you of a business reality. If you write about Hotel Mamie Stover in a widely read magazine, you may destroy the hotel. But you are finding much that you call good here. How can you destroy good without doing evil?"

Jesus reached for his wine glass, lifted it to his lips, and drank deeply.

Madison left Jesus's cottage and walked towards the general area. A full moon was cresting the mountain to the east. A fire was burning on the beach, and the ancient drummers, seated near the fire, were beating out their ancient rhythms. The guests who had arrived that afternoon had been introduced from the platform by Likelike, and the pairing game was being played. Perhaps a dozen men and women were sitting cross-legged in a partial circle around the fire. Somewhat apart, Madison sat down in this circle, leaned back against a palm tree, and stretched his bare feet towards the fire.

Madison's talk with Jesus had depressed him; now he wanted to feel at ease. He wanted to smile. What-the-hell, he thought, I'm not a moralist. I'm an enjoyer of life. I'm not a denouncer. I don't know anything to denounce except cruelty and war and poverty and hypocrisy and invasion of privacy.

Once in Beverly Hills a homosexual had said to Madison: "For Christ's sake, Jim, just because you don't do it yourself, don't go around knocking it!"

Madison wasn't a knocker. He felt that he was caught in the same lock-step towards death as other men and women. He was a practicing member of the human procession, not a withdrawer or a lamenter. What-the-hell, he thought, tomorrow I, too, will be dead! He exchanged smiles with the people who sat near him.

Elaine .Shelby came and sat beside him. She looked fresh and gay, in a yellow *muumuu*, with a scarlet flower in her dark hair. She took Madison's hand and stretched her bare feet alongside his.

"Have we met?" Madison asked solemnly.

"We have, sir," Elaine replied. "We have enjoyed advanced conversation in a· rendezvous lounge. Quite advanced."

179

"Not physical conversation!"

"Not yet. But we have a deal on that. The day after to-morrow. At romantic Waikiki. With the scent of Indiana apple blossoms. Remember?"

"Oh, yes, now it comes to me. In fact I recall a mistake I made last evening. For a mortal man to postpone physical conversation with a lady-lawyer from Richmond, Indiana, even for a few hours, is probably the unforgivable sin. If I miss Heaven that'll be the sin that keeps me out."

Elaine continued, "But what about that melancholy which would have overcome you had you proceeded with said physical conversation? Remember your quotation: 'Coitus makes the whole world sad'? What about that despair which would have seized you as you wandered lonely through the corridor? A despair so desperate that you might never have halted at the water's edge but might have continued headlong into the surf and surrendered to the undertow?"

They laughed together, and Madison felt thankful for Elaine. The only women he ever really liked were those who could make him laugh.

He said: "I have a suggestion. Mamie's program has encouraged me. I've ridden horseback. I've had three mas-sages. I've eaten four amatory meals. So I feel brave enough to defy post-coital melancholy. Suppose we go back to one of Mamie's more advanced lounges and correct my mistake of last evening?"

Elaine smiled mischievously.

"You tempt me, sir. But you have forgotten something else. You suggested a game for me to play. Remember? Operation Concern? I've been playing it. I'm meeting Mr. Whitaker at his cottage in a few minutes for more conversation."

"Oh, hell," Madison groaned. "Last night *was* my night for blunders. Well, how's the game going?"

"I believe you'll approve my moves. First, I was to have met him at 1 P.M. in the general garden. I kept him waiting ten minutes, then gave him an artful explanation for being late. I told him that I had gone to a lounge with you last evening, and that I had been shocked by the obscene atmosphere and by your abrupt and cynical conduct. That experience had made it necessary for me to consult the doctor again, and that was why I was late."

"And did that increase his concern?"

"It increased his curiosity. He started to ask me if I was still a virgin, then he realized he wouldn't believe me if I said I was. So there was no immediate way for him to relieve his curiosity except to say that he had remembered a telephone call he must make and would I excuse him for a moment."

"And he went and asked the doctor if you were still a virgin?"

"Exactly. Just as you had foreseen. When he returned I felt rather guilty. He looked so thankfully incredulous . . . as though he had received some blessing he hadn't deserved or expected. We walked awhile in the garden. He repeated how concerned he was about me, and that led him into his speech about how, since he was the manager and had to greet everyone who passed, he thought we should repair to a lounge where we could converse in privacy."

"Then what did you say?"

"I told him I wanted to be alone with him, but that the lounges were such obvious assignation rooms that if I went to one I was almost certain to become psychologically inhibited. So I thought we should stay in the general area until we could get to know one another. I told him I found him so interesting that I hoped he'd help me avoid any too-easy familiarity which might endanger our ripening interest in each other."

Madison chuckled. "You're learning fast . . . for a virgin."

"Well, after all, Jim," Elaine said, "I *am* a lawyer. And a good one."

"That's becoming apparent. Did he take you to his cottage?"

"Reluctantly. Only after I convinced him I'd never go to a lounge with him. He seemed pitifully afraid to take me to his home."

"Sure he was afraid."

"Why do you say that? Why should he be afraid?"

"It's a matter of risk," Madison explained. "Monty knows that taking you to his home instead of to a lounge increases his risk with you. Remember that old practice in China? A man finds a woman who is about to die, about to drown or starve or take poison, and the man rushes in and saves her life? What happens to the poor bastard? Is he thanked and decorated? Hell, no! The woman becomes his responsibility for life! Just because the poor bastard helps her he finds her on his hands. Well, a civilized man runs the same risk when he begins maneuvering with a woman for like-sex. Particularly with a virgin. The man's only protection is to move rapidly, to take her in her own bed, or to persuade her to meet him in a rented bed. In that way the woman gains no advantageous position. But if the man tolerates delay, if he allows the woman to visit his home and thereby confers status on her, the man is risking grave responsibility. The sight of you crossing his threshold must have sent shivers down poor Monty's spine."

Elaine laughed. "How you exaggerate, Jim!"

"I don't exaggerate," Madison insisted. "Monty Whitaker has never taken a sexual risk in his life. Even when he married he knew he could leave his wife at any moment with impunity. He is the product of a male sexual Heaven. The ideal sexual situation for a man has been to live here in Hawaii and take his sex in the bedrooms of women who must leave next week. In such a Heaven a man can perform miracles: he can be aggressive, dominant, zestful, and he can prolong his act with vigor and mutual ecstasy. That's why women who visit Hawaii go back to the mainland believing that men are more potent in the islands. That's why Hotel Mamie Stover is so successful: Mamie relieves men of responsibility so they can take women with irresponsible zest. That's why there is so much male inadequacy on the mainland. How can a man dominate a woman, give her zestful hours of intercourse, when he feels responsibility hanging over his backside like the Sword of Damocles? Monty Whitaker has never felt that sword hanging over him. So if he is allowing you to put him off, permitting you to maneuver him into a position of disadvantage, he must either be crazy or he is *really concerned* about you."

Elaine said: "Well, he isn't crazy. He acted very nice this afternoon after I had forced him to get his mind off sex. He played some beautiful records for me. He talked about his grandfather and his father and his mother. He told me about the old Lunaliho and about how lonely he often felt when he was a boy and after his mother died. He's really a very nice man, Jim. You said so yourself."

"Sure, Monty is all right," Madison agreed. "But I can't understand his taking such a risk. What do you expect to do at his cottage tonight?"

"Nothing much," Elaine said. "Just what you advised me to do. Remember? He'll play his records. We'll sit in the moonlight. I'll keep him talking. I'll keep listening. I'll keep saying no. We'll hold hands. Once or twice he can kiss me . . . if he wants to, and if he'll do it tenderly and not savagely. It's been done that way before, hasn't it? You told me yourself that men and woman once conducted themselves that way . . . back in the nineteenth century."

Madison shook his head. "It sounds unbelievable . . . even if I did suggest it. I was being facetious. It can't happen that way in Hawaii. Certainly not at Hotel Mamie Stover. Certainly not with Monty Whitaker. If Monty is allowing you to put him off in that fashion, he must be one flabbergasted sonofabitch!"

Elaine pursed her lips and looked into Madison's eyes. She tightened her hand on his. She suddenly wanted to force that sardonic smile from his face.

"Quit being facetious, Jim," she said. "How about your own treatment of me? Last night I went to a public bed with you. You put me off. Remember? You said you did it selfishly. Are you sure you didn't act unselfishly? Are you sure you didn't exaggerate your fear of post-coital melancholy? Isn't it possible that you wanted to put me in a more advantageous

183

position? Under our contract you are taking me to *your* home. Why? Are you crazy? I didn't demand that concession, you freely granted it. Is it possible that you want to confer status on me? Why have you agreed to help me with illusions and a few honest lies? I haven't flabbergasted *you*, have I?"

Elaine paused. She felt strong and assured.

"I'm afraid, Jim," she said, "that your conduct reveals a little weak, dangerous, foolish concern for me."

For about four seconds Madison dropped his guard. Then he regained his smile and said: "You can't convict me of concern, counsellor. If you'll read the fine print on our contract you'll see that I'm in the classic island position with you. I get you for nothing, I risk nothing. First, I'm a married man. You know this. I made full disclosure. The fact that with this knowledge you enter into a sexual contract with me discredits you before the court. Sure, I'll take you to my home. But not for sex. Just for meals . . . and because I like to think of you lying in my garden while I work. All the sex is in your bed at an hotel. My time responsibility is clearly defined: four days, no more. After four days you can't even expect a letter from me. My financial responsibility is limited: one hotel bill, plus one abortion in the unlikely event of a failure of both my will power and science. You are the visiting virgin who surrenders on my terms. Since you are also a lawyer you can't even claim that you entered into said contract without legal counsel. So you can't accuse me of being generous. You can't convict me of concern."

Elaine clung to Madison's hand and held his eyes with hers. She felt sadness brush across her heart, but it passed and she said: "I must go now. If I miss seeing you tomorrow, the contract calls for our leaving here together the day after tomorrow. At 2 P.M. I'll be ready. Even if the contract robs me of all advantages, I like it. I expect full performance from you."

"You'll get full performance from me," Madison said. "Since I'll be free of responsibility, I can be stronger, more aggressive, more dominant than any poor mainland bastard could be with you. My only concern will be my own selfish enjoyment."

Elaine swallowed and again felt almost frightened. She stood up, then she dropped back to her knees and put her lips close to Madison's ear.

"Are you quite sure," she said softly, "that you can spend four whole nights in my bed without taking any risks? Are you absolutely certain that I won't wind up as a responsibility of yours . . . of one sort or another?"

Then she rose and walked rapidly away.

After Elaine left him, Madison continued to sit in the sand. He felt comfortable and friendly, and he had no desire to do anything other than watch his fellow guests. The big circle around the fire began to fill. The rhythm of the drummers became more insistent. Couples began to dance. Madison exchanged greetings with everyone. He knew why so many of them had begun to notice him. The word had passed that he was a writer, so the author was now receiving attention. Madison welcomed this attention because of the one advantage it gave him: women, after learning he was a novelist, discussed themselves with him more candidly than they would talk to their psychiatrists.

The moon was now high. The surf pounded relentlessly. A breeze had risen . . . just cool enough to make the beach fire feel luxurious from a distance of thirty feet. When Likelike noticed Madison she left her pairing post to bring him a glass of *mobani* juice. She smiled down at him as she handed him the juice, and he thought she looked desirable . . . with her skirt of red ti leaves, a red silk halter around her breasts, a yellow flower in her black hair which was in a bun low on one side of her neck like Dorothy Lamour's.

Sally Rogers spoke to Madison. He had not seen her since the airplane ride, so he invited her to sit beside him.

"Sit down and tell me about yourself, Sally," he said.

She sat beside him in the sand. She wore sandals and a dark red *muumuu*.

"There isn't much to tell about me," she said. "A house-wife from Eugene, Oregon. Three months shy of forty. Two grown sons. A healthy husband. Twelve thousand dollars a year. A comfortable home near a modest country club. A few joys, a few sorrows."

"Why did you and Tom come here?"

"That could require a long answer. First, why shouldn't we come here? This must be one of the most beautiful spots on earth. Perfect beach. Breath-taking color. Good food. Good service. Wonderful sun. Salt air. Infectious music. Uniqueness. The excitement of non-conformity. A feeling of being on a remote island with nothing to do but enjoy. So part of the answer is: why shouldn't we come here?"

"And what's the rest of the answer?"

Sally Rogers hesitated, sighed slightly, felt her lower jaw slacken. Unconsciously she reached for Madison's hand . . . the gesture of one human being trying to feel closer to an-other, seeking warmth, or sympathy, or simple alliance against disillusion, decay and death.

She said: "I suppose some of the answer lies in my situation as of this moment. It's about 9 P.M. I'm on a 'romantic' island. I'm excited. I feel as though I look my best: I may never look this attractive again. I want to do something extraordinary . . . something I can remember when I'm dried-up and wearing a shawl and sitting by the fire during the long, damp Oregon winters. But my husband is now sleeping soundly . . . completely and healthily exhausted.

"He has been out on a fishing boat all day. Catching fight-ing fish. Soaking up sun. Inhaling salt air. Exchanging gutty vulgarities with other men. And during his delightful day he made at least one trip below deck and grappled a girl power-fully and excitingly in a bunk. He probably made two such trips . . . judging by his state of complete exhaustion. When he returned to the hotel he took a luxurious bath and massage. He ate a nourishing, amatory dinner. Then he summoned all his remaining strength, walked to the general area, greeted me, told me how pretty I looked, urged me to have fun, then asked me to excuse him because he was about to fall asleep on his feet, and he had to get to bed to be ready for boar hunting tomorrow. Would you say that my vigorous husband's delightful day might contain part of the answer you want?"

Madison wished he knew something to say. He didn't, so he held her hand and remarked: "That's a cruel situation. I suppose it must be the most ordinary form of human cruelty today. But at least your husband sounds like an honest son-ofabitch."

"He isn't a sonofabitch," Sally said. "He has many fine qualities. One of our troubles is that I started too young. I'm too young now to be as far along in life as I am. I was married on my eighteenth birthday. My first son came before I was nineteen. My second son came while I was twenty, so now my sons don't need me any more. My husband is a vigorous forty-four. I'm a vigorous thirty-nine. My husband and I have shared a bed almost twenty-two years. It's been a good bed. But not many beds can be exciting after twenty-two years. Can they? They can be warm and safe and secure. But they can't be very exciting."

Madison shook his head.

'So you see what my trouble is," Sally continued. "I'm not dried-up yet. My husband still has sex with me. But it's no more than a Saturday night chore for him . . . a pleasant enough duty but nothing to get excited about. Not nearly so exciting as the girl in the fishing boat, or in the lodge up in the timber. And because I know he isn't excited, I can't get excited. So it's an unexciting, dull, domestic encounter that in decency ought to be stopped. But neither of us has had the courage to stop it."

"So what have you done about it?"

"Nothing. There is nothing to do. We both want the marriage to last until death does us part. I just haven't been able to match his outside adventures. I haven't been able to sneak into cars at country club dances like some of my friends. I haven't been able to sneak into motels, or to sneak up in the

187

woods with some truant husband. I think adultery is shameful and sordid . . . as well as being a sin."

"Then I'm back to my original question," Madison said. "Why did you come here? You knew what this would be, didn't you?"

"I came here for two reasons," she answered. "First, to let him have his fun while I try, once and for all, to reach the point where I don't care. For fourteen years I've lived with the knowledge that I was his sexual second choice. I watched him go off to war in 1942. I saw how eager he was to leave me to rear our sons while he went to North Africa and Italy to save a world . . . and to take his soldier's comfort from the girls. It hurt then . . . it still hurts a little. Here . . . every day I expect to listen to his friendly explanations as to why he doesn't want me . . . each day I expect to care a little less, and when I leave here I expect to have become the completely tolerant wife, the wife who never again will give a happy goddam!"

Madison laughed. Then Sally shrugged and smiled.

"And your second reason?" Madison asked.

"Well," she said, "I came here to do a little prospecting myself. Adultery is beyond me in Oregon: I'll never be up to it. But here I'm looking for a man. I need something. I know what it is. I need sexual reassurance. I need to feel a strong, aggressive, dominant, excited man in bed with me again. I want him to be more aggressive with me than my husband was with that girl on the fishing boat today. I want a man who, when he makes sexual contact with me, exults, and feels like he's conquering the world. And when he collapses, I want him to feel certain that he has had the best available at Hotel Mamie Stover."

Madison laughed, and Sally Rogers joined him.

"Do you think you'll find your man?"

"I know I will. I know how to get what I need . . . when I set my mind to it."

Madison looked at her and felt guilty for not wanting her. He wished that at that moment he could proposition her, meet her in the most advanced lounge, and reassure her thoroughly. But he knew he couldn't. He knew that a man can't reassure a woman when he feels too sorry for her.

"Answer one more question for me, Sally," he said. "Do you think Hotel Mamie Stover is a good place? Or an evil place?"

She reflected. "I think it's a good place. It's cruel, obscene and indecent, but life, too, is cruel, obscene and indecent. This is an honest place. It's remote enough so that we can shed our hypocrisies and stop fooling ourselves and take off our clothes and look life straight in the face. That's good. What I've said just now to you . . . I've enjoyed saying those things . . . I've never said them to anybody before. I'm sure I couldn't say such things anywhere but here . . . maybe not to any man but you. I've read your books. You're not afraid of life. I feel better for having talked with you. I expect to feel better when I leave here than I have felt in years."

Sally paused, then: "And I'll add this. Since those Hawaiian princesses could give such 'indescribable sexual delight' until they were sixty, Mamie can count on me being back every year for at least twenty more years!"

There was a glint in Sally's eye as she left Madison and went to the Pairing Post where a newly arrived man was anxious to begin elementary conversation with her.

When Mary Ferrell sat down in the sand beside him, Madison guessed that she'd spark no laughter for him as Elaine and Sally had done. He guessed, correctly, that Monty's neglect had galled her, and that she was now seeking Monty's replacement.

Mary said: "Jim, last night during our elementary conversation, why didn't you tell me you wrote books and pictures?"

"You didn't ask me. During our few minutes in the garden you seemed quite preoccupied."

Mary had expected Madison to be cool. She understood why. He was listed in *Who's Who*. He was accustomed to attention from women. Because she hadn't known who he was, and because she had already arranged her rendezvous with Monty, Mary had been inattentive to Madison during their first conversation. That, she understood, was why Madison had not asked her for a rendezvous. Mary knew about male egos : she had come to feed Madison's. She fluttered her long lashes, tried to look distressed, and said : "I'm sorry, Jim. Please forgive me. I didn't mean to appear preoccupied. I was just . . . well, we all have our troubles, and I was having mine last evening."

She kicked off her sandals and squirmed in the sand to get comfortable. She also adroitly employed the squirms to tighten her sea-mist *muumuu* in the right places, just to remind Madison what luxury was now within his reach.

Mary had had a frustrating day. At 1 P.M. she had gone to the general garden to arrange an afternoon rendezvous with Monty. She had seen him preoccupied with Elaine. She had then spent the afternoon sunning on the women's beach, reading *Lady Chatterley's Lover*, watching several women play with the beach boys, and picturing Monty with Elaine in a lounge. At eight-thirty she had met Bob Ferrell in a lounge for one of his ridiculous efforts to impregnate her. Now Bob was asleep, and Mary, after hunting another hour for Monty, had turned her attentions to Madison. And she had to work fast : curfew was only two hours away.

"I read a great deal, Jim," she said. "I haven't read your books but I intend to. I read a novel this afternoon."

"Really?"

"*Lady Chatterley's Lover*. I lay on the women's beach for hours, luxuriously naked, and read every line."

"You must have liked it?"

"Well, naturally I'd like it."

Madison raised his brows.

"Is it possible, Mary, that you are revealing to me that you and Lady Constance Chatterley have something in common?"

Mary smiled, trying to hold his eyes on her while she maneuvered to interest him.

"I doubt that I have much left to reveal to you, Jim. I saw how you looked at me yesterday in the car and on the airplane. I puzzled you at first. You wondered why a husband in his right mind would bring a wife like me to Hotel Mamie Stover. Then you guessed the answer. I could feel your eyes looking right through my *muumuu* last night while you were talking to me in the garden and you didn't think I was being attentive. You are a very wise man about women."

Madison smiled at her efforts.

"You overrate my wisdom," he said. "I looked at you. I looked at your husband. I concluded that you were just like Tom and Sally Rogers . . . just another husband and wife bored with one another."

Mary bit her lip. For Madison to say that her husband was bored with her was hard to take. But she took it. She shook her head sadly. "No, Jim. My husband hasn't found me boring. That isn't our problem."

"Then I have it!" Madison snapped his fingers. "How stupid of me not to have seen it! You and Lady Chatterley! Your husband, *too*, is inadequate!"

Now Mary employed silence against sarcasm. She sat there looking distressed, helpless, inviting Madison to look at her. She put her hand on his. "I didn't sit down here to fight, Jim. Not at 10 P.M. at Hotel Mamie Stover . . . with a moon like that . . . and drums beating around a beach fire. I'm not the first woman to have to live with the tragedy of an inadequate husband. I don't think it's funny. Why do you make fun of me?"

"What did you marry him for? If he was inadequate?"

"I didn't know he was inadequate. I was a virgin bride. I knew nothing about men, adequate or inadequate."

"A point against virgin marriage. Why haven't you divorced him?"

"That's easier said than done. Marriages involve money. Places in society. Homes. Ambitions. Not just sexual adequacy or inadequacy. Marriages sometimes must be maintained.

191

Some smart people even say they should be maintained at all cost."

"So you're maintaining yours. And you travel all the way to Hawaii looking for gamekeepers. Aren't there plenty of gamekeepers in the Great North Woods around Eau Claire, Wisconsin?"

Mary didn't reply. She dropped her eyes and noticed that Madison's hand was still in hers. After a moment she looked back into his face, waited for his eyes to fasten on hers, then asked softly: "Now that you have made your speech I have a question for you: how are you in the role of the game-keeper?"

"No good at all," Madison said. "If I must compete with a husband I want him to be thoroughly adequate. I prefer not to race against cripples."

"You're quite sure you wouldn't like to adjourn this meeting to a lounge and drink *mobani* juice and see if we can't become more attractive to one another?"

Madison held her hand for a moment, then he replied: "I'll answer that with an observation about you and a revelation about me. You're the most beautiful woman on this beach. You are also the most selfish one I've met. Never in your life were you attentive to any man you didn't want something from. So I can't like you, and if we had sex together it damn sure wouldn't be like-sex.

"Now about me. I've adventured with my share of women around the earth. But barring a few adolescent trips to whore-houses, I've never had sex with a woman unless I loved her or genuinely liked her. Along with the aggression and domin-ance, I've tried to give a little admiration and tenderness and concern. So I haven't hurt women, and I haven't hurt myself. I've avoided one popular variety of sex. *Dislike-sex*. Dislike-sex is where a man, and sometimes a woman, uses sex to express hostility or contempt. Dislike-sex is trophy-hunting sex . . . the brutal act to reduce instead of elevate. I could do that to you. I could meet you in a lounge and do to you approximately what Monty did to you last night . . . though

Monty is heavier, stronger and seven years younger than I am. But that's sick-sex. It eventually makes a man sick, and you're already sick with it. So you can become inattentive to me again, Mary. There are plenty of men here who will jump at you, figuratively and literally. Attend them. All you can ever get from me is my good wishes."

After a moment Mary moved away. Madison watched her go and was sorry.

At ten-thirty Becky Sanders sat down beside Madison. She was in a sky-blue *muumuu*, and her ash-blonde hair was in a bun low on the side of her neck resembling Likelike's. Madison thought she looked like the soft, libidinous woman who, after an evening rendezvous, showers and slips on something and comes back to the group to listen to music for an hour before trying to sleep. Becky, too, kicked off her sandals and squirmed in the sand, but only to make herself comfortable.

"Since we have a mutual friend, Jim," she said, "I assume you've heard as much about me as I have about you. So we're no longer strange to one another."

"No friend of the doctor's is strange to me," Madison said. "The doctor and I are old horseback and massage-table confidants."

"And I guess there really aren't many secrets at Hotel Mamie Stover," Becky observed. "Despite all the secret passages and absurd disguises."

That Doctor Anderson had acclaimed her talents to Madison didn't bother Becky. She had achieved a melancholy acceptance of life.

"Tell me more about you, Becky?"

She replied: "There is nothing distinctive about me. Except maybe the year I was born in. Nineteen twenty-one. That's a distinction shared by a million or so American women. All it means is that by nineteen forty-one I was in love and married. My husband went overseas in nineteen forty-two, and he was one of those who didn't come back."

"And where did that leave you?"

"It left me in a city with two distinctions. Both before and after his death I worked in Washington, D.C. And besides being the capital, Washington has one other distinction : it's the easiest city in America to make a sexual arrangement in, and the hardest to make a marriage in. It's the easiest community to become a mistress in, the hardest to become a wife in. I guess you know the reason. A lot of superior men come to Washington, but they feel they are there temporarily. Even if they stay twenty years, each year is temporary duty. Their wives only visit them, and they visit their wives, because the wives are maintaining the establishments back home. And, like the Constitution, those wives *must* be preserved, because to discard one would be to risk political disaster."

"So you became a 'Washington Wife'?"

"In a modest way. I loved him and I'm a slave when I love. I'd like to have lived my life in a Blue Ridge Mountain cabin, having a baby every year, working my fingers to the bone every day, and sleeping with my man every night. And I'd have wanted my man to shoot any travelling salesman who dropped his eyes below my chin. I'm that sort of woman. Instead I became a mistress . . . for ten years ! You know what it means when you get hooked like that ? Heaven or Hell . . . nothing in between. Four nights with your man followed by four weeks of jealousy and loneliness. You swear every day you'll end it tomorrow."

"It's hard to break, isn't it ?"

"It's like getting off dope. Maybe it's harder than getting off dope because you can hide from the dope-seller while you're trying to shake the habit. You can't hide from a bed-partner who has you hooked. He keeps finding you in your agony and 'comforting' you and hooking you again. You have to fight him more desperately every year because you know you must shake him while you still have the looks to make that marriage-for-security."

"I gather you finally shook him ?"

"A year ago," Becky said. "I was able to shake him at thirty-three because I'm also a coward. I was afraid to risk waiting another year. Willowy ash-blondes like me begin to look washed out earlier than other women. We fade faster. I knew I had to move while there was still sheen in my hair, lights in my eyes, while my skin still felt moist and looked rose-tinted, and before I started bulging at the waist. I shook him, and after I had gone six months without him I knew he could never hook me again."

"Then you began stalking Mr. Security?"

"We call him the Security Man down in the Blue Ridge where I come from. Yes, I began stalking him. And that brings a new agony, you know. You feel dishonest, calculating, obscene. You have to keep talking to yourself. You have to stand naked before your boudoir mirror and say: 'Listen, Lady. You've been doing it for love since you were eighteen. Now you must do it for security . . . for money just like any other whore. So you'd better adjust right now for a long winter. This Security Man you're stalking is much older than you are. He'll die or divorce you, and there'll be another Security Man or two to stalk. And while you're stalking these Security Men, you damn sure better get enough security to take your dried-up carcass decently to the grave. Remember that women live for ever now, with all these miracle drugs, so you'd better learn to shake that tail with purpose and calculation, because the shaking years are short and the security years are long.' "

Madison held her hand while they listened to the drums and watched the dancers.

"Tell me, Becky," Madison said, "is the agony ended?"

"Just about," she said. "I'm now in the final stages of adjusting from love-sex to security-sex. I've found my Security Man . . . he's a good catch. I'm going to marry him very soon, and I think I'll be able both to endure him and to give him an acceptable substitute for love."

"Are you glad you came to Hotel Mamie Stover?"

She reflected, and Madison thought he felt her hand tighten on his while she was thinking.

"Yes," she said. "This is a good place . . . for me. Women

who live orderly, one-man lives should never come here. Not even those women who live orderly two-or-three-men lives. But for those of us who foul up, and who have to shift from love-sex to security-sex, Hotel Mamie Stover helps us make the shift. It's easier here to take that first man you don't love. Remoteness helps. The sensuous red and yellow colors, the drumbeats, the erotic dancing all help. The nakedness and the massages and the callous talk about sexual techniques and prowess . . . they help. Above all, the general attitude. Maybe it's no more than misery loves company . . . and that here nobody pretends to love anybody else. Maybe it's a form of group therapy. Maybe it helps a woman like me just to be surrounded for a week by a hundred other women, all of whom are compromising and adjusting and trying to do the best they can. Maybe it helps a woman like me to listen to Mamie explain how love isn't really necessary for sex . . . that sex can also be a simple festivity of the flesh, no more and no less. Perhaps a woman like me can never really believe it, but I've damn sure got to try."

At 11 P.M. Likelike's duties at her Pairing Post were ended for the evening. The last pair had been formed, the last rendezvous lounge had been assigned. She went to her room and freshened herself. She freed her black hair from the bun on her neck and let it fall halfway down her graceful back. She pinned two fresh, red-and-yellow hibiscus blossoms in her hair. She uncovered her breasts, like the women in the *Folies Bergère* or in the Las Vegas gambling halls. She removed her long skirt of red ti leaves, and replaced it with the brief Tahitian skirt. She kicked off her sandals. Then she returned to the fire to dance. Perhaps fifty men and women were now sitting in the circle, and several were dancing. As Likelike began dancing, the rhythm of the drums picked up, and the other dancers sat down so that everyone could watch her.

"She's lovely," Becky Sanders said to Madison. "Her body looks like Dorothy Lamour's. Her face is pure Polynesian sensuousness."

Around and around the circle Likelike danced, while the ancient drummers beat their drums and the watchers clapped hands and chanted. On her second time around she singled out Madison, smiled at him, danced before him, and beckoned to him. The other watchers shouted for Madison to dance with her.

Madison, also barefooted but wearing the duck pants and the red *aloha* shirt, laughed, jumped up and began dancing. He couldn't dance like a native, but he could dance better than the other white men. He had been in the islands seventeen years. He had danced at many a *luau*. He knew music, he played the piano, so he had a sense of rhythm. Moreover, he understood that such island dancing requires unquestioning surrender to the drums. Madison knew that his and Likelike's dancing was unashamedly erotic . . . that such dancing at midnight around a beach fire can have only one decent result.

As he danced Madison began to feel elated and he said to himself : "Likelike I'll take. She's lovely. She's the only woman here I've really wanted. For me not to take her after this dance would be both foolish and indecent. Somewhere in one of those rendezvous buildings she has a room where there is no midnight curfew . . . no curfew at all except sunlight streaming through the window. So this night I won't spend in the men's barracks. This night I'll spend with Likelike."

As they danced, his flushed face moved within five feet of Likelike's. His eyes were on hers. Then suddenly, imposed on Likelike's lovely, sensuous face, Madison saw the face of Jesus Portales.

"That sex-selling sonofabitch!" Madison thought. "This isn't a spontaneous dance! This woman doesn't want me! She's only performing a chore ordered by a whoremaster!"

As he continued dancing, Madison told himself that he might be wrong, that Likelike had chosen him because she liked him, maybe because he was in *Who's Who*, or because she had read something in his novels which made her feel close to him, or for no other reason than she was lonely and wanted to like him and wanted him to like her.

"What-the-hell!" Madison continued to himself. "I'll take her in any case. I want her. Who am I to look such a lovely gift horse in the mouth? I'm not turning her down this night even if she *is* only performing a whore-chore for Portales!"

The drums stopped: it was midnight. Madison, breathing heavily, took Likelike by the hand and walked with her to a palm tree.

"You're lovely," he said. "So graceful . . . lovely."

She said nothing. She stood waiting for him to ask her where and how soon. She didn't intend to tell him where; she intended to lead him straightway to a *cabana* on the men's beach.

Madison opened his lips to speak, but before he could say anything he thought he heard Likelike's voice, next day on the telephone to Jesus, reporting mission accomplished . . . that she had spent the night, as per instructions, weakening Mr. Madison's will, rendering him harmless.

"You're lovely," Madison repeated. "Thank you for the dance. We must dance some more together."

She knew what he meant. She dropped her eyes, waited a moment, then said: "Would you like to dance with me . . . tomorrow afternoon, on a very private portion of the men's beach?"

"Yes," Madison said. "I'd like that. And thank you."

As he walked towards the men's barracks, he kept wondering if he had been wrong, if Likelike had been acting on her own, if she had *really* liked him and *really* wanted him to spend the night with her.

"Oh, hell, I should have gone with her," he said, almost audibly.

Then Madison remembered that tomorrow was to be a busy day. He had, not one, but two commitments. He was dancing with Likelike during the afternoon, and Mamie was taking a holiday to entertain him for the evening.

"Goddam," he thought. "I better get some sleep."

CHAPTER THIRTEEN

The third day: in which we watch
catastrophe strike at Hotel Mamie
Stover.

AT 10 A.M. ON the third day Madison felt no presentiment of
catastrophe.

High up on the grassy slope of the volcano, he and Doctor
Anderson were riding horseback. They both felt wonderfully
lighthearted. They had been running the horses. They had
stopped several times, to admire the hotel grounds spread out
below them, to chuckle over sexual developments and expectations. Madison, now fully rested, expected to spend the
afternoon with Likelike and the evening with Mamie. Next
day, his research completed, Madison intended to leave the
hotel and return home to work, taking Elaine with him. Not
in years had he felt so reassured.

Then it struck.

Riding as if the dam had broken, an Hawaiian horseman
came racing towards Madison and the doctor.

"Mistah Madison! Mistah Madison!" he yelled. He tore
up whole square yards of turf reining in his horse.

"Good God, what is it?" Madison yelled. "Fire, flood or
murder?"

"Miss Mamie!" the horseman yelled. "She say please you
come hurry!"

Madison threw a perplexed glance at the doctor, who shook
his head, electing not to join a cavalry charge. So Madison
and the Hawaiian took off like a posse trying to intercept
rustlers at the pass.

From the stables Madison sprinted and jogged to Mamie's cottage, covering three hundred yards faster than he had moved since he crossed Omaha Beach under fire.

"What the hell, Mamie?" he gasped. She was waiting on the *lanai*, wringing her hands.

"I'm sorry, Jim," she said. "You used to let me turn to you when I needed you. I need to turn to you now. Even *she* wants to see you. So we need you."

Madison could only throw up his hands and wait for the dust to settle.

"Sit down, Jim," Mamie said, "and I'll try to explain. "We've got to protect the hotel. We've got to protect the Luau. We've got three million dollars invested, and we've got to protect it. So this must be handled *very* carefully. We must smuggle them out as fast as we can."

"Slow down, Mamie," Madison insisted. "What's threatening the hotel? Is it on fire?"

"Jim," Mamie said gravely, "they want to get *married*! At once! Now! They've both gone crazy. I got back here an hour ago and they hit me with it. He wants to sell the hotel . . . or his part of it! They want to leave Hawaii before sundown! They want to go to Niagara Falls on a honeymoon. They're even babbling some nonsense about planting apple trees in Indiana!"

"Mamie, you mean Elaine Shelby and Monty?"

"Who else? She's the only virgin around here, isn't she? Probably the only white virgin who ever came to Hawaii! She and Monty stayed at his cottage all last night. They talked all night. Sometime in the dead of night . . . just like that! . . . they decided they're in love. But they say they didn't do anything about it. Except just kept talking. They insist she's *still* a virgin! That's why they have to move so fast. They want her to be a virgin bride. So they want to marry *now* and race for Niagara Falls at three hundred miles an hour. They say it has something to do with illusions."

"Good God!" Madison said.

Mamie sighed and continued: "Now, Jim, this is some-

200

thing I don't know much about. Since I was seventeen I've lived only in Hollywood and Hawaii so I've never met anybody who was in love. But I do have some sense of propriety, and I know it's just not proper to call in a preacher or a justice of the peace and perform any marriage ceremony at Hotel Mamie Stover! It's not proper and it's not good business. Is it?"

"God no," Madison said. "This is no place to sing *Oh, Promise Me*. And mentioning vows around here would be worse than mentioning rope in a house where a man has been hung."

"That's what I think. Just imagine how it would make our guests feel! They didn't come here to think about marriage!"

"They sure as hell didn't."

"And think what publicity could do to us! The manager of Hotel Mamie Stover deciding to get married! And marrying a virgin! This is the sort of thing which if it isn't handled just right can cost people money, Jim."

"It sure is, Mamie. A rumor sometimes can topple an empire."

Mamie was calming down. For sixteen years she had cultivated the illusion that she was safe as long as she could turn to Madison. Now, just talking with him, she began to see her way clear.

"Here's what I think must be done, Jimmy. See if you think I'm right. First, we've got to keep this secret. Only four people know about it now. You and me and Monty and her. She's upstairs trying to compose herself. Monty is over at his cottage packing, and telephoning Jesus and Leo Hirshman. That'll be six who know about it. We've got to fly them to Honolulu just like nothing is happening. We've got to get them a marriage license and hush that up. Jesus can handle that. Then we hide them some place for a couple of hours while we get them married. Then we put them on an airplane and start them towards Niagara Falls. How does that sound, Jimmy?"

"Looks like about all you can do, Mamie."

Mamie sighed deeply. She came over to Madison, sat on the floor at his feet, leaned against him, and took his hand. She sat there for a moment, just holding his hand and resting her cheek against his thigh.

"Then as soon as we get them shipped off," Mamie said, "well, I've got to pick up the pieces. I've got to reorganize and buy Monty's stock and carry on. I just want to feel that you'll help me through it, Jimmy ... that I can turn to you, that I can depend on having your advice and your reassurance."

"I'll do what I can, Mamie."

Mamie thought his hand felt warm in hers. She rubbed her cheek against his thigh.

"I could never have been anything without you, Jimmy. I've known that for sixteen years.

"And Jimmy," she added. "I was just thinking. Since we must find a secret place for them to be married, I was wondering ... could you take us up to your house to have the ceremony performed there? Your house is sort of isolated, high up there in the Heights ... and nobody would suspect what was going on."

"I guess I can do that for you, Mamie."

"Thank you, Jimmy. I'm so worried. Now will you do this? She wants to see you about something. Will you go upstairs and talk to her for a few minutes while I run over to Monty's cottage and go over things with him?"

"Sure, Mamie," Madison said. "You go over and calm Monty down, and I'll go upstairs and calm her down. Though I can't imagine why she wants to see me."

Upstairs Madison found Elaine in her *muumuu*, on a chaise, in the act of swallowing a tranquillizer.

"Come here, Jim," she said, "and pinch me and tell me whether this is really happening or not."

"You tell me," Madison said.

"It's a miracle."

Elaine reclined and Madison sat on the foot of the chaise.

"How did it happen?"

"Nobody knows how a miracle happens," Elaine said. "It must have been about 2 A.M. I was doing what you told me to do. He was talking. I was listening and saying no. And bingo! He decided he couldn't live without me any longer. And, believe it or not, just about that same time I felt my heart jump up in my throat and I knew I had loved him from the minute I walked into his office at the Luau."

Madison smiled.

"Now don't give me that disbelieving grin, Jim," Elaine protested. "You *must* believe. This is a real, honest-to-goodness, modern miracle."

"So it's a miracle," Madison said. "What I can't understand is what all the hurry is about. Why am I running horses across mountains risking my neck? Where is the fire? There is such a thing as love-sex, you know. When you decided you loved him, why didn't you quit saying no, jump into bed with him, then sleep it off? And get married at leisure? Love should bring tranquillity, not a hell-for-leather race for a preacher and Niagara Falls!"

"Well, Jim," Elaine said, "that's another miraculous thing. Once I decided I loved him, that's exactly what I tried to do. I surrendered completely. I quit saying no and led him over to the bed. But you know something? By that time I had oversold him on virginity. He had remembered that his mother, forty years ago, had been a virgin bride when his father went to fetch her from Ireland. So it was Monty who decided that since we had waited that long we ought to wait until I have the ring on and we reach a honeymoon hotel."

"Good God!" Madison said. "The sexual troubles you have! And that's why you are in such a hurry?"

Elaine was feeling calmer: the pill was tranquillizing her. She sat up.

"Well, that's only part of it, Jim," she explained. "As soon as we realized how much we love each other, both of us suddenly felt afraid. We are afraid of Hotel Mamie Stover. We are afraid to stay here one minute more than it takes us to get away. This is a very obscene place, you know. It's no place for lovers. And I guess we're just plain afraid of Hawaii. Monty has lived an undisciplined life out here. He's known a whole procession of undisciplined women looking for excursion-sex. For twenty years he's been surrounded by cynicism, war and immorality. Now he feels a terrible urgency! He wants to make up for all those lost years. He wants a completely new life. He wants a real home and a real wife and a real family among real people. That's what I want for him. And I got scared when I remembered what I came to Hawaii for. You know what I came here for, Jim. I didn't come here looking for a husband. . . . I didn't think I had a chance to find one. I just came out here to . . . to . . . for excursion-sex! And I almost threw away my chance of all this happiness. I'm not kidding myself! I know that I wouldn't be on top of the world right now if I had lost my virginity before I met Monty. And I shudder when I think of my two close calls! If that man who tried to rape me had been a little less excited . . . or if you hadn't been afraid of post-coital melancholy . . ."

Madison laughed. Then Elaine laughed in tranquillized contentment.

"Maybe, in our excitement," Elaine said, "maybe Monty and I have exaggerated our fear of Hawaii. But Monty says not many people ever think of coming here for a honeymoon, and maybe an island atmosphere is not conducive to devotion. Maybe it's more conducive to sexual adventure. So for Monty and me, with so many lost years to make up, it just seems like we ought to flee from Hawaii towards the mainland and Niagara Falls and some illusions."

Madison pondered the situation.

"I guess I should call this to the attention of the Chamber of Commerce," he said. "Maybe the time has come to change the public image of Hawaii from like-sex to love-sex. Now that statehood is assured, maybe the Chamber of Commerce should hire a public relations expert to invite more virgins to Hawaii and fewer fornicatrices."

Madison and Elaine sat there, looking out over the roofs of the rendezvous lounges, towards the sea.

"Tell me this, Elaine," Madison said. "What's Monty going to do after this illusion-building flight to Niagara Falls? He's never lived anywhere but in Hawaii."

"I know," she said. "But I'm convinced he wants to leave forever. He says Hawaii is no place to live any more. He wants to *belong* on the mainland. And this morning about sunrise while we were talking, I remembered your jokes about apple blossoms. And I understood what you meant. There is something encouraging about the smell of apple blossoms . . . a lot more encouraging than the smells of ginger and hibiscus and frangipani. And I remembered that Senator Byrd, of Virginia, makes money growing apples. So Monty and I are going to buy land along the Wabash, and build a big, comfortable farmhouse, and we're going to raise kids and apples."

Madison found it hard to believe that only sixty hours had passed since he first heard Elaine's voice on the intercom as she talked with Monty at the Luau.

"Here's an irony for you, Elaine," he said. "About four hours from now you're going to get married. And you know where? Standing beside my pool on the very spot where you would have sunned yourself had a certain verbal contract not been automatically cancelled when the Party of the First Part received a more substantial offer."

Elaine smiled.

"That is an irony, isn't it? I think I might have enjoyed fulfilling that contract if a miracle hadn't happened."

As Madison rose to go downstairs, Elaine said: "There's one last question lurking in the back of my mind. About that contract. I wonder if the Party of the Second Part . . . when he suggested Operation Concern to the Party of the First Part, when he imparted such wisdom on the conduct of said Operation, and when he kept emphasizing his own selfishness . . . I wonder if he thought that a miracle just might happen?"

"Hell, no," Madison said. "I don't believe in miracles. Why do you think I've been riding horseback so much? I've. been getting into shape to fulfill that contract . . . aggressively and dominantly."

Madison went downstairs and telephoned his housekeeper to prepare food and drink for a dozen poolside guests at 2 P.M.

When Mamie returned from Monty's cottage she told Madison that Monty wanted to see him. So Madison walked over. He found Monty, with his servants, packing his bags.

"Damn nice of you, Jim," Monty said, "to let us use your place this afternoon. I wanted to tell you how much I appreciate it."

"Glad to do it, Monty," Madison said.

"I suppose you think I've gone crazy?"

"I wouldn't say that. But the reversal seems sudden. A few hours ago you were telling me what a good place Hotel Mamie Stover is, how mature adults have so much fun here learning sexual prowess and sexual longevity. Now you are chucking it all between sunrise and sunset."

"Nothing so strange about that," Monty said. "The hotel is still a good place . . . for people who need to come here. Suddenly it's not my personal cup of tea. The right woman can make a helluva difference in a man's outlook."

"Yeah, I guess so," Madison said.

Monty shook his head.

"I don't think you understand it, Jim. You're a cynic. You think everything's ridiculous. You're not capable of real devotion to anything . . . certainly not to any woman. You chase around the world, cheating on your wife, lying up in hotels with adventuresses. Every time a good piece crosses your path you expect to slap her on the tail and throw her in bed. But a man like me can get tired of all that . . . when he finally finds the right woman."

Madison still couldn't decide whether Monty amused him or exasperated him.

"What the hell you want to leave Hawaii for, Monty?" Madison asked. "You can devote yourself to your wife here, can't you?"

"I don't want to risk it, Jim," Monty replied. "Maybe it has something to do with my age. I'm not a teenager, you know. I'm thirty-five. I've thrown away an awful lot of years out here. I want to make up for it, and I don't feel like I have a minute to lose. Elaine and I are going to buy a good farm down in Indiana and plant acres and acres of apple trees. We want to live where it snows in the winter and gets hot in the summer . . . where spring is spring and fall is fall. I'm tired of the sameness of Hawaii. And I never expect to look at another woman as long as I live."

With effort Madison suppressed his grin. What the hell, he mused, it's Monty's wedding day. And all drunkards, when they think they are quitting, become prohibitionists.

"There's one more thing, Jim," Monty said. "It's about Mamie. My only regret is the way I'm treating her. She's a damn fine woman. She's been a real partner to me. And I guess I'm running out on her. The next few weeks will be hard on her. She'll have to carry the whole load. She'll have to replace me with one of the assistants : and she'll be in a hurry to pay me off . . . she doesn't like to owe anybody. So how about going easy on her, will you? She likes you. You could help her a lot if you'd drop around every now and then and let her talk things over with you."

"I'll do what I can, Monty," Madison said. "Since you're re-investing your fortune in apple orchards, I hope Mamie can give it all to you fast. I'm sure she will."

At high noon the wedding party left Hotel Mamie Stover. The *muumuus* had been discarded, the bare feet shod. Elaine was back in her white dress with tan pumps, tan straw handbag, and pigeon's-blood necklace. Mamie was in a stylish white dress, white gloves, pearls, sheer stockings, pink pumps, pink bag, and pink picture hat. Monty was in a white linen suit, white shirt with French cuffs, a maroon tie, even a planter's straw hat. Madison was back in his orange-colored slacks, blue silk sports shirt, sandals, and sun glasses. They rode to the air strip in a white station wagon driven by an Hawaiian man. Mamie's private plane was waiting: a seven-passenger, all-white, twin-engined Cessna, with a Japanese pilot. Quickly Monty's bags were transferred to the plane, the party boarded, the pilot taxied to the end of the runway, gunned the engine, and took off.

Monty and Elaine sat forward, pensive, holding hands. Mamie and Madison sat well back of them, in lounge chairs, also pensive.

As the plane flew over green water in bright sunlight, Mamie rested her chin on her right hand and gazed through the window. Madison sat in a similar position but he stared at Mamie. His eyes moved from her graceful feet, up her long, graceful legs, over her luxurious body, to her bony, fashion-model's face.

"God, she's a beautiful woman," Madison thought. "If only she had had a break in Hollywood! If only she had met some-body who loved her!"

Madison reached over, took her gloved left hand, and smiled at her. "It's a cock-eyed world, isn't it, Mamie?" he said.

She smiled forlornly. "It sure is, Jimmy."

At the Honolulu airport the pilot parked the Cessna beside the white C-46 which shortly would be flying the afternoon's new guests to the hotel. Two white station wagons had met Mamie's plane. In one of them Monty left to buy a ring and handle his last business chores. In the other Mamie, Madison and Elaine drove to Waikiki to pick up Elaine's baggage, then to Madison's home on the hilltop.

Elaine rushed upstairs with a Japanese maid, to open a bag, and have her tan silk suit and her red silk blouse sponged and pressed. Mamie and Madison walked through the house, through the cathedral-ceilinged living room with the paintings of his wife and his children on its walls, out on the *lanai*, past the pool and the flowers, and they stood looking down on all the color of Honolulu.

"The last time I visited this house was in 1940," Mamie said. "The night you returned the first twenty thousand dollars I earned out here. The war boom was just beginning. That seems a long time ago."

"Fifteen years," Madison said.

"Your house has been enlarged."

Madison nodded. "I built it in 1938. In 1946 she began rebuilding it, and expanding it for children. Now it's a mixture. There is still some of South Georgia in it...some of the Chattahoochee Valley. There is a great deal of Kent in it. There is a little of London in it, a little Rome, a little Inland Sea, a little Beverly Hills, a little Hongkong. Now maybe it's more hers than mine. But then she's mine."

"You have everything, don't you?"

"More than I deserve."

While the servant worked on her clothes, Elaine came downstairs and looked around. She stood with Madison before his wife's picture.

"She's made a citadel of this place, hasn't she?" Elaine said. "A citadel for her own permanent protection."

"That's a speciality of English women," Madison said. "Building citadels. For centuries they've been travelling about the earth building citadels to protect themselves...in jungles, on beaches, on high plateaus, even in deserts. Now they aren't building many citadels, because there aren't many places left where the natives will tolerate citadels."

"I'm going to build a citadel for Monty and me."

"I'll bet you are."

"But there will be one difference between me and your wife."

"What will that be?"

"You remember you explained that you doubted if your wife would be hurt much by an activity you and I were contemplating?"

"I remember."

"Now that I have seen this house I understand what you meant. But ..."

"But you'll never be that generous?"

"Not on your life," Elaine said. "But then I won't have to be. I'm not marrying a travelling man like you. I'm marrying a one-woman man who's tired of adventuring and who will want to spend every remaining night of his life with me."

"Of course."

Elaine was surprised: she had expected Madison's disbelieving grin.

"You don't believe that, do you?" she asked.

"Today, Elaine," Madison said, "I'm feeling extraordinarily charitable. Today I'm believing everything."

A big, shining, black Cadillac sedan, chauffeured by a Japanese girl in white, pulled into Madison's driveway. Out of it stepped Jesus Portales, elegantly attired in white linen. With him was his wife, a stout, fiftyish, tastefully dressed Portuguese woman with a face smiling like the moon coming up over Lisbon. Madison and Mamie greeted them, then introduced them to Elaine.

Madison and Jesus stood beside the pool, drinking whisky. Madison said: "Somehow, Jesus, I never thought of you as a family man."

"I'm the biggest family man in Hawaii, Mr. Madison," Jesus said. "Us Portuguese believe in only two institutions: matrimony and the Holy Roman Catholic Church."

"You are really devoted, are you?"

"For thirty-two years I've been a devoted husband. My wife and I have eight children and twenty-three grandchildren. The Portuguese are the greatest family people on earth. How else could a poor Portuguese like me survive out here in this cruel Anglo-controlled world?"

"And the Anglo trust officers let you move this whole brood ... all these generations ... out to Kahala?"

"Every last one of us," Jesus said. "We have all been officially proclaimed to be of Caucasian descent. We are as white as you are, and the Portuguese will some day inherit Hawaii."

"I'm afraid you're right," Madison said. "God help us poor, retreating Anglos!"

After refilling Jesus's glass, Madison dropped his voice to a conspiratorial level and said: "Jesus, what do you think of this apple-growing venture of Monty's?"

Jesus moved closer to Madison, lowered his voice also.

"Since I'm enjoying your hospitality, Mr. Madison," he said, "I'll share a secret prediction with you, just between the two of us. This morning Monty calls me and tells me he's getting married. I congratulate him. He says he's leaving Hawaii and wants to sell his stock to me and Mamie so he can re-invest in apple orchards in Indiana. I tell him sure, Monty, just give me and Mamie thirty days to get up the money and we'll pay you a cool million dollars."

"That was being friendly," Madison said.

"Oh, but I was even more friendly," Jesus went on. "Except Monty don't know it yet. There is one last beautiful house site in Kahala . . . about two acres with the best view left in the islands. Just as soon as I hang up the telephone with Monty, I go over to the bank and lease that site for fifty years. Because you know what's gonna happen? Monty will be a fish out of water in Indiana. In less than thirty days he'll telephone me that he don't want to sell out . . . that he's bringing his little lawyer-wife back to Hawaii. I'll transfer that home site to him, his little lawyer-wife will build a big ranch-style house and raise kids . . . and Monty will be right back running Hotel Mamie Stover."

Madison reverted to his South Georgia drawl.

"You reckon that's the way it'll happen, Jesus?"

"I reckon, Mr. Madison," Jesus said. "In Indiana Monty Whitaker will never plant one apple tree."

Leo Hirshman arrived with his wife, a petite woman about forty, with salt-and-pepper hair. She reminded Madison of Sylvia Sidney. She greeted Mamie and Mrs. Portales, then Elaine.

Madison and Leo stood drinking together.

"So press agents have wives, too?" Madison observed.

"Of course, Jim," Leo said. "Why do you think I dropped out of Northwestern in '32 to start plugging a fan dancer? I had to support my wife. We've got a grandchild, and Hannah is still not forty."

"Amazing."

"Nothing amazing about it. You know the Jews..."

"Yeah, I know," Madison said. "The Jews are the greatest family people in the world. That's how you've survived... and that's how you'll inherit the earth. I just heard that story from Jesus."

Madison drained his glass: whisky tasted good to him after three days of abstention.

He said: "As a good press agent, Leo, I suppose you have invited the press to cover this domestic rite?"

"Like hell," Leo said. "As a good press agent I've made sure that not a line of type will be set, not a word spoken on radio or TV. We've got three million dollars invested here in disillusionment. We'd be fools not to hide all efforts to find Values-and-Illusions."

Leo lighted a cigarette, then dropped his voice to the confidential level and asked: "You were over at the hotel, Jim. How do you account for this sudden decision by Monty to search for the Holy Grail?"

"From what he told me," Madison said, "it was like Saul of Tarsus on the Damascus Road. Suddenly he was struck down by a Great Light."

Leo shook his head.

"I think it's simpler than that," he said. "Remember the old story about the swordsman who goes around saying: 'Some day, Boys, I'm going to run into a woman who won't give it to me. Then I'm going to marry her.' I think that's what this is. This little woman is a lawyer and probably has a lot of peasant cunning. She probably just kept saying no until she had him flabbergasted."

"Well, maybe..." Madison said.

"What really beats me," Leo said, "is this bit about Monty

chasing off to Niagara Falls! That place has been dead for years. Nobody goes there any more. Press agents for the New York Central built up the Falls as Honeymoon Heaven back there when people travelled on trains. But Good God! Niagara Falls must be nothing today! The hotels must be shabby and run-down. And everybody sees the Falls every week on TV. Why doesn't Monty go to Tahiti? Or if he must go to the mainland, to Vegas? Or Arrowhead? Or Acapulco? Not Niagara Falls! You got to admit, Jim, that's strictly from corn!"

"Yeah, I guess so," Madison said. "But Monty couldn't go back to Tahiti... he took his nympho first wife there. And who the hell can find an illusion at Vegas? Or Acapulco? When you start looking for illusions today, Leo, who knows where to go?"

Just before Monty arrived with the Air Force chaplain, Madison and Elaine played a scene which neither had anticipated. Madison invited Elaine into his office and said:

"Elaine, I believe it's customary for a bride to ask a lady to stand up beside her during a wedding ceremony. A gracious little gesture. Which of these three women are you going to ask to stand up with you?"

"I thought I'd ask Mrs. Hirshman," Elaine said.

"Why?"

"Well... she's respectable, isn't she?"

"What's wrong with Mamie?"

Elaine felt a slight shadow fall across her. She had been feeling so joyful... and now she sensed the approach of something unpleasant.

"Jim," she said, "this is to be a religious wedding ceremony. We will stand up before a preacher. This is the beginning of a new life for Monty. It is the end of any relationships which might not have been too respectable."

"Then why didn't you take him to Indiana for the marriage ceremony? Or to Nevada before a justice of the peace? Why are you marrying here, with Jesus and Mamie present?"

"You know why. I'm to be a virgin bride. Today is the proper day for us to marry. We want to travel together, and it's more respectable to travel as man-and-wife."

"Then don't you feel you can include Mamie in this little ceremony here in my garden? She's respectable enough to have been your husband's business partner for five years. She picked him up when he was a lost ball in high weeds and made him a millionaire. Much of the money with which you'll build your citadel was made for Monty by Mamie. Mamie was respectable enough for you to visit. For you not to ask her to stand up with you, and to pointedly prefer a woman you've just met because she's a wife, don't you feel that would be an unnecessary affront to Mamie?"

Elaine's eyes still sparkled with happiness. She was still trying to smile. But she could feel her uneasiness growing, and with this uneasiness she felt the first trace of resentment.

Madison said: "At this little party I hate to see Mamie treated like the bastard at the family reunion. It's so simple for you and Monty to include her. Such a small gesture. A virgin who is sitting on top of the world should be capable of some generosity. So as your friend and present host, Elaine, I'm asking you to be generous. Go to Mamie pleasantly and invite her to stand beside you. Tell her that both you and Monty want her. It will mean a lot to her, and it's something so easy for you to give."

Fighting for restraint, Elaine warily weighed her words.

"Jim," she said, "you're a very generous man. You've been kind to me, so of course I want to do anything you ask. But please continue to be generous with me. This 'little ceremony' may look insignificant to you, perhaps a little ridiculous. But it's the biggest day of my life. It's the only marriage ceremony I'll ever have. I'll always look back to it. And surely you can understand that I don't want to remember that the day I stood before a preacher, in your beautiful garden in Hawaii, standing on my right was . . . was . . ."

"Was what?"

Elaine's restraint slipped a notch.

"Was . . . one of the most notorious whores in the world!"

Madison felt his own good nature recede. His jaw tightened.

"If Mamie is a whore, Elaine," he said, "I must remind you that your marriage wasn't made in Heaven. It was made in a whorehouse."

Elaine felt as if Madison had suddenly slapped her across the face. This man who had treated her compassionately, who was the host at her wedding party, was now staring hard-eyed at her, injecting harshness into the happiest day of her life. She bit hard on her tongue to keep from replying in anger.

"Why are you treating me this way, Jim?" she asked. "You have completely startled me. I can't believe this is happening. Why have you suddenly turned on me? Why are you trying to deflate and hurt me?"

They eyed one another: two people, once friends, now caught in a grinding conflict of wills.

"I'm not mistreating you, Elaine. I'm asking you not to be unkind to Mamie. If you and Monty can reach out your hands and accept a million dollars from Mamie in the next thirty days, why aren't you capable of reaching out your hands to her today?"

Elaine Shelby was a stubborn little woman. Only once before in her life, during the attempted rape, had she faced a stubborn man.

"I won't discuss it further, Jim. You are trying to debase me. You're sardonic and cynical, and you want to see me standing there before a preacher with a long-legged whore towering ten inches over me. *I won't do it!*"

Madison dropped his eyes. Unconsciously, the sole of his right foot tapped the floor. "What if I decide to compel you to do it, Elaine?"

"What do you mean?"

"What if I tell you that if you don't do it I'll wait until the chaplain asks that question which ends 'or for ever hold your peace.' And then I'll object to this marriage on grounds that it has reached this point by fraud . . . by a woman playing a game for her own amusement, a game suggested by me. As proof that I suggested it, I'll refer Monty to that charming little birthmark just south of your appendicitis scar!"

Elaine felt as if she was suffocating with hurt and anger. She had felt like this when she was fighting rape.

She gasped: "What sort of man are you, Jim?"

"Opinions differ," Madison replied. "You misjudged me. You called me kind. I'm kind only up to the point when I suddenly feel stifled by hypocrisy. Then I become the unkindest sonofabitch between San Francisco and Singapore."

"You must be inhuman . . . to treat me this way . . . on my wedding day."

"Well, you can relax," Madison said. "The treatment is over. You can let your blood pressure go down. I won't compel you to do anything. You are right: it is your wedding. It's my business to suggest . . . perhaps even to urge. It isn't my business to compel. I only wish that while you were collecting the Jackpot you could have demonstrated that you can also give."

Elaine's chin was quivering. "Do we have to part this way?" she said. "As enemies?"

"Not as enemies," Madison said. "Just as strangers . . . like we began. I hoped I could watch your wedding ceremony and feel encouraged. Instead I'll watch it and feel just a little bit sadder for the whole damned human race."

That's how it happened that the wedding of Elaine Shelby, of Richmond, Indiana, to John Charles Fremont Whitaker, of Maui, Hawaii, was not an entirely joyful occasion. The weather was perfect. The setting was ideal. The bride looked wistful. The groom looked proud. Everybody present looked healthy, well dressed and affluent.

Nevertheless there was tension: anyone would have felt it.

There were nine people in the wedding party, but they didn't stand together as one happy and hopeful party. They stood apart in two consciously separated groups.

In one group stood the Air Force chaplain, with Elaine and Monty before him. At Monty's left stood Leo Hirshman; at

Elaine's right stood Hannah Hirshman. The Hirshmans were not happy; they were embarrassed because they knew they were being used to protect the bride and groom from having to stand beside Jesus Portales and Mamie Stover.

In the second group the four other people stood smiling, but they were not easy because they knew that Mamie and Jesus had been deliberately excluded. In this group were Jesus Portales and his wife, Jim Madison and Mamie Stover.

The two groups stood in this manner, associates in an ancient rite, but self-consciously and embarrassingly apart. And they stood this way while the chaplain recited ancient words of hope and illusion ... *for richer, for poorer ... in sickness and in health* ... and while the bride and groom exchanged vows which would bind them until death.

And because he knew that deep inside her the six-foot-tall blonde woman was feeling hurt at being so pointedly excluded, Madison moved very close to Mamie, slipped her arm through his, and warmly held her hand.

At the airport the happy bride and groom said goodbye to the entire party, and there was laughter and a limited exchange of kisses. Only Leo Hirshman kissed the bride ... though all the women kissed the groom. Then the departing couple raced up the ramp, and the Pan-American Clipper took off for Los Angeles and Niagara Falls.

As the plane faded over the Pacific, Madison and Mamie stood with Mr. and Mrs. Hirshman and with Mr. and Mrs. Portales. All six swallowed and felt some of the loneliness which every human being feels at departure. Madison broke the silence. He took both Mamie's hands in his, and in a voice which all could hear, he said:

"Mamie, let's you and I go on a honeymoon."

Mamie smiled and said: "Are you kidding?"

"Hell, no," Madison said. "I'm not kidding. Let's let Jesus and Leo mind the stores. Let's you and I get in your airplane and fly to the Big Island ... to Kona. For four days and nights. We'll take the hotel's Honeymoon Suite. We'll fly around those damn volcanoes and look at them. We'll visit that little grass shack at Kealakekua. We'll go fishing for fighting fish ... and when I go below deck for a nap after lunch I'll go with you and not with a Woola Woola girl. We'll fabricate our own goddam illusions. We'll convince ourselves that we're the only two people on earth. We'll pretend that a voyage begun sixteen years ago never ended. We'll pretend that we're still aboard that freighter ... and that I still need to find your hand when I wake up in darkness. After four days we'll return to reality. I'll get back to work on a novel which I've suddenly decided is pretty good ... and you can get back to work displaying that gorgeous rump to all these lonely, disillusioned sex-hunters who'll be coming to Hawaii as long as ships sail and planes fly."

The Hirshmans and the Portaleses broke into applause and merry laughter. Suddenly everybody felt good again ... the tension had been broken.

Mamie beamed and squeezed Madison's hands. "Let's hurry, Jimmy," she said. "We can reach the hotel at Kona in an hour."

CHAPTER FOURTEEN

The seventh day : in which we watch
Madison reach conclusions and con-
trive a letter affecting Hotel Mamie
Stover.

AT 7 A.M. on the seventh day Jim Madison was back at his
desk. He had returned from Kona the previous evening. He
was trying to order his thoughts so that he could discharge his
obligation to *Vacation* Magazine. He began to write.

THE QUESTION : Why do ten per cent of all civilian visitors to
Hawaii transfer from Waikiki hotels to Hotel Mamie Stover?
PARTIAL ANSWERS : They are seeking activity which will make
them feel alive, and the only activity which can enliven most
of them is sexual activity. They yearn to participate . . . to
feel included . . . and only in sex can they feel participation
and inclusion. They long for drama, yet the only drama which
can stir them is the elemental drama of sex.
    Sally Rogers said to me: "It's about 9 P.M. I'm on a
'romantic' island. I'm excited. I feel as though I look my best:
I may never look this attractive again. I want to do something extraordinary . . . something I can remember when I'm
dried-up and wearing a shawl and sitting by the fire during
the long, damp Oregon winters."
    What could Sally Rogers have experienced at that moment
which she would have considered extraordinary and which
she would have remembered? Suppose I had played a Brahms
concerto for her? Suppose I had recited *Andrea del Sarto* for
her? Suppose I had invited her to dance or to play chess?
None of these would have satisfied her longing. She was
perceptive enough to define what she could consider

extraordinary and what she could remember: "I need sexual reassurance. I need to feel a strong, aggressive, dominant excited man in bed with me again. I want a man who, when he makes sexual contact with me, exults, and feels like he's conquering the world."

A more complex individual, Doctor Anderson, said: "You know, Madison, this is the first morning in years I've felt like a real man. You know why? Because last night for the first time in years I got what I needed from a woman. Never in my life have I been as strong with a woman as I am with her. It's something that makes a new man out of a man . . . gives him new confidence . . . new assurance."

Elaine Shelby said: "But something *has* gone wrong for me. Virginity at twenty-eight is wrong, isn't it? That's why I decided to come."

Becky Sanders said: "This is a good place . . . for me. When reality compels women like me to shift from love-sex to security-sex, Hotel Mamie Stover helps us make the shift. It's easier here to take the first man you don't love. Remoteness helps. The sensuous red and yellow colors help. The drumbeats help. The erotic dancing helps. The nakedness and the massages and all the talk about sexual techniques and prowess . . . they help. Above all, the general attitude helps. Maybe it's no more than misery loves company . . . maybe it's a form of group therapy."

And Mamie said: "Jimmy, whether you or the missionaries like it or not, the people who come to me *do* need sexual adventure. I try to help them."

MY CONCLUSION: Hotel Mamie Stover flourishes because it caters to human need; and, given the human condition in 1955, the hotel is more good than evil. In a fashion, perhaps it's as good as the leper colony which its guests fly over. The problems described by the hotel's guests are misery-causing problems, and in her crude fashion Mamie Stover is trying to help relieve misery. There is a breath of honesty at Hotel Mamie Stover, there is a measure of relief from hypocrisy, and what evil is done, adults do to themselves.

Therefore, it is my clear and present duty to *assist* Hotel Mamie Stover, not to *damage* it.

MY PROBLEM: Hotel Mamie Stover is vulnerable. It is built on land controlled by men who are themselves vulnerable. Their names are on church rolls. They are community leaders. If challenged, they must conform. If preachers get excited and denounce a serpent in the garden, these men must rise and try to slay said serpent.

Therefore, if I write anything at all about Hotel Mamie Stover, in the Statehood Edition of *Vacation* Magazine, I will excite preachers and thereby damage or destroy the hotel. So I must write nothing. But my writing nothing may not be enough. If I report my honest conclusions to the Editor of *Vacation* I may so excite him that if I refuse to write the story he will assign another writer and the damage may still be done. So, to protect Hotel Mamie Stover, I must take positive action. I must convince the Editor that this story is not publishable in his magazine. I must make him believe that any report on Hotel Mamie Stover published in *Vacation* would damage both the magazine and its editor.

To accomplish this, I'll resort to the cynical chuckle. Such chuckles never fail to dismay both editors and publishers.

Pondering this decision, Madison walked about his office for several minutes. He walked out in his garden and stood looking down on Honolulu. He wanted to write about Mamie Stover and the people who travel so far to become her guests. But he knew that, at that time and in those circumstances, any story would only damage what he wanted to help.

He went back to his typewriter and wrote this letter:

Dear Nick,

Regarding our proposed story about Hotel Mamie Stover for the Hawaiian Statehood Edition of *Vacation* :

I have today returned home after completing my research. I spent three days at the hotel. I interviewed representative guests. I personally participated in much of the hotel's program, including a healthy amount of horseback riding. Then, to free her of distractions so that I could enjoy her undivided attention, I went with Mamie to Kona where I interviewed her aggressively for four days.

After all this work, Nick, it is my considered opinion that

this story is not publishable in a mass magazine. As an established author, I don't think I should risk writing it; and even if I were reckless enough to write it, I feel sure that an editor of your eminence would never publish it in a magazine with the prestige of *Vacation.*

Because, goddamit, Nick, there is no way to write about Hotel Mamie Stover without becoming OBSCENE!

Any way you look at it, the hotel is no more than a new-model whorehouse. Abortion is practiced; contraception is medically assisted; and covert sexual encounter is encouraged by cleverly designed assignation rooms which one can visit without being observed.

Under the guise of "sex education" there is constant instruction in sexual technique, sexual prowess, and sexual longevity. After you have been at the hotel a few hours, you find yourself suspecting that the most important question in the world is not Co-Existence but how readily and how often a woman achieves sexual climax!

Beautiful, sixteen-year-old girls, carefully chosen from the islands of Melanesia, are exploited by being placed at the disposal of middle-aged men from the mainland. These are nubile, compliant girls who have never been taught the evils of sexual congress. And on the other side of the coin, middle-aged women from the mainland are invited to play naked on the beach with grinning Polynesian youths to whom coitus is like sandlot baseball!

For men, much is made of the "athletic program." The fishing is perhaps the best in the world. But what do you suppose the Added Attraction is on the fishing boats? You're right! The fisherman, at the first approach of ennui, is invited to go below with a girl for a siesta!

With such goings-on it is patently unnecessary for me to describe for you typical guests. Just bored, middle-aged, middle-class mainlanders who watch TV, buy too much soap, and drive Chevrolets and Fords along Main Street. But it may surprise you to learn that, among the professional groups, doctors dominate the guest list. These men-of-medicine are using cash they squirrel away from tax collectors to fly to Hotel Mamie Stover for a week of indefatigable tail-chasing.

My closest associate at the hotel was such a doctor . . .

from Sioux Falls, South Dakota. He devoted each morning to horseback riding to make himself "potent and demanding," and he devoted each afternoon and evening to sexual association with an attractive, erotic, ash-blonde "Government Girl" from the sedate community of Bethesda, Maryland.

I could continue at length, but I'm sure this is more than enough to convince you that Mamie Stover and her activities are not proper copy for *Vacation* Magazine.

You and I, Nick, are both too old and too secure in this business to start mailing FILTH and OBSCENITY into five million decent American homes.

Sorry this one didn't work out, but try me again soon.

All the best,

                                                              Jim

Four days later Madison was sitting beside the pool reading his letters. He found this reply.

Dear Jim,

Your letter, of course, brings gloom to all of us here at *Vacation*. It means that we shall have to put the Hawaiian Statehood Edition to press with no more than the same old crap about grass skirts, hula girls, Yankee missionaries, surfboard riders, etc.

But we bow to your wisdom. You are 100 per cent correct in your report. No story about Mamie Stover is publishable here, and I'm grateful to you for saving us from what might have been a débâcle. Such a story could have got us into a hornet's nest with the Church, the Post Office, perhaps with some of our advertisers. No doubt there would have been a tide of subscription cancellations.

For your indefatigable work, and to reimburse you for out-of-pocket expenses, I enclose our check for one thousand dollars.

However, Jim, I must say that you have not dispelled my personal curiosity about Hotel Mamie Stover. I feel that this is a phenomenon which those of us who mold public opinion should watch. I had expected to go to Europe next month, but I have changed plans and will travel to Hawaii instead.

So I'd appreciate your keeping in contact with Mamie so as to insure me an invitation to her hotel.

Also, in mentioning it about the club today, I learned that a number of my friends are planning Hawaiian trips soon. Each one asked me to ask you to expect a telephone call from him.

Finally, I happened to visit my doctor this afternoon for my semi-annual check-up. He expressed intense medical interest in what may be happening at Hotel Mamie Stover, and you may expect him out there most any day.

Again, I'm sorry it didn't work out, and I appreciate your saving us from publishing error.

Until I see you soon,

Nick

Madison smiled. He went inside to dress. He was feeling good because he was due at the airport in an hour to collect his wife and children.